By Shamini Flint

Inspector Singh Investigates:
A Calamitous Chinese Killing

Shamini Flint

piatkus

PIATKUS

First published in Great Britain as a paperback original in 2013 by Piatkus

A CIP catalogue record for this book
is available from the British Library.

ISBN 978-0-7499-5779-7

Typeset in Caslon by M Rules
Printed and bound in Great Britain by
Clays Ltd, St Ives plc

Papers used by Piatkus are from well-managed forests
and other responsible sources.

MIX
Paper from
responsible sources
FSC® C104740

Piatkus
An imprint of
Little, Brown Book Group
100 Victoria Embankment
London EC4Y 0DY

An Hachette UK Company
www.hachette.co.uk

www.piatkus.co.uk

For Usha Cheryan, Ben Singam
and Jon Singam – family when it counts . . .

Seek truth from facts

實事求是

Deng Xiaoping

Prologue

Justin Tan stood at the main junction of the old *hutong*, a neighbourhood of old courtyards dating from Imperial times, and stared down narrow alleys that disappeared quickly into darkness. It was after midnight and the street lighting was limited in such a poor neighbourhood. The lanes were too narrow for cars so no headlights lit up the gloom. Households had gone to bed but a few lamps glowed at courtyard entrances, little bubbles of light that deepened the dark around them. The air had cleared somewhat after a particularly unpleasant Beijing day, where the pollution index was off the charts, children were kept home from school and adults wore ineffectual face masks. Justin drew a deep breath and decided that he could still smell the soot particles mixed with rotting food from a nearby dustbin.

The young man reached for his mobile and dialled a number.

'Professor Luo?'

'Justin, is that you? What is it? Do you know what time it is?'

'I've made my decision about what to do ...'

'What is it?' asked the professor.

Justin hesitated and looked around. Had he heard something? Soft footfalls in the darkness?

'Justin, are you there?'

'I'll call you back.'

'Wait! Where are you?'

'At the *hutong* ... I needed to see, needed to think, but now I know what I have to do.'

'I'm so sorry I dragged you into this,' said the professor. 'There's something I need to tell you,' he continued, but Justin had terminated the call.

The young man stood still and strained his ears. It was not his imagination, he could hear footsteps in the distance. It sounded like more than one person, maybe two or three. He tried to dismiss the cold fear that settled in his chest. He was being silly, paranoid, it was just some workers heading home after a late shift. Or maybe Wang Zhen was making good on his promise to exact revenge. Justin turned and hurried away towards the main road, there would be people there even at such a late hour, and traffic – safety in a crowd, in numbers. He wasn't sure but he thought the people behind him had escalated their pace too. Justin broke into a run, panic taking hold. He was fit, he was fast, would it be enough? He'd sprinted fifty yards when he came to an abrupt halt. There were three men strung across the alley in front of him. Two of them were holding truncheons. He thought he could make out a dark sedan behind them, parked to block the narrow exit, the front window wound down and a pale face looking out. Impossible to identify from such a distance but Justin didn't doubt who it was; the net was closing.

He thought he caught sight of a shadow in the darkness and he shouted, 'Is anyone there? Can you call for help?' There was no answer, his desperation was providing him imaginary would-be rescuers. The three men started towards him with a calculated, deliberate step. His hand went to his pocket and he pressed a few buttons on his phone at random but it was too late to call for help. One of the men shone a torch into his eyes and, for a few seconds, he lost all vision.

Justin turned and ran again, feet pounding on pavement, heartbeat keeping frantic time. This time there was no mistaking their intent. As he glanced over his shoulder, all three were in hot pursuit. He was back at the junction where he'd started. He stopped, panting, trying to decide which way to go. It was no use. The original pair were waiting in the shadows. They stepped out and started closing the distance. Behind him, the other men arrived. He whirled round, turned back, knew he had nowhere to go.

'What do you want? Why are you following me? Do you want money?'

The front man slapped the truncheon into his palm. 'When the dog chases the mouse, there are always consequences.'

One

'Chinese!' said Mrs Singh.

The inspector, her husband, suspected that this was not merely an observation. No one above the age of fifty in Singapore, who was not ethnically Chinese, ever uttered the word without implied criticism. It was inevitable in a country the size of a pocket handkerchief where the Chinese dominated every aspect of business and politics. The other races foraged around the fringes for an identity and, if they were like Mrs Singh, sniped from the sidelines.

'These "made in China" things don't even last for one day before they break!' His wife held up a cracked plastic bucket as evidence. Maybe she thought a policeman would not be satisfied with her uncorroborated testimony. She'd be right about that too. Inspector Singh, plump pursuer of the truth, did not find his wife a credible witness. She was too prone to exaggeration, imagination and misplaced conviction. The sort of person who picked suspects out of a line-up with certainty even though they'd only had a fleeting glimpse of a perpetrator on a dark night.

'Why do you buy it if you think the quality is so poor?'

'Cheaper,' she responded.

Singh scowled and thrust out his pink full lower lip. His upper lip was obscured by the moustache that skirted his mouth and then expanded into a full beard, now liberally speckled with grey. 'You get what you pay for,' he pointed out.

'That's what my father said when I complained about you.'

She was referring, of course, to the dowry her family had paid all those decades ago when he married her. Singh decided to ignore her remark. It was his default position and for good reason. Despite his successful battles of words with senior police officers, hardened criminals, high court judges and highly paid lawyers, he'd never won a verbal encounter with his wife.

Besides, he was not in the mood for generalised criticism of China, the Chinese or 'Made in China' products. Singh had just returned from a harrowing trip to India. Say what you liked about the Chinese, at least they made something other than Bollywood movies, babies and skin whitening cream. Even the statues of Hindu gods and goddesses sold outside temples in Mumbai – Ganesh with his elephant head and Kali with her surfeit of limbs – were all made in China. Furthermore, one could walk down the street in Beijing without tripping over the bodies of the homeless, the destitute and, on occasion, the dead. Or so Singh assumed anyway. The foremost criminal investigator in the Singapore police department, in his own, but not his wife's or boss's estimation, had never been to China.

'You know what else they did?' continued his wife, taking victory in her stride and opening up a new flank.

Who were 'they', wondered Singh? The Chinese? The government? Mrs Singh was a great believer in conspiracy theories. Nothing bad ever happened, as far as she was concerned, that did not have the guiding hand of the rich and the powerful.

Singh felt a mild stirring of curiosity, like the taste of cumin in fish curry, just enough to whet the appetite. What grievous historical event was Mrs Singh going to lay at the door of China or the Chinese? He was in a relatively placid mood, just after lunch and before he had to drag himself back to the office. He was prepared to be amused.

'What have the Chinese done to provoke your ire aside from manufacturing low quality buckets?' he asked.

'They're all coming here!'

'All?' He had a sudden vision of a billion Chinese citizens queuing up at Changi Airport. A sight that might be visible from the moon, like the Great Wall.

'Yes, the government is letting them all in – permanent residence, citizenship – whatever they want they can get.'

Singh thought he understood. He clasped his hands and rested them on his belly and adopted his familiar 'Buddha-in-repose' attitude. 'You've been talking to Mrs Chong?'

'She says that they're all coming here. You know, taking jobs, stealing husbands.'

Mrs Chong was the neighbour on the right side of the Singh residence if you stood on the porch and faced out towards the road. The two houses were separated by a bright green chain-link fence. An attempt to imitate nature's colour on the cheap – Mrs Singh made Scrooge look like a philanthropist – had resulted in a shade that suggested the sort of toxicity usually associated with a nuclear accident. A very large heavy mango tree that grew against the boundary provided a rich carpet of fermented rotting fruit underfoot.

Mrs Chong spent her days worrying. Firstly, whether her children were coping with Mandarin and maths in school and secondly, whether her husband was secretly maintaining another family on the side, sucking much needed funding away from extra Mandarin and maths tuition for the kids. She spent a good part of each morning communicating these fears to Mrs Singh across the garden fence.

'You shouldn't believe everything Mrs Chong says,' said Inspector Singh.

This was a mistake. Mrs Singh was prepared to put up either with unconditional support or a position of Swiss neutrality from her husband but not a contradiction of any of the views she or Mrs Chong held dear. She straightened her skinny back and trained a basilisk glare at her husband.

'Not just Mrs Chong – everyone knows!'

'Everyone knows that *all* the Chinese are coming here?'

'Maybe not all,' she conceded. Mrs Singh trying a new role, the voice of reason. She wouldn't get past the first audition.

The Sikh policeman knew that his wife was merely expressing a widely held opinion. The citizenry was convinced that the government, determined to boost population numbers, was handing out residency permits like free chopsticks at a Chinese restaurant.

'The China girls come here pretending to work but actually they're only looking for husbands. And they don't care if they're married already or not.'

China girls. Not Chinese girls. A convenient way for the Singaporean population of nervous wives to maintain pride in their Chinese roots while distinguishing themselves from these brash, husband-snatching newcomers.

'Is that what Mrs Chong says? I'm sure most of the girls are just trying to find a better life . . .'

Mrs Singh's grimace suggested she had suddenly bitten into a piece of lime pickle. 'It depends whether the plan for a better life is to quickly catch a Singaporean man. You know what Mrs Chong says about the China girls? "*Up to no good until proven otherwise!*"'

Singh sighed, inserted a finger under his turban and scratched above his ear. 'Up to no good until proven otherwise.' It could have been the slogan for the entire nation. It was certainly the attitude of the police towards anyone who strayed from the norm, whether it was to appear un-shirted in public or graffiti a wall. Banksy wouldn't have lasted a week in Singapore. The Singaporean equivalent – a young woman who had painted the words, 'My grandfather's road', on a few thoroughfares in Singapore – had been arrested. As a man on the street had said on the news at the time, "Our society has no place for such impromptu creative acts."

The rotund detective's gut compressed as he leaned forwards, reaching for his white sneakers, and he gasped for air like a fish in a bucket. Slowly, he put the shoes on – another new pair – he'd been unable to face wearing the ones he'd brought back from India. Singh liked his trainers comfy and clean. A couple of weeks tramping through Mumbai suburbs had left him very suspicious of the undersides of his footwear and he'd binned them the moment he made it home.

9

'I'm going back to work,' he muttered.

'Chasing criminals? Should be chasing those China girls.'

'I thought the problem was too many Singaporean men chasing China girls.'

'I'm not worried about you,' snapped Mrs Singh. 'They only want Chinese men. Or at least men with a good job for good money.' She rose to her feet, collected his mug of half-drunk tea and marched off to the kitchen, colourful caftan billowing like a main sail in a high wind.

Inspector Singh levered himself out of his chair with both arms and headed to the car that was waiting outside to ferry him back to work although he would be the first to admit that his wife was quite right – it could not exactly be described as 'a good job for good money'. He experienced a moment that hinted at regret, his rotund form was indeed safe from the attentions of the China girls.

The beatings were the worst he had ever experienced which, he acknowledged quietly, was ironic. After all, he was the son of a man denounced as a capitalist running dog during the Cultural Revolution. But the Red Guard had consisted of enthusiastic amateurs while the prison guards at the correctional facility were experts at hitting a man to inflict maximum pain. And yet they broke no bones and the next day always pronounced him fit to work. Professor Luo Gan shuffled along towards the quarry with his fellow inmates, wearing the regulation grey uniform and rubber shoes, scratching at welts from the bed bugs in the crowded dormitories, grateful that he could still walk.

One of the other detainees whispered to him, 'Why do you

provoke them? You know how they will answer you. It is better to be prudent.'

'Is it provocation to stick to one's values and principles?' he retorted, carefully pushing to the back of his mind the reason he was there in the first place.

His response was met with a shrug from the intellectual, shakily adjusting his fragile glasses. The young drug addicts were indifferent to his actions while a couple of middle-ranking Party officials, arrested no doubt for some act of petty corruption, gave him a wide berth. There were so many ways to end up on the wrong side of the security apparatus in China that his companions were a cross-section of the entire population.

'It is remarkable that you reached such a ripe old age before ending up here!' said another fellow, recently interned, who still had some spirit left.

At the quarry, Luo broke rocks using a heavy hammer that he swung over his shoulder in a uniform excruciating rhythm. Breaking big rocks into little rocks and little rocks into rubble and carting the debris away in wheelbarrows. A metaphor for what he was experiencing – this so-called 're-education through labour'? He doubted it. The Chinese authorities tended to be very literal minded. 'Re-education through labour' had been one of Mao's favourite forms of control and punishment. But it had been maintained long after Mao was laid in state at Tiananmen Square as a convenient way to deal with the discontented and the rebellious.

Deep down, the professor had always known, always feared, that he'd end up in one of these black holes of the Chinese state. He straightened his back and felt it creak like the wooden slats of his bed back home. He shut his eyes tightly – it was important not to think of home or the little strength he had left would drain from his body like dirty water down a sinkhole.

He looked around, trying to regain his composure. The quarry presented a bleak, ravaged landscape but the surrounding mountains were covered in lush greenery and silhouetted against a pristine blue sky untainted by the yellow filter of smog that hung over Beijing. It reminded him of the delicate brush stroke paintings of a master calligrapher. He had no idea where he was although the landscape put him in mind of the area around the Mutianyu section of the Great Wall, absent of course, the thin snaking line of ancient defences that followed the contours of the hill. He doubted he was that close to Beijing. It was an incongruity really, that China's greatest architectural feature, designed to repel enemies of the state, was now of no use whatsoever. He glanced at the guards standing along the perimeter of the quarry, dark silhouettes against a bright sky. How could it be when the greatest threat to China now came from within?

Superintendent Chen was ensconced in Singh's chair and fiddling with his BlackBerry. He did not look pleased. As Singh sauntered in, reeking of the cigarette he'd stopped to have in the car park, the boss looked at his watch – Rolex, of course – and then back at Singh.

'You're late!'

'I would be if there was a fixed time that I was supposed to be here,' said Singh, sitting down in the plastic chair fronting his own desk. He wondered why his boss was making himself comfortable in the seat that Singh had spent so many years shaping to fit his own ample contours.

'I thought you were desperate to get back to work after your Indian adventure,' growled Chen.

'I am ... but the citizenry has become strangely law-abiding in my time away,' complained the inspector. 'Not a single juicy murder all month.'

'Low crime doesn't mean no crime,' retorted the chief, quoting one of the Singapore police department's posters.

'Low crime does mean no work. Which is why I can be late – I have nothing to do.'

'I can fix that for you,' said the superintendent.

Singh sat up straighter, a glint in his eye, nostrils flaring. 'We have a murder?'

The other man paused.

'We don't have a murder?'

His superior remained silent.

'You'd like me to commit a murder?'

Superintendent Chen's expression suggested an outpouring of gastric juices had made contact with the resident ulcers in his stomach. Ulcers, he assured anyone who would listen, that were not caused by the criminal underclass but by his recalcitrant Sikh inspector. 'I don't think you're the man for the job.'

'You never do,' Singh pointed out. He left unsaid that he still had the best solve rate in the department. Probably even better than the numbers suggested if you took into account the possibility that his colleagues frequently incarcerated the innocent.

'And I'm not in a position to venture an opinion as I don't

know what you're talking about,' he continued.

'Unfortunately, tales of your latest Indian escapade made the newspapers here in Singapore.'

This was true. The local press loved nothing better than a juicy story that had no Singaporean political implications.

'They called you the "curry cop",' continued Superintendent Chen, thin eyebrows – did he pluck them? – drawn together in irritation.

'And the "poppadum policeman",' agreed Singh equably, not bothering to suppress a wide smile. He'd enjoyed the coverage, his wife had been offended which had added piquancy to the pleasure. He'd even come up with a few nicknames himself, the "dhal detective" and the "sag sleuth" but his wife had forbidden any anonymous calls to the papers with these suggestions. 'Reuters picked up some of the coverage as well,' added Singh.

'Why were you solving murders in India anyway? You're supposed to be a Singapore cop!'

'You wouldn't let me come back to work after my Cambodian mishap,' pointed out Singh.

'That was typical of you. We sent you to be an observer at the war crimes tribunal and next minute you're chasing murderers across minefields.'

'I went to India for a family wedding. It's not my fault that my wife's family is full of murderers!' Singh paused. 'Although maybe I should have expected that ...'

'You don't take the job seriously – that's the problem with you.'

'I catch killers. What more do you want?'

'Sensitivity to surrounding issues,' retorted Chen. 'You don't

14

care about stepping on toes with your big feet in your non-regulation shoes!'

Singh glanced down at his feet and wiggled his toes inside his sneakers.

'I run faster in these,' said Singh, a man who had not voluntarily broken into a trot in twenty years.

Superintendent Chen began to massage his left arm and Singh wondered whether he was about to have a heart attack.

'If we did things your way, there'd be a lot of murderers walking the streets of Singapore,' continued Singh. 'Everyone sleeps better at night because the "curry cop" is on the job!'

'That's not *my* view,' muttered his superior.

Singh trained the point of his turban at the other man. It sounded like Chen had been overruled from above. But as far as Singh knew, he was even less popular further up the police hierarchy.

'So . . . are you interested?' demanded Chen.

'What's the case?'

'The murder of a young man.'

Singh hauled himself to his feet. The time for baiting Superintendent Chen was over. There was a crime to solve. A murder. A young life truncated through the act of a fellow human being. Singh felt his senses heighten. He had a case. And the fact of the matter was that there was nothing the corpulent copper liked better than a juicy murder to solve. After all, pursuing justice was his only form of exercise.

'I'll get to the scene. Send me whoever's on duty and we can decide on staffing once I've had a look,' said Singh. He hauled himself to his feet, ready to get to work.

Chen relapsed into a taciturn silence.

'Have we identified the victim? Someone important, I assume?' asked Singh.

'Why do you assume that?'

'Because you're sitting behind my desk and wondering whether it's worth the risk of assigning the case to me.'

Chen's lip twitched, indicating a direct hit. 'Things are not going to be as straightforward as you think.'

'What do you mean?'

'The young man in question was killed three weeks ago.'

'What? You know the first few hours are critical! The crime scene would have been totally contaminated. We won't find physical evidence that will stand up in court.' Singh was livid. Was this what happened when he was on medical leave or moonlighting as a Mumbai private eye? The police department gave up on basic protocol?

'Was it not obvious that it was murder?' he demanded.

'Actually, the young man was badly beaten – no doubt as to cause of death.'

'What are you people playing at? You know very well that most crimes are solved within the first forty-eight hours or not at all.'

'We don't have jurisdiction,' said Chen.

Singh's heart followed a downward trajectory until it was nestled next to his ample stomach and he slumped back into his chair. 'What do you mean we don't have jurisdiction?'

'I'm afraid this was a bludgeoning in Beijing.'

As evening eased into twilight, the guards huddled around a fire smoking unfiltered cigarettes. Luo Gan leaned on his hammer, lost in his own thoughts. It was difficult to fathom

16

his route to this so-called correctional facility with rebellious intellectuals, petty thieves, corrupt officials and prostitutes. His lips twisted and it was difficult in the half-light to determine if it reflected amusement or despair.

'You're Professor Luo Gan, aren't you?'

The professor blinked and peered at his questioner. He realised it was the bespectacled intellectual who'd urged him to be less provocative earlier in the day.

'I recognised you from the newspapers.'

'Does it matter?' asked Luo Gan. 'Here we are all the same.'

'Just interested, that's all. There are not many who are safe from the attentions of the security forces if someone with your profile can end up here.'

Luo Gan blinked rapidly, trying to focus on the past, on a time when he had been a respected figure.

'Why are you here?' asked the other man, lowering his voice until it was just a breath of sound, like the gentle rustle of willow in a light breeze.

The professor considered the question objectively. There were so many potential answers. Some of them even had the virtue of being true. He decided on the simplest response.

'*Falun gong*,' he answered even though it was a tiny part of the whole explanation.

Luo Gan had been one of the earliest adherents of *falun gong*. Truthfulness, compassion and forbearance – the three pillars of the movement. It had seemed such a simple yet worthwhile pursuit, manifested in the simplicity of measured exercises and spiritual contemplation. Hardly, one would have thought, capable of controversy. It was something that gave shape and meaning to an otherwise ordinary life teaching at

17

the University of Peking where he was just another professor bewildered by the present generation of students. And he wasn't the only Party member who'd found peace and solace in the movement – his own boss was a devout *falun gong* pupil. The two of them had often gathered with like-minded officials and workers and performed the slow-moving *qigong* exercises on the campus at lunch hour.

But in 1999 the Communist Party decided, some said that the edict was from Jiang Zemin himself, that the *falun gong* movement was too popular and had to be suppressed. With hindsight, the decision was not entirely surprising. Matters of the soul, spirit or faith lay outside the Marxist ideologies of materialism and atheism. And *falun gong* had a spiritual leader, which increased the sense of threat. The movement was outlawed for advocating superstition, creating disturbances and – the last and most serious accusation – jeopardising social stability. It was the same language that had been used during the crackdown at Tiananmen Square a decade earlier.

The yard exercises stopped and Luo Gan did not make eye contact with his boss for two years. He continued his *qigong* exercises in the privacy of his home but he made sure the curtains were drawn.

'Many here are *falun gong*,' agreed his companion. 'You are brave to protest the edicts of the Party.'

'Brave?' asked Luo Gan. 'Or foolish?'

The other man shrugged and then, sensing they had drawn the attention of the guards, returned to swinging his hammer. The professor followed suit, trying to answer his own question in his mind. Brave or foolish? Did it depend on the action or the motive?

He'd woken up that morning three weeks earlier as if it was one just like any other. But instead of going to the faculty office, Luo had dressed in a simple pair of drawstring trousers and white T-shirt and taken the train to Tiananmen Square. He stood all the way, swaying with the motion, lost in the cacophony of underground travel, oblivious to the chatter of other passengers, the music from the headphones wrapped around youthful heads and the whiff of garlic and chilli from a thousand breakfasts. As he emerged with the hordes of tourists from the provinces onto the huge grey rectangle, he'd noted the security men dotted around the square. The other visitors were oblivious, snapping photos in front of the Martyrs' Memorial and the mausoleum that housed Mao's remains. His countrymen gazed up in awe at the vast flagpole from which fluttered the Chinese flag – revolutionary red except for one large star and four small ones in bright yellow, symbolising the Party and the people. Four stars to represent the people was about right, Luo Gan remembered thinking to himself with a grimace. The Communist Party seemed only to have the interests of a tiny elite at heart.

He'd wandered about, trying to find the perfect spot, hoping not to attract the attention of the security personnel until he was good and ready, when his eyes were drawn to the imposing portrait of Chairman Mao above the entrance to the Forbidden City. Luo hurried back underground and used the pedestrian underpass to cross to the other side of the vast thoroughfare. He heard a guide say in English, 'The portrait is replaced with a new one every year or if it is damaged.' He wondered if that was true and whether Chinese tourists were ever told the same thing. He suspected not. It was better if they believed that Mao and his likeness were both impervious to weather or vandals. Luo Gan rode the waves of people carrying umbrellas in all colours – the sun was bright in the sky now – until he was directly under the portrait of Mao. He gazed up at the fleshy smug face, so different from the drawn tired visage he'd glimpsed in the mirror that morning as he brushed his teeth. He turned to face the crowds, none of whom seemed to notice him. He was just another tourist come to pay his respects to China's glorious past. Among a billion people, it was hard to get noticed sometimes.

Slowly, he began the steps of the *qigong*, focusing on the quiet centre of his own body. At first he was ignored. And then he heard a sudden intake of breath and then another. The crowds streaming towards the gates of the Forbidden City stopped and gathered in a semicircle around him instead. He heard the shouts of security guards urging the visitors to keep moving. They hadn't seen him yet. He continued the slow gentle steps, feeling the peace flow through his body like a clear stream down a mountainside. He saw a few mobile phones held up and wondered whether any of the photographers would be brave enough to post pictures of his lonely dissent on the Internet. Luo Gan sensed rather than saw the security police force their way through the crowd. He was grabbed by two uniformed men and flung to the ground. One of them kicked him in a kidney, but he remained alert enough to hear the other warn him not to do it in front of witnesses. They hauled him back to his feet, handcuffed his hands behind his back and frogmarched him towards a police vehicle that had drawn up, sirens screaming, on the main road.

'Will you let them do this?' he asked the crowd.

The people, represented by the four stars on the flag, answered him in deed, quickly moving away, grabbing their children by the arms and turning towards the Forbidden City again. Some used their umbrellas as shields, shutting him from view, from memory. No one wanted to get involved, to get into trouble.

From there to the correctional facility for 're-education through labour' had not taken long.

Luo Gan raised his hammer and smashed a rock into pieces. A shard flew up and cut his cheek and Luo Gan paused to wipe away the blood. Brave or foolish? The truth was that it really didn't matter.

Two

Qing worked on the assembly line for thirteen hours a day with two breaks for meals at the factory canteen, usually a thin soup, rice and a dish of boiled vegetables soaked in soy sauce. She did the work mechanically, ensuring the covers were aligned with the bodies of the calculators, clipping them on and then sending them down the chain to the next woman whose job was to stack the finished product twenty in a box for export. Before her, on the assembly line, were dozens of women adding the component parts to the devices before they came to her. The women worked in silence; the factory floor supervisors disapproved of distracting chatter.

She wore long overalls over her clothes and a pair of Nike shoes that a friend who worked at the shoe factory had obtained for her for a few yuan, a lot less than the foreigners would be paying in their shiny shops in New York and Singapore. Qing's short curly hair, crimped in a salon, with one of her earliest pay cheques, was covered in a plastic cap as per company regulations. She was not sure why. Were the bosses worried that a consumer might discover dandruff in the depths of their 'Made in China' calculator?

It was usually the fresh migrants from the distant provinces who found themselves trapped in the lowest form of employment, assembly line unskilled work. It didn't take long for most of them to learn the ropes and make their escape – usually by developing more sought-after skills, more often by lying about possessing such skills. A factory worker Qing knew had impressed a potential employer at a job mart by speaking a few words of English.

She'd laughed as she packed her things, ready to move up in the world to an office job. 'You know, Qing, he did not understand what I said in English. And that is good because I have no idea what I said either – just a few words I picked up at the language centre!'

In the new China, Qing had realised, it wasn't the skills that mattered but how convincing one was in pretending to have them. She sometimes wondered if people with more important jobs, like surgeons and builders, adopted the same approach. A scary thought but not one she wasted much time on. It wasn't her problem.

As she clipped the covers on, Qing tried to decide what to do. She dreamed of getting a decent job, one that paid good money, perhaps as a filing clerk in an office in Beijing. A clerical job would almost double the wage she had here. Overtime might be paid on time and there would be only four to a dormitory unlike the stinking twelve at this factory. Bliss indeed. And she might have European bosses; everyone knew they were the best. The next were the Americans. Those from

Hong Kong were bad, but the worst were the Chinese themselves. They didn't care about the workers, their pay, the conditions – they were only interested in productivity, efficiency and preventing their employees from leaving for better positions by holding on to their wages and their papers as security.

Despite this, Qing knew she was lucky. There were hardly any factories left in Beijing and she had found work at a small one well outside the 5th Ring Road, next to a manufacturer of local cars, around ten kilometres past the airport. If she had not found this small place, she would have ended up in Dongguan where life was even worse for the rural girls trying to make a living. In Beijing, at least, she was close to her aunt – not many factory girls had the comfort of a relative close by. And, there was every possibility that she would be able to better herself, improve her lot in life, without resorting to lying about her abilities to potential employers.

Qing brushed her fringe out of her eyes with the back of her arm. She really needed to find some time and space to think, to decide what to do with what she knew and what she had seen. She would have to trade shifts and free up some time despite the risk of being caught and sacked. The factory was freezing, air conditioned to prevent damage to the electronics, so her fellow workers would have assumed that her sudden shudder was a product of the cold, not fear. But Qing had felt heavy feet in big boots dance on her grave for a moment.

The bell rang to indicate the end of the shift. The women rose as one and the sudden cackling of human voices reminded her of the hen house at the farm where her mother still collected the eggs and her father worked their half-acre.

Or at least, she assumed they were still doing it, she hadn't called home in a while.

Feeling guilty, maybe even hoping for some comfort from home, she slipped out to the small bare earth yard and extricated her mobile phone from her pocket.

She rang the number of her parents' home and listened to the distant ring. The echo captured the emptiness of the thousands of miles between them.

'Mama, this is Qing.'

'Where have you been? We've been so worried.'

'I'm fine, Mama. I was quite busy for a while and am also looking for a new job with improved conditions.'

'How can you find steady employment if you are ready to throw away every job? If one does not plough, there will be no harvest.'

'But I am still in Beijing.'

'That is good – at least your aunt can keep an eye on you. I hope you visit her every week.'

Qing decided not to mention that she had not seen her mother's older sister for a while. The last time she had been to visit had thrown up her present conundrum.

'Have you found a new job?'

'Not yet. But there are other opportunities. Things will get better soon.' She wondered which of them she was trying to convince.

'Surely you understand that we have great need here? To put your younger brother through middle school is not cheap. But he is a bright boy and deserves a chance.'

'At this moment I don't have much money, but I will send some as soon as I can.'

'Your father is not well, he needs expensive medicine for his cough. The government clinics have all closed down and we must pay for everything. And can you believe the neighbours have a new colour television, such is the generosity of their two daughters who are migrants.'

Her mother was getting to the crux of the matter. Farm families spent most of their time comparing possessions obtained through the toil of their faraway offspring. Success was measured in home extensions, electrical goods and extra helpings of meat at meal times. Qing knew that she had not delivered so far. She felt a stab of resentment at her mother's demands and then suppressed a sigh. She could not blame her parents. It was the only way they knew. Neither of them had been further than fifty miles from the village of their birth. How to explain the big cities, the temptations, the opportunities, the traps? It was impossible.

'Do not worry, Mama. I have a very good method to earn some real money soon and then Papa's cough will be better and you will both watch Chinese soap operas on the biggest colour television money can buy.'

'You are a good and dutiful daughter,' said her mother. Even across the distant line, Qing could hear the higher tone that signalled her improved mood. The factory girl grimaced as she rang off. Why had she been debating her next course of action as if she was one of those rich people who had a choice about what to do in life? The bottom line was the bottom dollar and she would have to seize this unexpected opportunity, however dangerous, with two greedy hands.

*

SQ800. Had the number been chosen because the Chinese believed that the numeral eight was lucky and symbolised good fortune and wealth? Were there any SQ444 flights to China? Singh doubted it. There would have been empty planes on the route as the Chinese words for 'four' and 'death' sounded similar to native ears. In fact, decided Singh as his plane reacted to turbulence like a small boat on stormy seas, he was pretty sure he wouldn't have caught flight 'death' to China either.

'Your Indian vegetarian meal is ready, Inspector Singh.'

The policeman smiled at the stewardess. The Singapore police department was flying him business class and it was a pleasure to find a seat big enough for him to house his posterior comfortably. And who would have expected a curry at thirty-eight thousand feet? Singh's enthusiasm waned when he saw the mountain of chickpeas in front of him. He'd been hoping for more variety – some pickles perhaps, or yogurt. Still, a man who eschewed food was a skinny man and the inspector was certainly not that. He gulped some beer and tucked in, slowly reviewing the rest of his conversation with Superintendent Chen.

'Beijing? The victim was killed in Beijing?' he'd asked. 'Surely you don't think I'd be of any use there! I don't even speak Chinese.'

The Singapore government had run a campaign called Speak Mandarin First. Singh had immediately decided to speak it last. After all, he was not a school-going child to be bullied into memorising an Oriental system of hieroglyphics so that his nation could find favour with the global superpower of the future.

'Believe me, I don't think you're the right man for the job,' said Chen. 'I put forward every single policeman above the rank of sergeant ahead of you.'

'What is the job? Who's dead anyway?'

'Justin Tan – the twenty-three-year-old son of the First Secretary at the Singapore Embassy in China.'

Singh steepled his fingers and stared at his superior. 'How important is the First Secretary?'

'Very important. China is a critical posting.'

'Then why is he getting me?'

'She – Susan Tan.'

'All right – why is *she* getting me?'

Chen didn't pretend to misunderstand. His most successful crime solver was only sent abroad to keep him out of mischief or if a scapegoat was necessary. The fact that trouble, in the form of mysterious corpses, followed him wherever he went was an unhappy coincidence. Singh suspected that Chen half believed that he killed them himself just to have something to do.

'You wouldn't have been my choice –'

'You mentioned that already.'

– 'but the First Secretary demands it and she has the backing of the Ambassador.'

'The "poppadum policeman"?'

'Exactly. Your exploits have been well documented in the press and the First Secretary seems to think that you're the man for the job. She insisted we send you.'

Singh exhaled slowly and licked his pink pouting lower lip. Maybe he shouldn't have been so chuffed that the story of his Indian exploits had been picked up by the international newswires. Not if he was going to be summoned by various Singaporean diplomats to investigate the death of their offspring in foreign parts. Where next? Kazakhstan? Venezuela? North Korea?

'How was her son killed?'

'Bludgeoned to death in some back alley.'

'Wasn't there an investigation?'

'The Chinese police concluded it was the work of unidentified ruffians during the course of a robbery.'

'But the mother is convinced there's more to the story?'

'Yes.'

'So? The mothers are always convinced there's more to the story . . .'

'She's an influential woman at an important post – you're the cavalry.'

Singh picture himself galloping to the rescue astride a horse. Poor horse.

'I don't have to tell you that relations with China are very sensitive right now . . .'

'Why right now?'

'The Chinese authorities are not happy about the bad press Chinese migrants are getting in Singapore.'

'Ahh – the China girls!'

Chen looked surprised that Singh was so well informed about tensions between citizens and newcomers but he nodded. 'Yes – we've had to cut back on people from the mainland coming to Singapore and the Chinese government is offended.'

'Am I on some sort of secondment to the Chinese police?'

'No, this is off the record. The First Secretary is cashing in a lot of favours to get you to China.'

'If it's not official, why are you worried?'

'I'm afraid that you'll somehow find a way to cause a diplomatic incident. Isn't that what you usually do?'

'We aim to please,' said Singh, smiling cheerfully.

'I'm giving you a week,' said Chen, 'and not a minute more.'

Now, as he wiped his plate with a slice of bread to ensure that no drop of gravy went to waste, the inspector regretted that flippant remark. A young Singaporean man had gone to China to die. And now Singh was being sent to find out who had done it. Three weeks too late, in a country he knew nothing about, where he did not speak the language and where people with power and influence would be watching his every move. If he annoyed someone important, they'd probably send him off to a work camp and he'd spend the rest of his life breaking rocks with a pick and eating Chinese food. This case was precisely the sort that he would have crossed several streets to avoid. Maybe crossed several streets, skipped lunch, the accompanying cold beer and even forsaken his post-prandial cigarette.

Still, he decided, closing his heavy lids and gently letting sleep claim him, all he had to do was back up the official Chinese version. Killed by unidentified ruffians in the course of a robbery. It sounded perfectly plausible to Singapore's leading criminal detective. After all, who would have a motive to kill the son of the First Secretary? This Justin Tan had been an unlucky young man. Not the first, and certainly not the last. He'd be in and out of Beijing in twenty-four hours if he stuck to the script.

*

Anthony Tan, husband of the First Secretary, could still remember a time when the future had looked bright. A time when his son was still alive and he'd been on the cusp of the sort of financial breakthrough that would have allowed him to hold his head up, to stand tall as a man and not merely be the husband of a successful woman.

'Where are you going?' asked his wife, the disdainful tone a provocation in itself.

'I have a meeting.'

'With whom?'

'Do I ask you which country's diplomats you are meeting? No! So why must you know whom I see?'

'Because your business dealings have the capacity to embarrass me as well as the Singapore government.'

'That is only your prejudice – my work allows Singapore companies to take part in the Chinese economic miracle. I do more for Singapore interests in China than you do.' It was an old argument. Both protagonists uttered their lines by rote but much of the feeling had gone. That was what happened when you lost a son.

'Many of the business practices here do no pass the smell test. You should be careful which projects you become associated with.'

'I become "associated", as you say, with the profitable ventures.' Crooked fingers traced the inverted commas.

'That cannot be your only criteria. Some of the Chinese parties are basically criminals, pure and simple.'

'Entrepreneurs and nationalists,' he retorted.

It was too much of a clue for someone of his wife's insight. 'You are going to see Dai Wei, aren't you?'

'Why do you object to him? He's a brilliant deputy mayor of Beijing. He's cracking down on organised crime in the city. The people view him as a hero.'

'When a turnip is pulled out of the ground, some soil will inevitably come with it,' was his wife's cryptic response.

Anthony Tan walked out of the residence without bothering to respond. Her suggestion that Dai Wei would eventually be tainted by association with the same people he was cracking down on was the common view among the supercilious elite. The First Secretary's husband took the Embassy limo that was assigned to his wife. Strictly, he was not permitted to use the vehicle for non-consular activity but he didn't really care. Who was going to stop him anyway? Everyone knew that rules were made to be bent if not broken. The only martinet was his wife – she, who saw life in black and white. No shades of grey. No compromise.

Anthony Tan's meeting with Dai Wei was at his business offices, the penthouse of a gleaming new building in the heart of the business district. He knew it was his last chance to persuade Dai Wei to play along. The question was – would it work? It had to. The money he'd borrowed from the money-lender to grease the wheels was overdue. And Anthony Tan knew that his life would not be worth a bucket of warm spit if he did not get the deputy mayor to fast track the planning permit, receive his commission from the developers and pay the fellow back.

The Singaporean stepped out of the car, walked to the elevator at a slightly heightened pace and adjusted his tie in the mirrored walls. He looked, he decided, like a man who knew what he was doing. A dark, conservative suit, the hair well-combed and trimmed, the good-looking face, thinner than it had been before Justin's death and lined enough to suggest maturity, gravitas. There was no doubt about it in Anthony Tan's mind – he belonged in the big time. He exited the lift, patted his hair down and announced himself to the secretary cum supermodel at the front desk. He wondered whether she could type or whether she was purely for show. He suspected the latter. Dai Wei was famous for having an eye for beautiful things – his wife was a perfect example. Anthony Tan bit back his resentment that a short, pushy man like Dai Wei should have as many badges of success as an enthusiastic Boy Scout while he, Anthony, blessed with so many natural gifts, was reduced to the role of supplicant.

'Mr Dai will see you in ten minutes,' said the supermodel, smiling sweetly to reveal implausibly perfect teeth. 'He's on a conference call.'

Great. He would have to kick his heels and pretend he didn't mind. It was the privilege of the powerful to keep lesser beings waiting and Anthony knew from experience that Dai Wei was a wielder of power who enjoyed every petty display.

'Would you like coffee or tea?'

'Tea,' he snapped. His nerves were already getting the better of him.

In a few minutes, tea arrived on a tray carried by another employee, this one dressed in dark trousers and a white shirt with a small bow tie at his neck. Anthony acknowledged the drink with a curt nod, scalded his lips on his first sip and tried to decide what he was going to say to the man who held his future in his hands. Despite the financial hole he was in and the fact that Dai Wei was the one who had wielded the shovel, he knew he would have to proceed with extreme caution.

The heavy door behind the secretary opened and Dai Wei himself stood there in his platform shoes and Italian suit. Socialism for the twenty-first century.

'Anthony, very good of you to visit. Come in. Come in!' The bonhomie was theatrical and the smile did not reach his eyes.

'Thank you for making time to see me.'

'I always have time for a good friend.'

He led the way into the office and Anthony blinked at the gold and red interior. They sat down, not on the sofas like the first time, but behind the big desk and across from it. He remembered how his wife did not bother to come round her desk to speak to him either. His fists clenched and he had to will his hands open again.

'So what do you need from me, an important man like you?'

'I was wondering how things were going with my proposal?' said Anthony. 'My backers are getting anxious.'

'Your backers are getting anxious – I can understand that. But you know these things take time – Rome wasn't built in a day!' He added this last in English, smiling with pleasure at his use of an idiomatic expression.

'Ahhh . . . but we all know that the Chinese are better and harder workers than the Romans,' said Anthony.

'Unfortunately, it is not as easy as it once was to issue permits for new projects,' explained Dai Wei. 'The people are starting to protest in large numbers at being forcibly moved from their homes. It is always on these uncontrolled websites – sometimes even in the *People's Daily*.'

'The consortium backing this venture will build the best shopping mall in all of China. It will be the biggest, contain the leading brands and be a wonder of the world.'

'That is capitalist talk. We are a socialist nation – the people come first.'

Anthony bit his tongue.

'As you know, I am leading a Maoist revival here in Beijing to ensure that the people participate in the growth and success of China!'

'Your efforts are an inspiration to everyone,' said Anthony. He'd have liked to punch the other man. His ghastly choirs and orchestras playing tunes from the Mao era, his distribution of flyers with Mao revolutionary slogans, his insistence that television programming contained suitably laudatory historical segments and not just games shows and dating shows – all an attempt to cement his own grip on power.

'But you need the land,' pointed out Dai Wei.

'Yes, we need the land and it has to be the spot we identified because of its location in a high population area of Beijing,' agreed Anthony.

'It is even more difficult for me to issue permits for the *hutongs* because they are those who say they are part of our history.'

'The imperialist past – not the great socialist era.'

'That is very true,' said Dai Wei.

'So can you help?' asked Anthony, the edge of desperation in his voice like a suicide's ledge.

*

35

Qing sat on the kerb, knees demurely pressed together in tight blue jeans, waiting for the bus that would take her into the city. She was resting because she knew that she would probably have to stand all the way to the centre of Beijing. There were a lot of people who wanted to experience the big city on the weekends. She had a half-day off that Sunday and had traded the other half to a girl who was keen to maximise her working hours. That meant she had one full day. Enough to go shopping, meet a friend, have a cheap meal, have her nails and hair done. Not that she was going to do any of those things. She still felt guilty after her call with her mother. The family was depending on her and she had let them down. Tempted by what the city had to offer, she had spent hard-earned money that was earmarked for home.

She remembered a conversation with a senior worker at the factory back in Dongguan where she had stood twelve hours a day sticking the eyes on teddy bears. She had learned to hate the soft toys, destined for some privileged child's bedroom. She had never had such a thing in her life! And the glue fumes made her feel nauseous. Despite this, she had waited for payday with bated breath and received her small wage – less deposits, payment for her cot in the dormitory, lunch money and other miscellaneous items.

'Where are you going?' asked the older girl who had the top bunk and was lazily painting red onto her pouting lips with the use of a small hand mirror.

'To send money to my family,' she replied.

'You newcomers are all the same.'

'What do you mean?'

'Sending your hard-earned money home. Why should you do it? Are you their slave?'

Qing was troubled by the mockery she heard in the other girl's voice.

'You know what I say to my family?' she continued.

'What is that?' asked Qing.

'I say that if you want this money, there is a train that will bring you from Yunan province right here to Dongguan. Then you too can earn the same.'

Qing had wanted to protest but could not find the words to contradict the worldly creature now rummaging under the bunk for high-heeled boots.

'What do you use your money for then?' asked Qing.

Her friend held out her hands so Qing could see the painted nails, and the legs so she could admire the knee-high boots. 'I buy myself nice things so I look pretty and can find a husband who is not too short, at least one hundred and seventy centimetres or "need not apply"!' She laughed at her own joke but Qing felt a frisson of worry for her younger brother whom she loved very much but who was still shy of that magic number that would make him desirable to both the women and employers of China.

'So you see, I am investing my money in my future!'

Qing had learned to spend money on her clothes and hair, on her nails and shoes, pushing any sense of guilt to the back of her mind and learning to live in the moment.

In the distance, Qing saw the bus approaching and leaped to her feet. She had no intention of being forced to wait for the next one however many old women and children she had to trample to get on board. For some reason, the bus was not as full as usual and she found a seat towards the back next to a young man whom she instantly dismissed from her mind, despite his meaningful smile, because his teeth were crooked and his breath smelled. Her plan was to spend the day with her aunt in Beijing and decide how to maximise the knowledge that she had. Qing was quite sure that if she played her cards right, she would be able to send money home for her brother and parents as well as pretty herself up until she was of interest to young men less hideous than this fellow next to her. For once, she had the opportunity to obtain enough cash that she did not always have to make difficult choices. She smiled to herself at the thought and settled back for the ride to town.

The airport gave Singh his first inkling that he had stepped outside his comfort zone. Instead of queuing for the train, a horde of people pushed past him just as the doors opened. He was left clutching his small case to his chest as the train drew away from the platform. The policeman gritted his teeth. He would have to do better than that if he was to reach baggage claim. He sat down and waited for the next train, noting the sign that read, RELAX – TRAIN COMES EVERY 3 MINUTES. Easier said than done if one had to physically battle to get on. The next time, however, he was more successful, using his case and his bulk to achieve access. The inspector permitted himself a small smile. He was learning quickly. The question was – would he be such a quick study when it came to investigating this murder? In his own experience, painfully earned, a policeman out of jurisdiction was a fish out of water. And Superintendent Chen had only given him a week. He reminded himself that the Chinese police were most likely correct in their conclusion. He wasn't really on a mission to investigate a murder, but to comfort a mother.

The immigration queue was long but efficient and he whiled away the time reading billboards that mostly seemed to feature the Olympics, now some years past and various ancient buildings like the Summer Palace and Great Wall.

He dragged his small wheelie bag out through the glass sliding doors that separated passengers from those waiting for them. A smart young man in a long-sleeved, well-ironed blue shirt held a sign with his name on it, correctly spelled. Or at least the English bit was correctly spelled. He had no idea about the Mandarin. He looked at the squiggles. He assumed it was phonetic. Not that it helped.

'Inspector Singh?' asked the young man. The policeman would have been more impressed at his acumen if he hadn't been the only Sikh at the airport.

'Yes.'

'My name is Benson. I have instructions to take you straight to the Embassy of Singapore. It's in Chaoyang.'

'Certainly,' he agreed.

'Let me take your bag.'

Singaporean accent – did the Embassy import drivers as well? That seemed a waste of taxpayer dollars. Singh wondered if he should write to his MP.

He sat back and decided that such a smartly dressed and well-spoken young man was likely to be some junior member of the staff rather than merely a chauffeur.

'You know the First Secretary?' he asked, once he had

bisected his middle with the reassuring seat belt. They were overtaken aggressively on either side by taxis with their suspension a few inches off the ground. His own driver weaved between lanes like a fighter pilot avoiding enemy fire.

'Susan Tan?'

'Yes.'

'I'm taking you to see her now.' Benson noticed Singh flinch as a van veered to close for comfort. 'Takes a while to get used to the driving in Beijing,' he explained. 'Shanghai is even worse.'

'Let's not go there then,' growled Singh, whose life had flashed before his eyes three times already. A mosaic of hot curries and cold beers punctuated by murder.

'Tell me about Susan Tan,' he demanded, more to distract himself than anything.

'What would you like to know, sir?'

'Anything and everything.'

'She's been in Beijing for two years. She's married and has two children.' He corrected himself. 'One child.'

'Her son, Justin, was killed ... you know about that?' demanded Singh.

'Yes, sir. We were all very shocked.'

'Who's "we"?'

'The staff at the Embassy.'

They were now stuck in traffic, rows of stationary cars and frustrated drivers as far as the eye could see. 'Bad traffic,' grunted Singh.

'It's always like this, sir.'

All things considered, the policeman felt safer when they were inching forwards. There was less likelihood of becoming roadkill. On the other hand, he'd need the toilet soon. He noted the number of luxury vehicles. The Chinese economic miracle was clogging up the streets.

'What happened to Justin?' he asked.

'He was attacked by a bunch of ruffians . . . they beat him to death. Apparently it was a robbery gone wrong.'

Not a pleasant way to go – terrifying, agonising and always the knowledge of how it was going to end.

'Gone wrong?'

'Nothing was taken.'

'Is that sort of thing common in Beijing?'

'It is very rare for foreigners to be targeted.'

'They might not have known he was foreign? He's Chinese after all.'

'The locals can always tell, sir.'

Singh remembered Mrs Chong the neighbour. She seemed to have no difficulty distinguishing between China girls and the rest.

'So Justin was just an unfortunate young man?'

'It seems that way, sir.'

'So why does the mother think there's more to it?'

Benson drummed his fingers on the steering wheel as if considering his answer. At last, he said, 'I guess it is difficult for the family to accept what happened . . .'

The inspector nodded his great head. That was the crux of the matter. A grief-stricken family did not want to believe that their boy's death was nothing more than very bad luck.

'We're here! This is the Singapore Embassy,' exclaimed Benson, as if they had suddenly come upon one of the Seven Wonders of the World.

Singh rolled down the window and stared at the plain three-storey building with dark windows, obscured to some extent by trees and a high wall. A policeman stood to attention directly in front of the gate, narrowed eyes watching the car as if he intended to sacrifice his life rather than allow ingress.

'It's big,' remarked Singh.

'There are staff residences as well,' explained Benson.

He parked the car and opened Singh's door even before he'd managed to locate the seat belt ejector. Benson waved his hand with a flourish as if welcoming Singh onto Embassy grounds – 'some corner of a foreign field' that was forever Singapore? It didn't have quite the same romantic appeal. And the building was almost entirely lacking in character. Mind you, wasn't that what foreigners said about Singapore?

The inspector extricated himself with some difficulty from the car, wished that there had been time to supplement his breakfast on the plane with a snack at the airport and mentally girded himself to deal with the grieving mother.

Luo Gan looked up at the sky and decided it was around eleven o'clock in the morning, the time of his original arrest at Tiananmen Square a few weeks earlier – he'd already lost count of the exact number of days. He squinted up at the sun, feeling the crow's feet tighten around his eyes. Luo Gan carefully placed the hammer with its dusty worn head by his feet, stood up and walked away from it at a slow deliberate pace. He knew that numerous pairs of eyes, guards and prisoners alike, were focused on him – he was the rock in an eddy of work. They knew what was coming because he had done this every day that he had been well enough to return to the quarry after the beatings. In his mind, he could hear screams, shouts, a few coherent words begging for mercy, for life, and then a sudden silence that lasted mere seconds but felt like an infinity. He didn't know how it had happened, perhaps Justin had been trying to call for help, perhaps the 'last dialled' number had been accidentally depressed when he was attacked. All he knew was that he'd listened in on the slow death of a young man.

Luo Gan began the movements that formed the opening sequence of the *falun gong* spiritual exercises. He heard the guards shouting and their heavy-booted steps as they ran towards him but he ignored them. Around him, he saw other *falun gong* prisoners follow his lead for the first time and he felt pity and admiration for them. They were inspired by his courage in defying the authorities but only he knew that his own so-called bravery was built on a foundation of guilt and remorse.

By the time the guards reached them, more than half the prisoners were performing the ritual movements so that they looked collectively like an ill-trained ballet troupe. The other prisoners, petty thieves, prostitutes and corrupt officials, stood and watched in silence. Luo Gan knew there would be hell to pay. He'd been a rebel and that was bad enough. But now he was a leader.

Three

Susan Tan stood up as Singh came in and walked around the bureau towards him. As she reached him, she held out her hand and shook his. A firm handshake, almost masculine in the manner it conveyed decisiveness. Good body language all round, thought Singh – not a woman who needed protection or the implied authority of a big desk. She was not what he'd expected. Somehow, he'd assumed the First Secretary would look like a pen-pusher – small, bespectacled, bookish – or like a middle-aged headmistress of an all girls' school: matching twinset, skirt just below the knees, pearls, pursed lips and face powder. Susan Tan was a tall – almost six feet – ethnically Chinese woman who was also stick thin. She wore a trouser suit in some sort of shimmering grey material and a snowy white shirt. Her shoes added unnecessary height as far as he was concerned. She would have towered over the inspector from Singapore without them. Her dark hair was greying at the temples in a matching shade to her clothes. Her jaw was firmly set and dark shadows suggested that all was not well in her world. She must have been formidable once. Now she just looked exhausted.

'Inspector Singh, you're not what I expected.'

'Madam First Secretary?' said Singh, ignoring the comment. After all, what could he do? Apologise for being short, fat, scruffy and turbaned? For having chickpea curry on his tie? For wearing white trainers instead of the sort of glossy black shoes favoured by this woman and Superintendent Chen? Besides, he'd just come to the same conclusion about her.

'Call me Susan,' said the woman and ushered Singh to a section of the office where there was a deep sofa and an armchair around a glass table. Coffee and a plate of *paus* were ready and Singh fought the urge to grab one.

'Thank you for agreeing to come, Inspector Singh.'

Singh did not respond. He'd been strong-armed into coming to Beijing so it would be mendacious to claim credit for the decision.

A hint of a smile disappeared quickly. 'I don't suppose you had much choice?'

'I'm happy to do what I can,' said Singh cautiously.

'But you're not sure what help you can be . . .'

'Exactly.'

'My son deserves justice.'

'Tell me what happened,' asked Singh mildly. He sensed this woman might shatter into a million metaphorical pieces.

'Justin joined us here in China a few months back. He'd just completed his National Service in Singapore.'

At the raised eyebrow from Singh, she walked over to his desk, flipped open a large diary and said, 'Three months two days exactly.'

'What was he doing here?'

'He was attending a course at the University of Peking to brush up on his Mandarin and learn a bit more about Chinese history. He was due in Oxford to do PPE ...'

'PPE?'

'Politics, philosophy and economics. The same course I did many years back. It is good preparation for the diplomatic service.'

'So he was destined to follow in your footsteps?'

'He didn't seem that sure about what he wanted. He obtained a deferment from Oxford for a year while he tried to figure it out.'

'And you were comfortable with that?'

'I wasn't delighted,' said Susan, her clear brown eyes meeting Singh's. 'I thought it was high time he got on with things. But he seemed happy here in China and was reluctant to leave.' She closed her eyes for a long moment as if the memories were imprinted on the insides of her eyelids. 'If I'd forced him to go, this wouldn't have happened.'

'You can't blame yourself,' said Singh automatically. How many grieving mothers had he spoken to in a lifetime of hunting murderers? More than he cared to remember. All of them, without fail, found some way to blame themselves. Did it make it easier to do that? Was it better to assume some fault than to imagine that one's child was a victim of arbitrary fate, of capricious gods?

Susan Tan was struggling to master her emotions. It showed

in the way her jaw was working although she remained dry-eyed.

'What else can you tell me?'

'His body was found in a back street that runs along a *hutong* in Dazhalan Xi Jie, south of Tiananmen Square.'

'*Hutong?*'

'A sort of old Chinese residential area. Courtyards, homes, shops, narrow streets. Dating back a few dynasties. A lot of them have been torn down but a few remain. '

Singh nodded and tried to look as if he'd known all this beforehand.

'He was beaten to death,' she continued. And then, as if she expected scepticism, she added, 'That's what the autopsy report said. I have a translated copy for you.'

Singh nodded his thanks. 'And the Chinese police?'

'They said it was a robbery gone wrong – he was just in the wrong place at the wrong time.'

'And you accept that?'

'No,' her voice was loud, angry. 'I don't accept that at all.'

'Why not?'

'Well, for starters nothing was stolen.'

'They might have been frightened off before they had a chance to rob him?' suggested Singh.

'They had time to beat him to death but not to rob him?'

'It doesn't take as long as you might think to kill someone.'

She flinched at his words and the hairs on Singh's neck stood up along the base of his turban. Suddenly, it was as if Justin was a presence in the room, a wraith come to demand that the policeman from Singapore do his duty and not be so keen to accept the official version of events. It did not take

47

long to kill someone. But she was right, it took even less time to make off with a wallet.

'Do you have a picture of him?'

Susan Tan went to the desk. There was a framed shot on her table that had been facing away from Singh, for the eyes of the woman who sat behind the desk. She picked it up, hesitated, opened a drawer and recovered a file, and then walked over to Singh. She handed over the picture and Singh took the heavy frame. Justin Tan had been a handsome young man. One day he might have developed the gravitas of his mother, but in this picture he looked like a youth with the world at his feet, and as if he knew it. The grin was mischievous; the army cap pushed back, the green fatigues neat but a couple of buttons undone revealing a shadowed hairless chest. In uniform, but not constrained by it. He must have been a handful for a commanding officer. On the other hand, decided Singh, looking at the open, handsome face, he might have inspired loyalty. There was gravity about the eyes despite the wide smile. Officer material? Maybe, but it was not something Singh intended to extrapolate from a well-taken photograph. Although there was a strong physical resemblance to his mother, the open trusting expression was diametrically opposite to the shuttered face of the woman with him.

'The picture was taken the last time I was in Singapore, just before his term in the army was over,' said Susan.

'So he looked like this?'

'His hair had grown out a bit, but yes, that's how he looked the day before he died more or less.'

She opened the file and extricated another photo that she

dropped on the table between them. 'And this is how he looked the day after.'

Singh picked up the picture. He was not squeamish by nature and not even violent death in all its bloody glory could upset his equilibrium. Even so, he felt a pang of regret for a young life taken, and with such brutality. Justin's face was puffy and bruised. Both eyes were swollen shut. His cheeks were raised and darkened along the ridge of his cheekbones. His nose was badly lacerated. A patch of blood along his hair-line suggested that a fistful of hair had been yanked out. He would have been better off maintaining the army crew cut, there would have been no grip for his assailants then. Only his jaw, by accident rather than design, was unmarked and Singh saw that the son had a cleft chin. He looked over at the mother and saw that she shared the same feature.

'Are you really trying to tell me that that –' she gestured at the photo – 'was a robbery gone wrong?'

Singh put the picture back down carefully. He leaned back against the sofa and felt a sharp pain between his shoulder blades. Even in business class, a night flight was uncomfortable and he was too old for it – and much too old for this.

'The level of violence does seem excessive,' he agreed.

'So it can't just have been a robbery gone wrong.'

'There are other factors that might have played a part,' said Singh, as gently as possible.

'What do you mean?'

'I agree that the crime looks disproportionately violent but there are potential explanations for that of which the most likely are drugs or alcohol.'

Her shoulders slumped but she did not give any other hint

that she had taken his words on board. Was it because she recognised the truth of what he was saying or was she disappointed that he was toeing the official line?

'Do you know what I was doing the night he was killed?' she asked. 'I was hosting a function here at the Embassy. Can you believe it? I was at a party while my son was being ... assaulted ... murdered.'

'What do you want me to do?' he asked, although he could guess what the answer would be. It was always the same request, demand, order, plea – from the bereaved. This mother, unusual in so many other ways, did not break the mould.

'Find out who killed my son ... and why.'

Fu Xinghua was tall for a Chinese and powerfully built, nature having been enhanced by his own efforts. His suit was well cut and showed off the breadth of his shoulders and his tapered waist. The long overcoat he affected, a summer cotton but dark and with just enough buttons and flaps to suggest the military, flapped open as he strode forward. He did not break step but he did glance sideways into a shop window to check out the profile he presented. His lips thinned with satisfaction. It was impressive. And it needed to be. He had tipped off the press that the 'strike black' task force, set up to take on organised crime syndicates, the 'black' to which his campaign referred, was about to go into action again.

The policeman did not look back, but he knew that he was flanked on either side and behind by a cadre of officers, all wearing similar trench coats, marching in step, their boots stamping a rhythm on the pavement. He'd designed the coats and boots himself. He wanted his special force to have a distinct identity from the rest of the force. There had been some discontent when he had set out to do this – 'are we policemen or fashion designers?' – but he had gotten his own way in the end. He usually did. And few would deny that his task force had been powerful, effective and most importantly, popular. This last was in no small part due to his effort to manipulate his, and their, image for popular consumption.

His men were armed and ready to arrest the wealthy real estate mogul, Wong Kar Wai, who was in their sights that day. He had a filthy reputation and no tears would be shed when he was removed from circulation. As he approached, Fu could hear sirens as the police cars converged on the building. In the air, there was the regular thump of the police helicopter's rotors. The sky was clear and blue. Unusual in Beijing, usually so mired in filth that the air was like beef noodle soup. It was perfect weather for a televised confrontation. Fu didn't mind in the least that he was tipping off his quarry with their noisy arrival. This was another opportunity to burnish his image as China's leading crime fighter, a man unafraid to take on the criminal elements on behalf of the people. Even with his public profile and general popularity it was a dangerous business. Crooks in China were often well connected to powerful figures in government. Indeed, they were often *the* powerful figures in government.

Fu knew he would not have succeeded half as well if he didn't have political cover and support. The deputy mayor of Beijing, Dai Wei, was the political will behind his crusade against the Chinese mafia. What was the expression the press used for the two to them? 'Singing red' and 'smashing black' –

a reference to their Mao-era revivalism and crusade against organised crime. Fu was a policeman from the ranks who had hitched his wagon to a rising star. On his own, he was nothing more than another ambitious copper from the provinces with no real prospects for advancement. Dai Wei on the other hand was from the right sort of background. His father had been a right-hand man of Mao before he was purged and later rehabilitated. So he was a princeling, with all the power, prestige and privilege that suggested. Fu's lip curled – these fellows like Dai Wei were useful, but they would never understand what it was to be a success through sheer guts and hard work.

The policeman arrived at the front of the building just as the police vehicles converged, sirens wailing, tyres squealing. He saw the flash of cameras and suppressed a smile; it would not do to compromise his image as the hard man of the Beijing police force. Fu shrugged off his coat and a flunky caught it before it hit the floor. It was a well-practised move. He raised a hand and another member of the team handed him a loudspeaker. He held it up almost reverently, pausing as silence descended over the waiting crowds, all of them eagerly anticipating the denouement.

'Wong Kar Wai, we know you're in there. Come out now and face justice!'

There was silence from within the building, a shiny three-storey structure encased almost entirely in glass. It faced a crossroads and the glass sheath was probably the result of advice from a feng shui expert. The new generation of Chinese billionaires could afford to fund frivolous projects to protect their wealth even from the vagaries of luck.

'We know that you are an enemy of the people – stealing their land for your rich-man projects. Come out now.'

Still silence.

'This is your last chance, Wong Kar Wai. My men will enter the building in ten seconds – starting from now.' He raised his hand and dropped it like an official beginning a race.

'Ten, nine, eight ...' He could sense the anticipation in the police, the media and the gathering crowd of spectators drawn to the spectacle.

'Seven, six ...'

He did not speed up or change his tone. He could have auditioned for a talking clock.

'Five, four, three ...'

The glass door was pushed open hurriedly and a massively overweight man appeared flanked on either side by beefy characters in tight suits. Again, Fu suppressed a smile. The trio were almost a caricature of criminality. It was why he had picked this particular dodgy businessman for the big show-down. He'd known instinctively it would play well for the cameras. There was no point going for the skinny conmen who looked like accountants. This way, their crackdown on organised crime stayed in the headlines.

'You are under arrest, Wong. Tell your men to go back inside. No one will be hurt as long as you show good sense.'

In China, food was often equated with wealth. Wong must have spent the better part of the last decade on ten course dinners. Fu straightened his shoulders to preserve and emphasise the contrast with the grotesque creature he had come to arrest.

'This time you have gone too far, Fu.' The fat man had to

shout to be heard – he didn't have a loudspeaker and it diminished his authority.

'I'm just doing the people's work, Wong.'

'Do you know who you're messing with? Am I just a common criminal that you should come here with this –' his hand swept a wide arc – 'this circus?'

'A corrupt real estate mogul – you steal from the people and you destroy those that stand in your way. Why should you expect to be treated better than a common criminal?'

'You're nothing but a jumped-up policeman dancing to Dai Wei's tune! Do you think that you will get away with this conduct? I have many friends, even in the Politburo – all of them can send you to work on traffic junctions in Mongolia if I raise my finger!'

'I will do what is right,' insisted Fu. Inside, he was jubilant. This ridiculous man was playing into his hands, threatening to use his influence to find a way out. It was precisely that sort of behaviour that was inflaming public opinion and turning Fu and Dai Wei into the people's heroes.

'Out of respect for your seniority, I will give you one last chance to come out here and surrender. Otherwise, I will have no choice but to use force,' said Fu, authority once again magnified through the megaphone.

The gross piece of flesh in front of him was sweating through his suit. The men on either side looked uneasy – from where they were standing, the odds probably didn't look that good. The semicircle of men with gun and cars and flashing lights were an intimidating sight. Just like something out of an American movie, Fu's favourite form of entertainment. The policeman didn't doubt that the press was hoping that Wong would not give up easily. It made for better copy if there was a gun battle.

'You and I are both pawns in a great game, Fu.'

'My only desire is to serve the people in the fight against black,' replied Fu.

Out of the corner of his eye he saw the glint of sunlight on metal. He stared up at the roof of the building and saw the gleam again. This time he had no doubt what it was. The bright afternoon sun was reflecting off a gun barrel. There was a sniper on the roof.

'If you want to fight against black, my friend, you should look to your own soul and that of your boss,' screamed Wong, suddenly losing control and waving his fist in the direction of Fu and the police cordon.

The words had barely dissipated into the hush when the first shot was fired.

'I'll need to speak to your husband, of course, and Justin's sister.'

'Why? Why should you need to speak to my husband?'

The inspector looked at her, eyebrows forming two arches. It was interesting that she was more concerned about him speaking to the husband than the daughter. 'If you want me to find out what happened to your son, I'm going to have to speak to everyone he was close to, had a relationship with, anyone who might know what he's been up to this last three months in China.'

'Correct me if I'm wrong, Inspector Singh, but it sounds as if you're suggesting that my son was in some way *responsible* for what happened to him.'

Singh couldn't help admiring the First Secretary. The woman combined sarcasm, punctilious politeness and an over-all air of threat to perfection. No doubt she was a dab hand at commercial negotiations and bilateral trade deals. But she needed to leave the murder investigation to a pro.

'You have a choice, Mrs Tan. Either you accept that your son was the victim of an unprovoked attack, a victim of the fates, or you decide to look into the matter further with my help. If you choose the latter course, then you must under-stand that I decide what's relevant or not.'

There was a silence while Susan Tan debated the options as they had been presented. The inspector was mildly sur-prised that it should take her so long to make up her mind. She'd dragged Singh all the way to China to find answers. But now she was hesitant. There was only one possible explan-ation. The family had secrets. But Susan Tan was going to have to accept that a murder investigation was not laser-like in its intensity, following a certain path to the truth. It was a bright white beam that lit up hidden corners and dark cran-nies where the family skeletons were hidden.

'Very well, I understand what you're saying. I'll arrange access to whoever you think is necessary, including Anthony and Jemima.'

She opened her mouth to continue and then closed it again. The expression slowly ebbed away from her face until she was like those terracotta statues of Qing Dynasty soldiers. Singh waited, curious to see what the woman would say next. A request to keep discoveries confidential? A warning not to stray too far from his remit of finding a murderer?

In the end the diplomat thought the better of any of these

options. Not that Singh would have complied. His loyalty in a murder investigation was always and only to the victim.

Instead, she asked, 'What else do you need?'

'Access to his friends and teachers at the university.' Singh was ticking off his requirements on his fingers. 'Any girlfriend?'

'There was someone, I doubt it was serious. I'll see if I can find out who she was.'

Not a mother who felt threatened by the other women in her son's life.

'And the crime scene, of course,' he continued.

'It's been more than three weeks since Justin was killed. I've been back there a couple of times – there's not much to see.'

'Why would you go back to the place where your son was killed?'

'I don't know – I just feel drawn back there … if I just stand there … just stand there and look up and down the street, up at the sky, somehow, I'll get answers.'

'That's precisely why I need to go there even if the trail has grown cold,' he said.

'It speaks to you?'

'Sometimes.'

'It's a small junction, narrow streets with courtyards, not wide enough for a car. There are *hutongs* that have become tourist attractions, designer shops and bars for tourists, but this one is just an old-style, cramped, grubby dwelling place in a poor neighbourhood. I can't imagine what Justin was doing there in the small hours of the morning.'

'I'd like to see for myself.'

'You'll need an escort or you'll spend most of your time in

Beijing asking for directions. Your driver from this morning, Benson, will assist you. He's an intern here – learning the ropes before he goes into the diplomatic service.'

'And a translator,' said Singh. He had a sudden flashback to his time investigating the murder of a witness at the war crimes tribunal in Phnom Penh. He'd had a translator then, Chhean. He suppressed a smile at the memory of the stocky creature with the enormous self-confidence who had not hesitated to pursue any line of questioning as she saw fit regardless of his views of the matter. He added quickly, 'Someone who'll do what he's told.'

Susan raised her head and met his eyes defiantly as if she was expecting him to protest her next comment. 'I have asked an ex-policeman from the Beijing police force, Li Jun, to assist you.'

So he was going to be furnished with a babysitter cum spy. No big surprise – Singh would have done the same in her position.

'I look forward to meeting him.'

'But first we should get you to a hotel. I'm sure you need to freshen up and get something to eat. The red eye from Singapore can be draining.'

For a moment, Singh thought she was suggesting some form of conjunctivitis and he rubbed his eyes with both knuckles. Then he realised the diplomat was talking about the flight. 'Yes,' he agreed, 'I need a shower.' No need to mention the cigarette and room service.

'I'll have your Chinese escort pick you up at –' she glanced at her watch – 'eleven.'

Singh managed to keep the grimace off his face. That was

barely two hours. Susan Tan was letting him know in no uncertain terms that he was on a short lease. So be it – he had a murder to investigate.

'He is dead now but still you cling to him!'

The tone was accusing but the voice betrayed an underlying need. The young couple stood under the arc of a weeping willow just inside the ornate traditional gates that marked the entrance to Peking University.

'It is too soon,' whispered the girl, her voice heavy with tears.

'I understand that you are feeling his loss but he was never right for you!'

Dao Ming wanted to lash out, to say that it was Wang Zhen who had never been right for her despite the shower of gifts and the expensive restaurants. She had been this man's trophy, worn with the same pride as his original Adidas shoes and Tag Heuer watch from the shiny modern shops in Sanlitun district. Not for him – the fakes and 'third shift' products from the Silk Market. He was the son of privilege, a princeling, a high cadre child. There were so many nicknames in China for that whiff of privilege carried like a birthright.

'What could he give you that I can't?'

'It isn't about what he gave me, Wang Zhen. It's about how he made me feel.'

The boy frowned as if the words were blows and she suspected that they were. What she did not believe was that she was hurting his heart, she only had weapons to damage his pride.

'We were so good together. Everyone said so!'

She almost smiled as he betrayed his youth. 'Everyone said so' – that was his proof that their former relationship had been a success. It was true that, outwardly, they had looked like the ultimate student couple. The scion of a powerful family and a girl widely regarded as being one of the most beautiful and smartest on campus, the child of a leading if troublesome intellectual.

But then Justin had come along with his wide grin and irreverent spirit, so different from the mainland Chinese boys, and he had made her laugh. Made her feel needed. Made her feel special. And she had walked away from Wang Zhen without a second thought. She should have known it was never going to be that simple. These children of the powerful did not like it when their toys were taken away. Justin had never said but she was sure the two men had argued, maybe even come to blows over her.

Wang Zhen grabbed her by both shoulders, his grip so tight that it hurt.

'Let me go!'

'You belong to me. Now that he is gone you should return to your rightful place.'

'I don't belong to anyone. That's your whole problem, right there. You think of me as another trophy, someone to make you look good. Justin just wanted me to be happy.'

He slapped her suddenly and hard and then took a step back as if shocked by his own behaviour. As the tears rolled down her face, she covered her flaming cheek with a hand and warded him off with the other.

'I'm sorry, Dao Ming. I didn't mean to do that. I was just

so jealous for a second – it's because I love you, surely you can see that?'

'I don't mean to hurt your feelings, Wang Zhen. You insist that you really care for me. But –' her voice cracked into a sob that rested on the humid air between them – 'I know it hurts you to hear me say it but Justin was my destiny. A part of me ... a part of me can't believe he's gone.' She moved her hand and stared at the smeared blood on her fingertips. He had cut her cheek with his ring.

Wang Zhen turned away and kicked at a loose stone. His hair fell over his forehead and she was reminded again of how handsome he was – sought after by every girl on campus, except her. Was that why he had decided that no one else would do? It was the way of the privileged to always want what they did not have.

He looked up, eyes glittering like black diamonds. 'You are a dutiful daughter, are you not, Dao Ming?'

She thought of her father, remembered the ticking off she'd received because she was spending too much time with Justin. Her father had counted off a long list of reasons why she should keep him at arm's length. 'You are too young and so is he; he is a foreigner, here only for a short time; he is from a privileged background quite different from yours. There is no future for you both and the present serves only to distract you from your studies.'

'But you yourself like Justin, Father. Does he not help you with your research?'

'He is a good and diligent student and his heart is in the right place. But he is not for you.'

In the end, she had stormed out of the room swearing

that nothing would change her mind about Justin. Within a week, they had received the news that Justin was dead, killed. Even now, almost a month later, she couldn't quite believe it.

'What do you mean?' she asked Wang Zhen.

'I understand that your father's performance review at the university is coming up soon.'

Dao Ming exhaled, a quiet sound of relief, but Wang Zhen did not hear it. He did not know the situation with her father – not yet – so secrecy was still an option.

'*My* father can ensure that he never holds a post in a university in China again.'

She realised that Wang Zhen meant it. She was also sure that her father would not want her to cave in to threats, wherever he was, he would not want her to succumb to such pressure.

'Do you want to be responsible for the end of your father's career? He is a well-respected man. The scandal would destroy him.'

She knew that what he said was true. Her father loved his job almost more than his two daughters. But where was her father? What was the use of sacrificing herself for his job, for his happiness, when he would soon lose everything anyway, probably already had, with his long unexplained absence? A thought came to her, an idea. Was it worth the risk? She remembered Justin, the big smile and the big heart – willing to do what was right regardless of the consequences. She would honour Justin's memory in her own way, using the assets and advantages that she had. She pretended to think, turned away from Wang Zhen so that he could not see her face, the sudden hope that brightened her features like the sun coming round a mountain.

'Very well, Wang Zhen, you give me no choice.' She could not look at him, could not meet his eyes. This man who would rather have a songbird in a cage and silent than free to fly away and sing. 'I will be with you again. You have convinced me that your feelings are genuine. It is the best decision for my whole family.'

His voice throbbed with happiness. 'We will be so happy together, Dao Ming. I promise you that!' He really meant it as well. She could almost marvel at his inability to understand the human heart.

She said, trying to stop her lip from quivering, trying to project calmness and determination, 'However, there is something you must do for me in return.'

Singh focused on the autopsy report. He sat in the cool interior of the limousine and spread papers all over his ample lap. Benson glanced at him once and then left him to his own devices. The original report was in Mandarin, a sheaf of papers stapled together down the left-hand margin. The Chinese characters were tight complex works of art – they reminded the inspector of an Escher painting. Geometrical, repetitive, complex, and essentially pointless. Human beings had devised an alternative system in which a twenty-six-letter alphabet did the work of thousands of characters. As if to prove his point, the English summary was a good few pages shorter than the original. He hoped it didn't mean that information had been left out.

'Benson!'

'Yes sir.'

'Do you read and write Chinese?'

'Of course, sir.'

'Good – I'll need you to check a translation for me later.'

'Do you mean the autopsy result?'

'Yes.'

'I did the first translation.'

'Oh.' Singh pondered this for a moment. 'Left anything out?'

'No, sir.'

'Then how come your version is so short?'

'Chinese is an unwieldy language by comparison.'

The inspector's full bottom lip stretched into a smile. 'That's what I thought. So how come the whole world is learning Mandarin? Why don't we wait for the Chinese to learn English?'

'It's true that the Chinese are working very hard at their English. Every second building in Beijing is an English tuition centre.'

Singh stared out of the window and read the nearest sign-board out loud, '"Traveller from to get into by bus".'

'The quality of English is very mixed,' explained Benson.

Singh noted another sign on a construction fence which read, SLIP AND FALL DOWN CAREFULLY. It was good advice, he supposed.

Singh resumed his perusal of the report. He'd had enough of this discussion on linguistics. As always, when he was in some corner of a foreign field, he would have to rely on trans-lators and hope they'd caught enough of the substance not to obstruct the hunt for the truth.

Even in English, the language was complex but the conclusions were simple. Justin Tan had suffered multiple injuries including lacerations, bruising, broken bones and internal injuries. It was difficult to be certain which injury had ultimately been the proximate cause of death but the examiner speculated that a number of the blows to the head with the proverbial blunt instrument might have been fatal on their own. Also, a punctured lung, pierced by a snapped rib, would have led to death, but not immediately. Turning the page over, Singh noted that a number of blows had been post-mortem, the kicking and punching had continued after Justin's death. Some of the wounds had bled less than would have been expected if the victim had still been alive. Certain blows had not bruised despite the force used. In other words, his heart had stopped but his assailants had not. It bore out what he'd said to Susan Tan – it had the hallmarks of a drug-fuelled rage.

The inspector turned back to the file, looking for hints of the attacker or attackers. The pathologist had been convinced there was more than one. Singh couldn't disagree. The blows had been of different strengths, from different angles. The indentation of shoe prints on the flesh suggested at least two men, probably more. The pathologist was a diligent fellow; he'd carefully photographed the marks and then attempted to draw them as well. Singh wondered whether any progress had been made identifying the type of footwear. It wouldn't be much use until a suspect was identified, but at such a point, it might amount to one more strand of circumstantial evidence. No foreign DNA had been recovered from the body. He read the detail on Justin's hands. They were bruised and battered, he'd warded off the first few blows. But he'd never got his hands on any of his opponents. There was nothing under the fingernails that would lead directly to a killer or killers.

Singh leafed through the pile and found what he was looking for – an inventory of what had been found on or around Justin's body. A Tag Heuer watch with the inscription, 'Congratulations to my beloved son'. Perhaps it had been a present on his passing out from the army. Not graduation certainly as the young fellow had taken a year out. A wallet, leather calfskin Versace containing ten thousand yuan, various credit cards and a Singapore identity card. Singh assumed the credit cards – Visa, Amex and Mastercard – were supplementary to the ones of his parents. Susan Tan hadn't been concerned that Justin might go on an uncontrolled spending spree. Or maybe she and the father were just naive. It wouldn't be the first time successful parents had been blinkered about their own offspring. Singh stopped to wonder if he would have been foolish about a child – assuming the best, never suspecting the worst. He doubted it. He was too much of a cynic by nature.

The only other object that had been in Justin's possession was a ticket stub for a subway ride. From the East Gate of Peking University station to Beijing West Railway Station.

'Where are these stations?' he asked Benson.

'The first one is close to Peking University. The other is a few streets down from where Justin was killed. I would guess that he caught a train at the university and headed there.'

'How have they come up with such an accurate time of death,' demanded Singh, noting for the first time that the time of death had been set at twelve minutes past midnight.

'The watch was broken.'

'And they assumed it was broken in the assault?'

'It seemed a sensible conclusion.'

'Or he fell over the previous evening while going for a piss at night?'

Benson shrugged. 'Tiananmen Square is on your right,' he said, changing the subject.

Singh turned to stare out of the darkened window with interest.

'Pull over,' he said and Benson complied. Singh hauled himself out and took a deep breath despite the oppressive humidity. The place was an ode to grey cement. A few children flying kites in the foreground lessened the sombre appearance of the place but not by much. There were hundreds of tourists around, almost entirely Chinese. He wondered if they were from overseas, part of the Chinese diaspora, or local. He stared at a few tourists and they stared back open-mouthed. A few stopped so suddenly at the sight of him that others walked into them. A small girl in a party frock pointed at him and stuck out her tongue. Locals, he deduced. The diaspora was familiar with the turban-wearing segment of the population while these folk reacted as if they'd stumbled upon their first inter-planetary visitor.

'Tourists from the provinces,' explained Benson. 'They're ... umm ... not used to foreigners.'

Singh cast his mind back to 1989 and the television footage of angry students at Tiananmen Square, thousands of them demanding freedom and democracy. The inspector had been rooting for the students. He had watched with the rest of the world as soldiers from outlying regions were shipped in to quell the rebellion in Beijing. They had opened fire on Beijing residents without thinking twice. And now, more than two decades later, they and their children were back in the square as tourists.

The inspector's thoughts turned to Justin. He'd died alone – not part of a movement, not in pursuit of an ideal, not as a hero. Maybe the kids in Beijing in 1989 had the right of it. A life given for a cause was surely a death more worthwhile than the victim of a robbery gone wrong? Maybe even some cold comfort to the parents.

'That's Mao,' said Benson.

Singh stared at the portrait in the distance. He could make out the fleshy face and the swept-back pitch-black hair. The Great Leader wore a grey buttoned-up jacket of the type that had come to be known as Mao pyjamas.

'Do people still respect him?'

'The government pays lip service to his memory, but the hero worship of past eras is over.'

'And what about the ordinary people?'

'The so-called proletariat?'

'Yup.'

'They've found another god to follow.'

'Xi Jinping?' asked Singh, referring to the current leader.

'Money,' said Benson, as the two men continued to look across the vast grey blank towards the man who had been China's first communist leader.

Four

'You're making a mistake.'

'Don't you want to know what happened to our son?'

'What's the point? It's not going to bring him back!'

Susan Tan looked at her husband and tried to remember a time when she had loved him. She'd met him at university all those years ago and been swept off her feet – he was so tall, so handsome, so confident. She'd married him and they'd had two children in quick succession, Justin, now dead, and his sister Jemima, lurking in the residence somewhere, red-eyed and miserable over the loss of her brother.

'I need to know what happened,' she insisted, wondering whether all conversations on sudden death turned into clichés.

'I know what you need,' said Anthony. 'You need to think you're in charge, that this is just another problem that will go away if you bring that famous determination and hard work to bear. Well, I've got news for you, honey – there is nothing you can do to make this particular problem go away. Justin is not coming back.'

Looking at his mouth twisted in anger, Susan realised with a sense of mild surprise – and strangely, relief – that her husband did not care about her either. At least, she didn't need to feel guilt about the breakdown of their relationship. It wasn't just her, it was both of them. The closeness was long gone, the barriers between them as solid as the Great Wall. She wondered suddenly whether he'd had affairs, betrayed her with other women. He was still a good-looking man, had aged well. Greying temples and laugh lines down his cheeks. A number of colleagues had said to her that he looked like an ambassador. Was it just humour or had it been intended to hurt? She didn't really care, a career trajectory like hers was always likely to provoke envy.

She gazed at her husband as if he were a stranger. Was she naive to expect that he'd remained loyal to her? She'd never strayed, of course. She was one of those women married to her job. Working all hours, even weekends, missing children's sports days and prize-giving days – her country had needed her and she'd put it first. She realised now that she'd happily have binned every trade agreement she'd negotiated, every peace plan concluded, every diplomatic coup and newspaper headline for one more hour with her son. An hour to hear how he was doing at his lessons, to gossip about his new girl-friend, to find out what he thought about the world. Maybe just to give him a hug.

'Who is this policeman you've dragged down from Singapore?' demanded her husband.

'An Inspector Singh – he came highly recommended.'

'He won't have the first idea how to get anything done in this town.'

'You think we need someone Chinese? I have to admit I thought the same thing.'

'You've changed your mind?'

'Singh's a bit of a character, he might be able to see things that we can't.'

'You're talking nonsense.'

'I was reading about him, he has a nose for trouble and no respect for authorities.'

'In that case he'll be lucky not to wind up in prison.'

'I need to know what happened,' she repeated in a low whisper, as if reminding herself, not him, why she had summoned the inspector.

Anthony walked over to the raised kitchen table and sat down on a tall stool. He buried his face in his hands. His grey suit blended into the background. The whole residence was decorated in soothing tones of grey and white. Zen, Susan had explained, when she'd selected the design for their residence. Something minimalist. Looking around her, the First Secretary realised suddenly that the place was sterile. It lacked any colour, any sense that it might be the abode of a family. Even the paintings, selected by the highly paid interior decorator, were in grey tones – Chinese brushstrokes of mountains and cranes, a sop to their location. No doubt the embassy residences in India had Moghul miniatures. Had Justin found a home here? Did Jemima? She knew that she could not ask the latter, did not want to hear the answer. Susan Tan pressed her temples with her forefingers.

'He wants to see you.' She addressed her husband's back.

'Why?' He swivelled round to face her. His fingers had left white streaks on his cheeks where the pressure had driven away the blood under the skin.

'I don't know. He says he needs to talk to everyone who knew Justin well – who might be able to shed some light on this ... business.'

'How can I possibly shed light on why our son was unlucky enough to be set upon by thugs and killed in some filthy Chinese alley?'

'Is that what you really believe?'

'What else is there to think?'

Jemima sidled into the room. She was a thin shadow, flitting around the residence in a sort of sideways crawl with her eyes darting from side to side as if expecting trouble from any direction. Her mother felt her eyes grow wet with tears. She blinked quickly, her practised response to a thousand emotional situations. Don't let anyone see weakness. Keep your feelings inside where no one can exploit them.

'Is the policeman here?' asked Jemima.

Both her parents looked at her in surprise. A sixteen-year-old with only the lightest grasp of daily reality at the best of times, she had completely shut down after Justin's death.

'Yes – he's gone to the hotel,' said Susan.

'Where is he staying?'

'The Hyatt.'

'Will he find out what happened to Justin?'

'We hope so,' said her mother.

'The Chinese police have already done that,' insisted Anthony.

Jemima shook her head. 'They didn't try very hard.'

'What makes you say that?'

'They didn't even come here, talk to us, search his room, anything!'

'There was no reason to,' insisted Anthony Tan. 'This isn't a television show.'

Susan Tan said gently, 'Inspector Singh might want to speak to you, Jemima. He's trying to understand a little more about Justin.' Would Jemima be able to cope? She'd always been fragile, now she was brittle.

Again her daughter surprised her. 'Of course he must speak to all of us. He can't find out what happened unless he knows as much as possible about Justin.'

Anthony walked over to his daughter and put an arm around her. She flinched like a nervous foal but did not withdraw.

With a pang, Susan realised that the last of his family feeling, the last of his protective instinct, was available only for Jemima. Despite this, she felt her own attitude to him soften. It was something, after all, that Anthony cared for his children, although his reaction to Justin's death had been to bottle up his emotions inside. Not so different from her, really.

'I hope he finds out what *really* happened to Justin,' said Jemima as she extricated herself from her father's embrace. She spoke in a whisper but the strength of her feelings came through.

'What do you mean?' asked Susan, but Jemima had already slipped out of the door.

It seemed that her daughter, like herself, thought there was more to Justin's death than had been revealed so far. She wondered whether her surviving child had any evidence to back up the feeling and dismissed the thought. Jemima, inhabiting a world that existed almost entirely in her head, was not the sort to know anything useful.

The traffic gave him the opportunity to count every Starbucks and McDonald's – the advancing forces of capitalism sweeping Chinese food away? – that lined the major roads. Indeed, if these highways were the arteries of Beijing, the city was due a massive heart attack. By the time they reached the hotel and inched their way past luxury vehicles and dilapidated taxis to the entrance, Singh only had half an hour before he was due to meet the Chinese ex-policeman. He followed the circuitous corridor until he found his room. It was large and luxurious and the bed looked firm and inviting, but he regretfully eschewed such pleasures for later. Instead, he showered quickly. The water was steaming hot and refreshing, but the water pressure was not to his satisfaction. The inspector liked a shower to double as a massage and this one was more of a tickle. He wrapped a towel around his waist and then the turban around his head at lightning speed – his wife wasn't there to criticise the construction and the Chinese wouldn't know any better if it was more beehive than avatar of a warrior. He ate an apple from the fruit display without washing it and then hurried down and out the main entrance of the hotel, mentally urging the revolving door to move a little faster.

The doorman offered him a taxi but he shook his head and pulled a packet of cigarettes out of his breast pocket. He found a gaggle of swarthy-looking men sucking on their fags behind a line of limousines and joined them. A couple of them glanced at him and one said something in Chinese that provoked a titter. He couldn't blame them – they probably didn't come across that many short, turbaned Sikhs with a surfeit of facial hair and a smoking habit. This last trait engendered sufficient fellow feeling that when he stubbed out his cigarette one of the men tapped a packet on his wrist and offered the protruding death-stick – as his doctor called it – to the policeman. Singh glanced at his watch, shook his head regretfully. He inhaled deeply to ensure a good lungful of secondary smoke and wandered into the lobby in search of his Chinese sidekick.

An elderly man, as thin as he, Singh, was plump, was waiting for him. They were almost exactly the same height when the turban was taken into account, which meant the Chinese man was a couple of inches taller than him. He had lines of sparse hair arranged horizontally and with precision across his scalp. Singh suspected that a mild breeze would soon put paid to the military neatness. The inspector realised to his amusement that this was the first man he'd spotted in China with grey hair. The rest of the sixty-plus club sported ebony black helmets.

The Chinese gentleman was wearing a pair of black pyjamas with a high collar and cloth-covered buttons. It was the sort of outfit that a waiter might wear in a Chinese restaurant in Singapore. On closer examination, Singh noted that the outfit was faded and fraying at the collar and cuffs. A button three from the bottom had been replaced with one that did not match the rest. This man would not pass muster as a member of staff in the sort of posh restaurant that specialised in shark's fin soup and other endangered species.

'Inspector Singh, I am Li Jun, formerly of the Beijing police force.'

Singh stuck out a hand and shook the other man's appendage vigorously. On this man hinged his hopes of producing a result to satisfy Susan Tan in the shortest possible time.

'Thank you for agreeing to help, Mr Li Jun.'

'You may call me Li,' said the former policeman with a smile that revealed two missing incisors. It made him look like a rather forlorn rabbit.

'Shall we discuss the case over coffee,' Singh asked hopefully, banking on being able to supplement his coffee with cake. His stomach grumbled audibly and the other man's lips twitched.

'Certainly,' he said, 'and perhaps we might have time to have a light snack?'

Singh decided, as he led the way to the lobby café, that this might be the beginning of a beautiful friendship.

Fifteen minutes later, he'd eaten three croissants that flaked all over the front of his shirt and drunk two very sweet and milky coffees.

Li Jun sipped sporadically on a delicate cup of jasmine tea and seemed to have the infinite patience of those monks who sat on mountaintops seeking inner peace. The inspector gazed at his companion thoughtfully and then around the gleaming gold and marble lobby. He realised that not a single other man, Chinese or otherwise, was wearing anything traditional. Everyone was in a Western suit and tie. Li Jun's Mao suit stood out like a throwback to a past era. The ex-policeman from Beijing belonged in a grainy black and white photo of the past, not in the lobby of the present.

'What do you know of this case?' asked Singh.

'I have been informed of the facts by the First Secretary. I have also looked at the autopsy report.'

'And what is *your* opinion on this matter?'

'That the son of the First Secretary was killed by robbers.'

'Really?' Although it was Singh's preferred solution, he felt his usual desire to be contrary when presented with a fait accompli.

'All conclusions must be tested with a rigorous examination of the facts.'

'Of course,' agreed Singh, trying not to smile at the other man's circuitous conversational style. Was that what communism did to you?

'I think the *extent* of the injuries justify further investigation. The attack was very severe for a robbery attempt. As our great leader, Deng Xiaoping has said, "Seek truth from facts."'

'Was your great leader talking about a murder investigation?'

The initial puzzled look was replaced with that peculiar toothy smile. 'No, however his words have great application in many different situations.'

'The level of violence could be explained by drugs or alcohol.'

'It is quite possible. Chinese youth are also *flying upwards* these days.'

'What?'

'They have adopted the use of many drugs like ecstasy and marijuana.'

Singh tried to brush some of the crumbs from his shirt. 'Anything else?'

'I have heard that the father's activities bear further investigation.'

'Anthony Tan? I haven't interviewed him yet, only the mother.'

'He is a businessman here in China.'

'So? I didn't think he was likely to be a house husband.'

'He's more of what you might call a fixer. He puts people together, promises access to the powerful in exchange for a share of the deal or a cash payment.'

Singh wrinkled his nose. It sounded seedy, not the sort of thing that would meet with the approval of the First Secretary.

'He uses his wife's position to suggest that he is in a position of influence,' explained Li Jun further.

'Susan Tan sounded reluctant that I interview him.'

'There are rumours that one or two projects have not gone well, that he owes people money.'

'So? What has this to do with Justin's death?'

Li Jun looked over the rim of his delicate teacup at his counterpart. Singh noted that his nails had been cut to the quick and were spotlessly clean.

'Did Madam Tan explain how we met?' he asked.

'No.'

'I came upon Justin in some difficulty a few weeks back and was able to help him out.'

'What sort of difficulty?'

'He had been cornered outside a nightclub by some unsavoury characters. I . . . I persuaded them to leave him alone.'

Singh slashed through the air with flat hands. 'Let me guess – you're some sort of kung fu master?'

Li Jun laughed out loud, drawing curious glances from some of the other patrons of the lobby café. 'You have been watching too many Jackie Chan films, my friend. No, I merely suggested to them that I was still a policeman.'

'And that was enough?' Singh was prepared to admire such a law-abiding society.

'I also told them that I was the uncle of Fu Xinghua.'

'And who is he?'

'The most powerful policeman in Beijing. He is cracking down on organised crime.'

'What did Justin say about the incident?'

'He said that he had been overcharged for a drink and refused to pay.'

'You believed him?'

'It's not an unusual way of extorting money from foreigners and tourists.'

'One attack by a gang of thugs is unlucky, two is careless,' remarked the policeman from Singapore.

'It does seem to be an unhappy coincidence.'

'And you think Justin might have been killed as some sort of revenge for a deal involving the father gone bad?'

'There have been incidents of a similar nature in Beijing in the past. In China, family ties are considered very important – so if you want to hurt someone, you target the family.'

Singh's eyebrows made an effort to meet above his nose.

'"To be rich is glorious",' explained Li Jun. 'That is Deng Xiaoping's vision of a more prosperous China. But there has been much corruption and violence as the bonds that held society together previously are strained.'

'Sounds like organised crime is taking over,' grunted Singh.

'That is a *temporary* setback, of course,' said Li Jun.

'I guess you're wrong about that.'

'You do not support my hypothesis?'

'There's nothing temporary about death.'

Dai Wei's single greatest regret was that he had been born short. He stood looking at himself in the full-length mirror in the bedroom. His skin was good though, smooth and unlined so he looked ten years younger than he was. After further contemplation of his reflection, he sat down on the edge of the bed – covered in imported Egyptian cotton sheets, nothing was too good for the new elite of China – and pulled on his black shoes with the raised platform heels. With these lending him some important inches, he marched back to the mirror.

Dai Wei was perfectly certain that if he'd been a towering physical figure, like Fu Xinghua, his point man in the police department, he would have achieved his extraordinary personal success earlier. Although, to be fair, the conditions might not have been ripe. Deng Xiaoping had only made his trip to southern China in 1998. That had been the catalyst for the 'socialist market economy' or 'capitalism with Chinese characteristics' that had allowed Dai Wei to achieve his present prominence. It was true that he was only deputy mayor of Beijing but everyone knew that the senile fool in nominal charge was past his sell-by date. An old party cadre like him was difficult to oust and Dai Wei would have to wait for the next so-called election in three years for the mayor to gracefully refuse to run. In the meantime, Dai Wei was the power behind the throne and anyone of any importance in business or politics knew it. Even the Standing Committee of the Politburo knew very well that he was knocking on the door and would seek elevation to the body when the next leadership transition occurred in a few years.

His wife came in wearing a silk kimono that he had bought her from Japan. It was just as well that the people did not know that the man responsible for the promotion of Maoist revolutionary fervour and undying loyalty to China and its leadership – namely him – liked his wife dressed in the fashions of public enemy no. 1. The Japanese occupation, now six decades old, was still fresh in the public mind in no small part through the efforts of politicians like him. He quoted himself out loud, '"The past must not be forgotten, it must be avenged".'

'Mao himself would have been proud of such a slogan,' said his wife.

He smiled. 'You are looking very beautiful today – as you do everyday,' he said, reaching for her.

She ducked away from him and took her turn in front of the mirror. 'You are too good to me, dear husband.'

'Better even than you think for I have a surprise for you.'

'Oh! What is it?' This offer of a treat persuaded her to perch on the bed next to him.

Dai Wei reached into a drawer and retrieved a small box that he handed over, clasping both her thin hands in his as he did so.

She opened it, squealing with delight and then her face fell. 'Sapphires? I was hoping for diamonds – you know I need a new pair of diamond earrings.'

'This was just for a change,' he said quickly, heading off a tantrum at the pass. 'Here –' and he extracted another box from his jacket pocket – 'is your other gift.'

This time her excitement was real and she embraced him with enthusiasm before hurrying to the mirror to try on her new baubles.

'What do you think?' she asked, tucking her hair behind her ears so he could see the full effect.

'Perfect,' he replied and meant it. Dai Wei adored his wife, a young former actress with the beauty and delicacy of a Ming Dynasty vase.

There was a knock on the door and a servant came in to announce that his lunch was ready as was his lunch companion. Dai Wei nodded and rose to his feet. His wife twirled out of the room, still as delighted as a child with a new shiny toy.

He liked to entertain visitors at his mansion in an elite area of Beijing reserved for Party officials and their families. The experience of dining with him at the residence of his father and grandfather before him, except for the brief period when his father had been purged during the Cultural Revolution, would cement loyalty and enhance fear of his status and power.

Dai Wei sauntered down, enjoying the sound of his clicking heels on the tiled floor as he made his away across the main hall to the dining room. The senior policeman who was his guest was deputy head of the Beijing Public Security Bureau.

'Fu Xinghua, how does the crackdown proceed?' he asked, after the ritual greetings.

'Very well, Comrade Dai Wei.'

'I saw from the headlines,' replied the other man with a nod to the English and Mandarin papers by the side of his plate. Fu barely glanced at them and from this Dai Wei deduced that he had already enjoyed their portrayal of him before he had come for this meeting with his boss. His boss. Those were the key words, decided Dai Wei, and his pet policeman might need a reminder of it.

'You received good publicity for this takedown of Wong Kar Lai,' said Dai Wei.

'Yes, sir.'

'It was unfortunate that he was killed in the melee – it would have been better if he had faced trial.'

'Unfortunately, he had placed a sniper on the roof. When the first shot was fired by Wong's stooge, my policemen returned fire. You know the results.'

Dai Wei did indeed. The blood-soaked body of the fat real estate man was the front page picture in most newspapers except the *China Daily*, which had chosen instead to run a picture of Fu, eyes narrowed, cigarette dangling out of the corner of his mouth. His back was to a police car – the front windscreen shattered from a single bullet. There was no mistaking the heroic nature of the pose, a man getting the job done, indifferent to the fact that death had passed so close to him.

'The editorials have been very positive about *your* leadership in the crackdown against black,' continued Fu.

Dai Wei smiled. Fu had guessed what was bothering him, the fact that his underling was stealing too much of the limelight. Dai Wei decided to leave the issue of his police chief's fondness for the headlines aside for the moment. The man was still useful to him. Two persons with a separate destiny could still find themselves on a common path for a while.

'As they should be positive about my leadership – and yours,' agreed the deputy mayor. 'After all, this crackdown, as well as our dedication to Maoist ideals, has been very popular with the people.'

'There is one more thing,' said Fu. 'A small matter.'

'What is it?'

'One or two of the more influential online blogs have questioned why it is that so many of the businessmen we have accused of crimes have died resisting arrest.'

'Like your man yesterday?'

'Exactly. They are suggesting that it is very convenient that they are not being charged in a court of law where they can assert their innocence.'

Dai Wei nodded. It was typical of the Chinese way of thinking to see conspiracies everywhere.

'How can it be our fault when they open fire first?' asked Dai Wei.

'There is also a suggestion that Wong might have been murdered to keep details of his businesses away from the eyes of the public. Everyone knows that Wong had dealings with princelings.'

Dai Wei scowled and his face wrinkled like the surface of Lake Kunming on a windy day. He was a princeling after all, the privileged son and grandson of leading Party members. 'Wong had many interests outside real estate – I believe his factories also manufacture baby formula. Suggest that he was one of those involved in adulterating baby milk with melamine. That will ensure that the public is on our side and these bloggers abandon incorrect lines of thinking.'

Fu nodded at once and a smile spread across his face. 'That will do the trick,' he agreed.

They were interrupted by the appearance of Dai Wei's wife, dressed in finest raw silk, made up to perfection so that she looked like a porcelain doll, her diamonds catching the light and gleaming like small stars.

Fu stood up quickly and clasped her hand lightly in greeting. 'It is always an honour to see you, Madam Dai.'

Her laughter was light, like a stream in spring meandering through the countryside. Dai Wei loved the sound of it.

'You have a way with words for a lowly policeman,' she replied.

Five

'Where shall we go first?' asked Li Jun, as he courteously trailed after the fat man towards the lobby.

'Crime scene,' said Singh.

'That is a good decision.'

Singh slowed his pace so that they were walking side by side. He noted that his companion was thin to the point of fragile and remembered that he'd not had anything to eat while Singh had been replenishing his energy levels. He also noted that the heels of Li Jun's shoes were worn down to the ground. Chinese pensions for retired police officers were clearly not generous.

'At least now I know how you came to be involved in this case,' he said as they clambered into the car and Benson set off towards the *hutong* where Justin had met his death.

'The First Secretary was grateful for my help on the previous occasion – and as she knew I was formerly a policeman, she asked me to assist you in this matter.'

'I hope it's a paid position,' said Singh, conscious of the man's threadbare appearance.

'It is not appropriate to seek reward for doing one's duty.'

'I thought "to be rich was glorious"?'

Li Jun laughed suddenly. 'You are a dangerous man, Comrade Singh, to use the words of our leaders against us. But remember that Deng Xiaoping also said that "some people must get rich first". I might be part of the second wave.'

Singh decided to make it a point to feed his Chinese compatriot on his expense allowance – otherwise he might lose his own appetite.

'Was there an investigation into the assault?'

'Justin refused to report it.'

'Why not?'

Li Jun grimaced. 'At the time of the incident, I assumed he just did not want the attention. I think he was embarrassed to be rescued by an old man.'

'And now?'

'And now I am not so sure. Thinking back, it seems that he was hiding something.'

'Or protecting someone?' demanded Singh.

'That is also a possible interpretation. I have asked my former colleagues in the force to look into it.'

Within twenty minutes – traffic had been unusually light except for a brief hiatus behind a taxi driver who had abandoned his car at a red light to spit noisily into a drain – Benson pulled up.

'We're here?' asked Singh.

'As close as I can get,' he replied. 'You have to walk from here because the streets are too narrow for vehicles.'

Singh's disgruntlement was obvious in the sagging jowls. Misinterpreting its cause, Li Jun said, 'Do not be concerned – I know the way. I came here a week ago when Madam Susan first requested my help.'

It was typical of his misfortune, decided Singh, that he was always investigating murders in the most difficult circumstances – in slums in Mumbai, during floods in Phnom Penh, dodging terrorists in Bali. Wasn't he a member of the Singapore police department – the city-state famous for its sterility and cleanliness? He'd certainly never had to trek towards a crime scene on foot in his home jurisdiction because the roads were too narrow. There was always a six-lane highway leading precisely where one wanted to go in Singapore. And as concrete structures like flyovers, overhead bridges and retaining walls were screened with creepers, palms and shrubs, none of the residents seemed to notice that the island was basically a large car park. It beat walking anyway, thought Singh, as he stumped along grumpily, feeling the rim of his turban turn damp with perspiration.

They stopped before a busy street and Singh watched in amazement as Li Jun suddenly darted across the road, between cars, minivans and bicycles. The Chinese man reached the other side, looked around in evident surprise that his companion was not with him and hollered back across to Singh, 'You must cross!'

'It would be easier to dodge bullets,' shouted Singh. He was overcome with an uncharacteristic timidity when confronted with the aggressive driving. He noted that Li Jun was about to recross. What did he intend to do – lead Singh across by the hand like a child or a blind man? It would be too embarrassing. Singh set off at a remarkable speed for such a rotund runner and made it breathless to the other side.

'You see, it is easy,' said Li Jun.

'My eyes were shut,' retorted Singh.

The two men fell in step and headed down the street. Singh stretched out both hands and touched grey walls topped with tiles on either side. 'How do people get around in here?' he asked. 'Benson wasn't exaggerating, the streets really are narrow.'

'Bicycles or on foot,' replied Li Jun.

Singh peered into an entrance like a portly peeping Tom. The open area in front of the residence was piled high with tyres, old furniture and sacks of what appeared to be cement. A row of forlorn bicycles missing various parts stood against the wall, handlebars drooping with disappointment.

'Many of the *hutongs* have been cleaned up for tourists,' said Li Jun with an air of apology, 'but this one is still in an old state.'

'It has a certain charm,' said Singh and he meant it. The narrow cobbled streets, the flashes of colour – a flowering creeper in a crevice or a red bicycle – the sounds of children's laughter, the exposed wiring that hung like bunting from poles and most of all the smell of freshly cooked food. 'These are homes?' he asked.

'And places of business and restaurants, everything that is necessary for human existence is contained in a *hutong*.' As if conscious that he had been uncharacteristically enthusiastic, he said, 'I grew up in a similar place before . . .' He trailed off.

'Before?'

'It is not important,' explained Li Jun.

Singh was prevented from enquiring further because they turned a corner and he said, 'This is where it happened.'

They were standing at an intersection of four narrow lanes. It was a slightly bigger space and a single tree, leaves grey with dust, stood in a corner. The lanes themselves all looked the same, reaching a dark apex in the distance. Walled residences behind closed doors lined the streets for the most part. A few open doors revealed a glimpse into the otherwise hidden world. There was a steady stream of traffic passing through – bicycles being slowly pedalled by old men in white vests, washerwomen with baskets on their backs, a milkman with slopping tins attached to a rickshaw. A young man strode past and then spat into a drain with unerring accuracy and disconcerting volume.

Li Jun led the policeman from Singapore to a spot next to the tree. 'Just here.'

Singh looked down at the ground and felt a pang for the much-loved son who had been murdered on the spot. There was no mark, no hint of what had taken place. The stains on the road could have been from any source, nothing spoke of blood and death.

A bell rang as a bicycle struggled to find a way around the fat Sikh and his skinny companion. A teenager on high heels teetered past and stumbled over an uneven patch of ground into Singh's arms. He hurriedly righted her and she tottered away, stealing a backwards glance at her unusual-looking rescuer.

'No one saw anything?' he asked.

'It would have been less busy after midnight when the murder took place – maybe there was no one here at all except the killers and Justin.'

'Someone must have heard something ... no one gets beaten to death quietly.'

'The police files do not reveal any witnesses.'

'We need to go door to door,' said Singh.

'I'm sure the police would have done that,' pointed out Li Jun.

'And their conclusion was that Justin was beaten to death in the course of a robbery. Our task is to test that conclusion. And that means we can't rely on the same source material.'

Li Jun looked as if he wanted to say something about re-inventing the wheel but he wisely refrained and Singh warmed to him.

Turning away, his attention was caught by a poster that was pasted to the nearest wall. The same notice was randomly affixed to various surfaces all around the area. Justin Tan's picture, the one of him smiling in army uniform, was at the centre of each poster.

'What's this?'

'Madam Susan arranged it. It is a request for information about the death.'

Singh noted the currency symbol. 'And a reward?'

'Yes ... for anyone with good information.'

The residents of the *hutong* wandered past without sparing the posters a first, let alone a second, glance.

'Chinese people prefer not to get involved in matters that have nothing to do with them,' explained the other man.

'Not even for money?'

'It depends on how much money they have and how much money they need.'

'This looks like a poor neighbourhood,' Singh pointed out,

pirouetting on the heel of one trainer to take in the whole view.

'Yes,' agreed Li Jun.

'We can hope then,' said Singh, looking anything but optimistic. In his experience, murders were rarely solved so easily as with the timely appearance of a credible eyewitness.

'Is there any news?' whispered the young girl to her sister.

Dao Ming ruffled her hair and pinched her nose playfully. There was a gap of twelve years between them and sometimes she felt more like the little girl's mother than her sister. 'I'm afraid not, little sister. But you know Father, he gets so lost in his own world that he forgets to let us know what he is doing sometimes. That is what it is like if you're more interested in books than people!'

'But he has never gone away like this before.'

'Well, there is a first time for everything. I am not worried so why should you be?'

'Really? You're not worried?'

'Not at all!' This was accompanied by a quick smile and a big hug.

The little girl returned the hug with interest and then hurried off, her concerns assuaged by the certainties of her older, trusted sister. Dao Ming could hear her a few moments later, holding a tea party for her dolls, censuring them about their table manners like an old-fashioned mother. Dao Ming wondered how she knew to behave like a mother when her own had died in childbirth, bringing her – bouncy and healthy and motherless – into the world. Surely, it was not her example? She was certainly not so particular about behaviour as the imaginary mother of Dao Wu's make-believe world. The younger sister had always preferred an orderly structured life bound by routine on all sides, maybe to disguise the absence of a mother while Dao Ming, despite being the oldest, was a free spirit. Dao Ming glanced over at a photo on the mantelpiece of her father and mother on their wedding day, an earnest-looking couple wearing grey Mao pyjamas and holding the 'Little Red Book' in joined hands. The other photo of her mother was a studio shot in colour taken a few years before her death. The background had been mocked up to look like Venice. Her mother, hair done up in tight curls and *cheongsam* hugging her still attractive figure, stood against a gondola. If it had been real, her feet would have been wet. Dao Ming remembered laughing about it – 'Are you going for a swim, Mother?' – while her mother pretended to be offended at her lack of respect.

'Come and play with me, big sister!' Dao Wu was quick to notice that her sister had not moved from the spot she had left her.

'I have a few things to do, little one.'

Dao Ming wished that she was as easily distracted as a six-year-old girl. The truth of the matter was that she was worried sick. Their father had been gone for almost three weeks now. She'd watched him set off that morning, surprised that he was not dressed for work.

'Why are you not dressed for office, Father?' she had asked.

'I have some errands to run today, eldest daughter.'

'On a working day?'

'I can see that I am too predictable in my behaviour if even my eighteen-year-old daughter can question me about minor deviations.' He had smiled and she had been reassured until she noticed that the smile did not reach his eyes.

'Shall I come with you? My company will make the errands seem less burdensome surely.' She reached out her hand as she spoke and he recognised the silent plea because he drew her close and held her. Despite her best efforts, she felt the tears well up and spill over. She drew her head back and looked at the damp patch on her father's shirt.

'I still can't believe that Justin is gone, Father.'

'I understand your pain, Dao Ming,' and from the worn look on his face, Dao Ming could almost believe it was true.

'The police say it was a robbery gone wrong . . .'

'I know.'

'I can't believe it,' she said, voice raised and angry. 'It must have had something to do with the work he was doing . . . for you!'

'It is still best we accept the official verdict,' said her father and this time she heard the warning note.

'Times have changed, Father. In modern China, we do not have to just accept what we are told any more.'

It was as if a dark cloud had passed directly overhead. 'Have things really changed, daughter?' he asked.

'Of course. You always say so yourself,' she replied.

Her father was a man of deep principle and he used his position as a leading academic to make his views known. His work exposing illegal land grabs was particularly dangerous. It meant he was crossing swords with the most corrupt elements of the present hierarchy. His position at the university and his reputation as an important Chinese intellectual afforded him some protection but not much, certainly not enough.

'I fear my child that the changes are like the paint on a Chinese opera mask. The surface looks different, but underneath it is exactly the same as before.'

She was unable to respond. Was her father right? Was Justin's death to be ignored, forgotten?

'I must go, my daughter,' he said, flicking her under the chin gently, 'or I will be late.'

She had smiled and nodded and tried to get rid of the sense of foreboding that rippled through her consciousness. Her father's face had grown serious, the lines that etched his cheeks like trenches. 'Dao Ming, you must always remember, whatever happens, that your sister and you are my heart's delight. Everything I have ever done, ever thought, ever believed was to try and build a better society for the two of you.'

Dao Ming had watched him walk down the road towards the bus stop and wait there patiently, his umbrella neatly rolled and under one arm. He did not have his briefcase, she realised, which was a mystery. The bus trundled down the street and her view of her father was obscured. He was not there when it belched black smoke and went on its way again. She hadn't seen her father since.

She was completely alone – deprived of her father in her time of sorrow, deprived of her boyfriend in her time of need. She felt the tears well up yet again and she blinked them away fiercely. Justin was gone, there was nothing that would bring him back.

As if that was not enough, Wang Zhen was determined to revive their relationship, unused to not having everything his way. She sighed and tried to give the young man the benefit of the doubt. There was no doubt that he truly believed he cared for her. Anyway, she was in no position to refuse his attentions. If he did some sniffing around, her father's disappearance would become known.

As it was, she'd almost run out of excuses. That ghastly woman from the faculty office called everyday demanding to know why Professor Luo Gan had not come in to collect papers for marking. Dao Ming had insisted that he was unwell although her story was getting thinner by the day. Fortunately, it was semester break or she would not have been able to cover his tracks even for this length of time. But if he did not return soon the secret would be out and he would lose that which he cared about most after his family, his tenure at the university. Her thoughts turned to Justin and she felt the tears well up. She shook her head firmly and dashed them away with an angry hand. There had been no time, and there was no time, to mourn. Her immediate priority was her father, her immediate responsibility her sister.

Li Jun, formerly of the Beijing police department, was an orderly man. As such, standing at the junction of four alleys with the inspector from Singapore, he tried to decide the most efficient way to execute his task.

'Up and down each street twice, once on the left and once on the right-hand side, ending up back in the centre?' said Singh, lips drooping as he contemplated the distance that needed to be covered.

'Clockwise,' agreed Li Jun. 'What would you like me to ask the residents?'

'Whether they heard or saw anything that might have a bearing on the murder.'

Li Jun set off at a brisk pace with Singh trailing after, clearly intending to moderate the pace by failing to keep up. The Chinese man hoped that the undersides of his shoes would not give way. As the inspector from Singapore appeared to have guessed – he was sharper than his appearance suggested – Li Jun was struggling to make ends meet. And he certainly didn't have cash for a new pair of leather shoes at modern China's market prices. For reasons that were obscure, he did not feel comfortable shopping for fakes in the numerous markets. In the past, as a Party member and a policeman, he would have gone to one of the special stores with controlled prices where a pair of shoes for a diligent policeman would have been well within budget, but those days were long gone. As a former officer who had been forced to resign rather than be stripped of his post in disgrace, he had retained his pension. But that was predicated on a different world where the 'the iron rice bowl' could be depended on. In the present day, it was hardly enough to eke out a meagre living.

The first door he knocked on remain unanswered and the second and third. At this rate, they would be done quickly and finish empty handed. Li Jun bit down on his lower lip with his two lonely front teeth. For some reason, he wanted to prove himself to the fat policeman from Singapore.

'Perhaps the residents are out at work,' he said apologetically.

The policeman from Singapore did not respond. He was huffing and puffing sufficient to blow the next house down.

The fourth door was answered by a toothless old crone. Her hair was tied back in a tight small bun, bare scalp visible between neat furrows of sparse white hair. She was stooped over so low she had to crane her neck to look at him even though he wasn't a very tall man.

'*Nǐhǎoma, lǎotàitai*,' Li Jun said politely, addressing her as an elderly woman but in a respectful tone.

She immediately cupped her hand behind her ear and shouted at him to say it again. The inspector from Singapore stepped backwards hurriedly. It took them ten minutes to extricate themselves – she was obviously lonely as well as deaf.

'Someone could have been murdered directly behind her back and she'd have been none the wiser,' grumbled Singh.

At the fifth door they were met with a stream of abuse and an instruction to keep their noses out of matters that did not concern them.

'Err . . . they said that they didn't see or hear anything,' said Li Jun.

Singh's raised eyebrows suggested that he was not convinced that the torrent of angry words availed themselves of such a simple explanation but he did not protest.

Li Jun stepped back out on to the street and dabbed his brow with a handkerchief. As usual at this time of the year, the air was as hot and muggy as the tropics. The narrow lanes and high walls formed a barrier to any mild breeze that might have cooled him down. This was hard going without any authority behind them. Li Jun wondered whether he should lie about his position, pretend he was still in the force, but decided that his age and worn clothes would arouse suspicion. And if someone reported him – the Chinese people did not kowtow before authority as they had once done – he might find himself without even his derisory pension or in prison.

Up and then down the first alley, they were rewarded with impatience and flat denials that anyone had seen or heard anything or for that matter that they would tell them even if they had. They were outsiders, not to be trusted. Both men were chased out of a small courtyard by a mangy dog and Li Jun had to smile at his colleague's sudden change of pace. The mongrel was as moth-eaten as he was but much more aggressive, Li Jun decided, as he skipped away after Singh and slammed the wooden door in the nick of time.

'Maybe we should have asked for the police files,' said Singh, hitching up his trousers so that they circumnavigated his belly.

In the next lane, they found a gaggle of women gathered around a street vendor selling slices of roast pork. Li Jun could barely get the words of enquiry past his saliva glands. He explained, hoping to appeal to some maternal instinct, that he was on a mission for Justin's parents to find out more about their son's death.

'The boy who was killed?'

'That was a terrible thing!'

'To think that it could have happened in this *hutong*.'

'The thugs who did it must have come from outside the neighbourhood. Maybe even outside Beijing. We don't have such things going on here.'

'He was a foreigner, right? It must have been foreigners who killed him. Why would a Chinese do such a thing?' At the word 'foreigner', all the women turned and glared at Singh in unison. There was no doubt in their minds that the Sikh man fitted the bill as far as suspicious foreign characters with murderous tendencies were concerned.

Li Jun translated the gist of their remarks for Singh without the insults.

'But did they see or hear anything?' demanded Singh.

Li Jun repeated the question, an edge of desperation in his voice as he tried to interrupt the women. It was like being trapped in a hen house while a fox prowled outside.

'What do you mean?' asked a plump woman with pink cheeks and a heavily laden basket of fruit over one arm.

'It happened at night, when the streets were quiet. Did anyone hear anything? Screams for help . . . that sort of thing?'

As if he had suddenly brought the murder close, the women fell silent.

The hair on the back of his neck stood on end. Justin's spirit was waiting for their answer as much as he was, thought Li Jun, and then mentally castigated himself for such superstitious nonsense. Chairman Mao would not have approved.

'No, we did not hear anything,' said a tall, skinny young woman wearing an unfashionable straw hat. He guessed she was an unmarried daughter, left on the shelf because of her gangly height and now beyond the effort of making herself pretty. He wondered whether to share his character analysis with Singh and decided against it. The plump policeman, damp patches under his armpits and over his belly, was looking extremely impatient.

'Anyway, there are the posters everywhere,' she continued. 'There is a reward offered by the family. There is no need for you to go looking for information in this way, Lao Tse, because the information will come to you!'

'It is true,' agreed the plump woman who had spoken earlier, her good humour restored at the thought of a reward. 'There is no one who lives on this street who would walk away from such a thing,' she continued. 'We are all poor and I personally wish I knew something but I do not.' She sounded as if she meant it but Li was not convinced. It was a reflection on the state of Chinese society in this new era that none had suggested that a witness would come forward because it was his or her altruistic duty. Those days were definitely gone.

'It is not as if we don't have other things to worry about,' said a sharp-faced woman with a dissatisfied expression. Li Jun suspected she was a widow on a tight budget and then chided himself for being fanciful. 'This murder is completely unhelpful, it makes it seem as if this is a dangerous neighbourhood although we are good, law-abiding citizens who just want to be left alone.' She scowled at him. 'Left alone by everyone,' she added meaningfully.

'What sort of "other things" are they worried about?' Singh whispered and Li Jun dutifully translated.

'There is talk that they will demolish the houses here – all of them!'

'Who will?'

'Who do you think? The powerful men in big cars who want to turn our homes into another glitzy shopping mall.'

'Are you sure? This is an ancient *hutong* – I thought it was policy to preserve such places.'

The widow snorted. 'Policy lasts until palms are greased, old man. Are you so naive that you do not know this?'

The plump woman's cheeks sagged like a chipmunk's. 'No

one knows everything and yet everyone knows something – but we fear the worst.'

The ex-policeman nodded. It was the Chinese way. Whispers and gossip amongst the downtrodden, but not facts. Facts were for the elite. Rules about land acquisitions applied only to the rich.

'Hopefully, it is not true and you will remain here as will your children and your children's children,' he said.

There were nods and sad smiles at this and the two men made their escape.

'Does that happen in your country?' asked Li Jun.

'Gossipy women? I thought they were universal,' retorted Singh.

'Land grabs by corrupt officials,' explained Li Jun, allowing himself a smile.

The policeman's quick shake of the head was all the answer Li Jun needed.

Sighing, he led the way back to the junction. A motorcycle shot past and missed him by a whisker. He knew that if he'd been knocked down, in all likelihood he would have been left there to bleed to death, residents walking by with averted eyes while Singh begged for help. No one wanted to get involved in other people's business. A child had been run over recently and the citizens of Beijing had walked past her battered body with indifference. Society's bonds had frayed and snapped in the new China and it was every man for himself. Was it any wonder that young men were beaten to death in back alleys with impunity?

'Third time lucky?' asked Singh, nodding at the third street.

'That is the most likely outcome,' said Li Jun with an optimism he did not feel, appreciative of the fact that Singh had not remarked on the waste of their afternoon so far.

Li Jun intended to knock on every door although he did not expect any success. It was his duty to Justin. He had been there to prevent a beating or worse the first time. But it was well known that fortune did not come twice but misfortune never came alone. Perhaps he should have warned Justin, found some way to protect him, had a word with his parents – anything really that might have kept him from his rendezvous with death.

As he set off again, his narrow shoulders squared with determination, Singh tapped him on the shoulder and nodded in the direction of a grimy wall. He saw a slim girl staring at one of the reward posters. Li Jun's mood improved. It was always possible, he knew from experience, to get lucky in an investigation.

Qing stared at the picture, absorbing the features of the grinning young man who looked as if he didn't have a care in the world. There was no anticipation of death in the photo, no shadow cast over the future. The dead fellow – Justin Tan was his name, she read – looked young. It said he was twenty-three; he looked eighteen to Qing. What was that like, she wondered, to look young for one's age? It rarely happened in China except perhaps to the children of the elite, the high cadre kids. She ran a hand down her cheek, felt the dry skin. In her village, where she had grown up helping her father tend to the crops and her mother do the housework, there had never been a question of looking or feeling young.

Her earliest memories were of her siblings – carrying them around on her hip, wiping their faces in the evening, baths were a rarity, dressing them in everything they owned when the weather turned cold. Her happiest memories were of huddling in front of the television, watching dramas of Imperial China, admiring the rich costumes and fine manners. She was twenty-one, two years younger than the dead boy, and she knew well she could have passed for thirty. It wasn't so much that she looked old, although there were fine lines on her otherwise light peach skin, but that her face spoke of experience and responsibility. She reminded herself that Justin was dead and tried to feel some compassion, but she did not have the energy for it. Not after a twelve-hour seven-day shift. But today she had a whole day visiting her old aunt, the only family she had in Beijing, and a few free hours to decide what best to do with the information she had. She smiled – at least her TV watching habits had not been entirely wasted.

Qing gently prised the poster from the wall. She folded it in four and tucked it in her cavernous handbag, largely empty except for a bun in a plastic bag, her purse and a toothbrush. The wind picked up and she wrinkled her nose. These narrow streets channelled the cooking smells from every stove in the neighbourhood and it was tickling her taste buds. Qing hurried down the street, pushed open a door and entered the cemented courtyard.

Her old aunt was stooped so low that her horizon was entirely bounded by the dirt and cement floors. Qing grinned, she'd bet Old Aunt didn't stub her toe that often, not when she had no choice but to watch where she placed her feet.

'So you are back again, always to suit your own convenience and not that of your elders,' snapped her aunt in lieu of a more traditional welcome. Qing knew the old woman's impossible manner hid a warm heart.

'You know I work at the factory, Old Aunt. My time is not my own.'

'You need a hot meal, I suppose?'

'I come to see you, Old Aunt. As my father has said often, a family with an old person has a living treasure of gold.'

It provoked a toothless half-smile and a curt, 'Well? What are you waiting for? Do you think these old bones can stand to wait around at your convenience? Come in and close the door.'

Qing hurried into the dark gloomy interior of the small dwelling. It smelled of old people; carbolic soap and old soup. The girl shuddered and reminded herself that she was determined to find a future that had some brightness about it.

'What is the news then, Old Aunt?' she asked, by way of conversation.

'There are still rumours that this area will be bulldozed for the new development.'

'But surely there must be something official? You cannot just believe the gossip.'

'You think they will come and ask us nicely?' She mimicked an official tone: 'Your land is to be developed into a shopping mall, it is better you move now before you are buried under the rubble.'

'I have heard that such things happen in the countryside, of course,' agreed Qing. 'But not in Beijing surely.'

'Corrupt officials with their broad noses in the trough with the pigs – they are the same whether in the provinces or the cities.'

'But what do you plan to do?'

'There is a residents' association which is trying to find out the truth about these men in suits.'

'Will they have any success?'

The shrug of thin shoulders was the only response. She was old and had been shrugging since the dawn of the Cultural Revolution. 'I know that they will have to carry me out of here feet first if they want me to leave.'

Qing looked around the gloomy interior and a part of her wanted to ask why her aunt felt so strongly about this tiny piece of Beijing real estate, worth more to others than to her. Instead, she said, 'But the compensation might be quite good?'

'You are naive, child. Profits for fat cats are not made by paying a fair price to the likes of you and me. Besides, what do I care about money? This is my home and I will leave it when the time comes for me to take up residence in an urn on your father's mantelpiece.'

Qing tried to distract the old woman from her morbid thoughts. 'I think everything will be fine, Aunt. I will be visiting you here for many years to come, looking forward to a fine home-cooked meal.'

Her aunt was not easily placated. 'Well then you must be careful of your safety or you could end up dead in an alley just like that boy.'

'That was a very shocking thing. Have there been any developments in the case?'

'The police are happy to call it a robbery gone wrong.'

'You don't think so?' asked Qing and wished that her voice had not sounded so constricted.

Her aunt started to rummage around in the small cupboard where she kept her cooking utensils. She pulled out a small pan and placed it on the gas cooker, a luxury compared to an era of coal stoves that had left her walls and roof blackened. She lit the flame with a match and then carefully put the burned match back in the small box. Qing knew she would use it again if she had to light a candle from the stove. In China, amongst the poor, not even a used match was wasted.

'It is not for me to pass judgement. What does an old woman know about these things? But others are not satisfied. Someone was asking about him – the one who was killed. An old man who was almost as poor as I am.'

'How do you know he was poor?' asked Qing, curious about this deduction.

'I could see that his shoes were down at heel.'

'You should have been a detective, Old Aunt,' said Qing, feeling a sudden warmth of affection for the doubled-over, bad-tempered creature. She had not let her limited field of vision thwart her natural curiosity.

'I wonder why they are asking questions now, so long after the death,' she continued.

'I really don't know what the world is coming to,' said her aunt.

Was it necessary, when old, to trot out every single old person cliché in the universe, wondered Qing, fingering the poster she had hidden in her handbag.

'Weren't you here that evening he was killed?' asked her aunt.

'I might have been around the same time.'

'You should count yourself lucky not to be involved then.'

'I know how lucky I am,' said Qing and she meant it.

She was a factory girl from the provinces. Back home, her parents were like baby birds in the nest, waiting to be fed. Opportunities to do anything other than eke out a living were few and far in between. She had assumed that she would work hard, study hard and better herself through tiny incremental steps. But now she had an opportunity. Her silence about what she'd seen the night of the murder would have to be bought and paid for – and she was sure it had a far greater monetary value than years spent on a factory floor. Qing nodded her head vigorously so that her curls bounced. 'I know how lucky I am,' she said again.

Six

'You see – we're only looking at two possibilities.'

Singh was back in the limousine with the blacked-out windows, grateful for Benson's smooth driving and the air conditioning. It was like being shoved in the fridge after being stir-fried in a hot wok. Going door to door down those narrow streets had left him melting like an ice cream. Singh paused to wonder why all his mental metaphors were food related and then decided it was likely because it was getting close to teatime.

'What are those possibilities?' pressed Li Jun.

Singh nodded his great head approvingly. This fellow had the attributes of a good flunkey. Asking the right questions when prompted and not venturing his own opinions on the murder case. Singh much preferred to form his own views. All he needed was someone to agree with him from time to time when he uttered his thoughts out loud. He pursed his lips thinking back over his investigations. The worst was the most recent in Mumbai. Between Inspector Neejha with his dodgy syntax and his own wife with her definitive opinions unsupported by evidence, it had been hard going. Precisely the sort of sidekicks he didn't need.

'You said there were two possibilities?'

Singh scowled. Did Li Jun think he'd lost his train of thought? Or as Neejha had said to him once, that 'his mind was derailed'?

'Either Justin was beaten to death by a gang of unknown thugs in a robbery gone wrong . . .'

'Or?'

'Or he was beaten to death by a gang of unknown thugs for some *other* reason. So the only real question is motive.'

'Meaning he was killed on the orders of someone?'

'That's right.'

'So he had enemies?'

'It could be,' said Singh, thinking out loud. 'Or, as you suggested earlier, it wasn't his enemy but an enemy of someone else in the family.'

'I believe the First Secretary is widely respected,' replied Li Jun.

'It's not going to be the sixteen-year-old daughter so the husband is the best bet.'

There was nothing Singh liked better than annoying rich men with questionable business practices. Besides, he was curious to meet the man who had married Susan Tan. 'Let's head back to the Embassy and ask Anthony Tan about his dodgy business associates,' he proposed cheerfully.

'Benson!' he barked. 'We want the First Secretary's husband.'

'I'll call and find out where he is,' said Benson, reaching for his phone. After a quick, quiet conversation, he rang off and said, 'He's actually not far from here, Inspector, and says he'll meet us at a tea shop around the corner.'

In five minutes, he drew up on the main highway and pointed at a small outlet in a row of shops. 'That's the one. And that's Anthony Tan going in now.' He indicated a tall man with a slight stoop around the shoulders ducking into the tea shop.

'Do you wish me to accompany you?' asked Li Jun.

The other man shook his head. 'I've got a better idea – why don't you try and rustle up some old buddies from the force?'

'You wish me to check the progress of the murder investigation with my former colleagues at the security bureau?'

'That's right,' agreed Singh.

He hopped out, waved the car on, dodged a motorcycle at the last moment and walked over slowly. The entrance to the shop was narrow and the interior gloomy after the bright sunshine outside. Singh blinked rapidly a few times to clear his vision. The premises were panelled in dark wood and filled with the pungent smell of a thousand types of tea. A thousand at a minimum, decided Singh, looking at the boxes piled high on shelves and side tables. He sneezed as the various competing scents tickled his nostrils, reached for the neatly folded handkerchief in his breast pocket and wiped his nose vigorously. Anthony Tan was sitting at a table at the back, the only customer in the shop as far as Singh could tell, and he waved a greeting at the policeman. Singh shook the outstretched hand although he noted that Tan did not get to his feet.

'My condolences over the loss of your son,' he said, as he sat down on a carved jade-coloured stool. To his consternation, he realised that the glass table revealed red and white carp swimming just beneath the surface. He tapped his fingernail on the glass but the fish ignored him.

'Thank you,' said Tan. 'It was a great shock to all of us.' He poured some tea from a clear pot in which floated individual blossoms and pushed the small cup over to Singh.

'What do you think happened?' asked Singh, sipping his tea and deciding that it tasted like boiled grass, or the way he imagined boiled grass would taste.

'Justin was killed by a gang of thugs in a robbery gone wrong.'

'So you don't share your wife's opinion that there is more to it than that?'

'What else could there be? He was twenty-three and had only been in China for a few months.'

'Not long enough to make enemies?' Singh was not convinced. He himself could set up blood enmities within minutes, especially with his wife's relatives.

'Exactly!'

They both sipped their tea and watched the circling carp for a few moments.

Anthony Tan, hands still cupping his tea, said, 'Inspector Singh, I hope you don't mind if I'm frank?'

'I don't mind.'

'My wife is devastated by the loss of our son. She's not thinking rationally. Justin's death was a terrible tragedy, but no more than that. The Chinese police have the matter well in hand and you're wasting your time here.'

Although that was precisely what Singh thought, he found himself growing defensive. Anthony Tan's dismissive tone was getting under his skin.

'She seems convinced.'

'But where's the evidence?'

'I guess that's what I'm supposed to find ...'

'And how would you go about it? It's an impossible task, especially if you're not Mandarin speaking!'

'What would you prefer I did?' asked Singh.

'Go home.'

'I expect I will soon,' agreed the inspector, 'but as I've come all the way, do you mind if I ask you a few questions?'

The handsome face across from him was marred by a scowl. 'If you must.'

'If – hypothetically speaking – your wife is right and this was a targeted murder, who do you think might be involved?'

Anthony Tan's eyes crinkled around the edges as he tried to give the question some consideration. 'I really don't know,' he said at last. 'I can't think of anyone. Justin was a popular boy. He worked hard. I know that professor of his, Professor Luo, thought highly of him. No one would have wanted to kill him. I'm certain of that.'

'And yet he is dead.'

'It must have been ... random.'

'Or maybe it was a murder to send a message to someone else,' said Singh.

'What do you mean?'

'Have *you* any enemies?'

'What are you trying to say?'

'I'm not *trying* to say anything,' snapped the policeman. 'I'm asking you if someone might have killed your son as revenge or as a warning to *you*. I hear you're a businessman.' He managed to make the word an accusation. 'Any transactions gone pear-shaped recently?'

Anthony Tan's elbows were on the table and now he covered his face with his hands. When he looked up again, his eyes were bloodshot.

'Did my wife put this ridiculous idea in your head?'

Singh ears pricked up but his only response was a non-committal shrug. Anthony Tan seemed to treat this as confirmation and his face reddened with anger.

'It's about Dai Wei, right? That's what she's insinuating! She has no idea how business is done in this country.'

'But you do?'

'I know how to make things happen to everyone's advantage.'

Singh remained silent – the best approach in his opinion when dealing with angry spouses.

'How could she even think something like that? None of my business dealings had anything to do with Justin's death. Dai Wei is the deputy mayor of Beijing, for God's sake!' He slammed his hand on the table and the fish shot out in different directions. 'Do you believe her accusations?'

'I'm just exploring different avenues.'

'Let me be as clear as possible then – this so-called avenue of yours is a dead end.'

'That's all I needed to know,' said Singh with equanimity, although his mind was racing to absorb the implications of Anthony Tan's tirade. He opened his wallet and took out a business card. He slid it across the table to Tan, who picked it up automatically, staring at his own shaking hands as if surprised that his appendages were behaving in such an unpredictable way.

'Call me,' said the inspector, 'if you think of anything that might help us find the killers of your son.'

Anthony Tan didn't look up but he nodded once in assent.

Professor Luo huddled in his bare cell. He was in solitary confinement now so had his pick of four filthy corners. He tried to keep his teeth from chattering by clenching his jaw. It didn't work. Another lesson in life – the involuntary and instinctive triumphed over the best of intentions. He wondered what would happen next. He'd been badly beaten when he'd led the *falun gong* exercises in defiance of the guards. So had the rest of them who had foolishly or bravely followed his lead. Despite this, Luo had a sense the wardens were holding back. The way they had gone about the assault had been professional, aiming for his back and shoulders. They had consciously avoided permanent damage. He was still able to walk and nothing was broken. His body was a kaleidoscope of bruises but those healed. Anyone who had lived through the Mao era knew that. It gave him some hope that they might release him, didn't want to inflict the sort of injuries that would cause an outcry if he went public about his incarceration and torture. He clenched his fists, trying to prevent his heart from exploding with anticipation at the possibility, however faint, that he might be free to see his children again.

He wondered what they were doing and then shied away from the thought. It was too painful – the memory of an outdoors, of two young girls in bright clothes, of laughter on a crisp spring morning. But still his head filled with images as if there was a movie theatre in his brain that could not be switched off. He thought of Justin and Dao Ming, an attractive young couple with so much to look forward to in life. He'd been against the relationship. It was not that he hadn't approved of Justin, quite the opposite, but no one who was not a Chinese citizen, being ethnically Chinese was not enough, could fully understand what it was to be a native of this, the most populous country in the world. That poor boy had not realised the consequences of what he was doing, had believed that the truth gave one protection. Singapore did not train its people, despite its reputation for authoritarianism, for the reality of confronting power. There the closed fist was wrapped in glossy paper and ribbon from the shiny shops on Orchard Road. Not so here in China.

Professor Luo heard footsteps down the corridor, boots on cement, and tensed. He realised how afraid he was. Afraid of never seeing his daughters again. Afraid of living in a world without justice. But, most of all, afraid of what they had in store for him in the next half an hour. It was an interesting psychological phenomenon. How fear narrowed the parameters of the imagination until one was completely focused on the here and now. No longer concerned about the externalities that had led to the existence of fear in the first place. Luo Gan willed himself to think outside his terror and remembered that hunger was the other great attention grabber. He focused on the memory of the gnawing emptiness of his stomach all those years ago when, as a teenager, he was sent to the provinces to correct his bourgeois leanings by working with peasants on the land. He smiled at the irony, back to square one after forty years. Those Western scholars who thought history was linear should visit China. Here, fate travelled in circles.

The bolts were shot and the door swung open.

'Luo Gan, come with me.'

The old man slowly unbent his stiff legs, felt his knees crack and rose to his feet. 'Where are we going?'

'The director is concerned that you have been injured as a consequence of your rebellious behaviour.'

'That is very kind of him.'

'He wishes you to receive medical attention.'

'I would prefer to be released.'

'That is not possible at this time.'

Luo Gan considered the middle-aged man in the PLA uniform. How had he ended up at this post? Did he mind that he was the jailor of Chinese citizens who had been incarcerated without due process? Did he feel sorry for an old man with severe bruising who might look just like his father or an uncle?

'I have two daughters,' he ventured. 'I would like to see them again someday.'

'There is no reason why you shouldn't, old man. But you must show some remorse for your anti-Party activities.'

'It is not anti-Party or anti-anything to practise *falun gong*. It merely allows for the clarity of mind that promotes moral and spiritual awakening. The community included many high-up officials before it was blacklisted by Jiang Zemin.'

The soldier did not respond. Instead, he held the door open and gestured with an impatient hand. There was to be no discussion of the rights and wrongs of his imprisonment with this sad-eyed, stiff-jawed soldier.

Professor Luo hobbled towards the door. There was no point inviting another beating. 'Where are we going?' he asked. 'Where are you taking me?'

'To the hospital.'

Benson rapped on the door once and then again, louder. He turned to Singh apologetically. 'It seems that Jemima is not in, Inspector Singh. Would you prefer that we returned later or tomorrow?'

Singh's stomach growled its concurrence before he had a chance to speak. He was peckish. More than that. He was famished. Was it time to suggest ferreting out a curry? He decided that, remarkably, he was prepared to eat more Chinese food. What was happening to him? Next, he'd have to call himself a food tourist and write a travel book.

'What would you like for tea?' asked Benson.

The sound of a bolt being drawn back interrupted his response. Singh's jowls drooped. It seemed that someone was home after all.

The face that peered around the door was thin, young and very suspicious.

'Jemima, Inspector Singh would like to have a few words with you,' said Benson.

'Are you the policeman from Singapore?'

'Yes,' he replied. 'Your mother asked me to look into Justin's death.' Singh's policy, when dealing with children, was to be as honest as possible.

Her eyes filled with tears and turned bright red around the

rims at the mention of her brother. Singh did not have to be a highly rated detective to know that her grief was still very raw. 'I'm sorry for your loss,' he said gruffly.

'Sorry no cure . . .'

'That's true,' he agreed.

'Have you spoken to the rest of my family?'

'Your father and your mother, yes. It's what we do in an investigation – speak to everyone connected to the case.'

'And now you want to talk to me?'

'Yes.'

'My mother doesn't believe it was just a robbery.'

'And you?'

'I'm not sure.' She spoke cautiously but thoughtfully, as if she had given the matter a lot of thought.

'Is there something you want to tell me, something I should know?' asked Singh, watching Jemima's eyes dart from side to side as if she expected a non-frontal attack from some third party. Was it the death of her brother that had made her so nervous?

'I'm not sure – I don't know what's important, you see.'

'That's always true, but the more information we collect, the more likely we are to find the pieces of the puzzle.'

'I could tell you about Justin?' she offered tentatively.

Singh was reminded of a puppy laying a ball or a stick at its owner's feet.

'We'd love to hear about Justin. Especially from you.'

She pushed the door open and he stepped into the front room.

'I'll wait in the car,' said Benson, retreating rapidly.

Maybe he didn't want to hear what his employer's daughter

had to say about his employer's son. Or what his employer's daughter had to say about his employer or her husband. He was definitely walking a fine line when it came to long-term employment. The inspector, on the other hand, was looking forward to a basketful of dirty laundry.

As he stepped into the residence, Singh was struck, as Susan Tan had been earlier that day, by the coldness of the interior despite the temperature being regulated at a pleasant twenty-four degrees. The grey walls – he'd bet an interior designer would have called the colour 'slate' or 'mist' – were downright depressing.

'Nice place,' he said and his voice seemed loud, as if he'd shouted in a mausoleum. Who needed to visit Mao's tomb when you could just hang out here?

'Would you like a drink? Coffee?' The question was formal as if by letting him over the threshold, Jemima was now obliged to conform to a certain standard of behaviour.

'Coffee would be good,' he answered and followed her into the modern kitchen with the high table in the centre. He perched nervously on a bar stool – his feet didn't reach the floor. He'd probably slide off and end up in a Beijing hospital.

She pressed a few buttons on a coffee machine that looked like it would facilitate time travel.

'How many sugars?'

'Two. No, make it three. Heaped.'

Jemima bit her bottom lip as if preventing a comment or a smile, but Singh was not embarrassed. If he had to delay his next meal to talk to this girl, then he needed something to tide him over.

'So how come you're in China? Shouldn't you be in school?'

'I'm waiting for exam results.'

'How long have you been here?'

'Two months.'

So she had overlapped with most of Justin's stay.

'Are you doing some part-time study here?'

'Like Justin? No. I just hang around the house.' He liked the tone of her voice – quiet and even. She came across as a thoughtful girl, unusual for a teenager, but that last sentence had smacked of bitterness. Was she resentful of her sibling?

He hazarded a guess. 'You wanted to do a course like Justin?'

'No. I prefer to be on my own.'

He gave up trying to elicit personal information. 'Tell me about Justin.'

'He wasn't like me at all.'

'What does that mean?'

'He was fun – he had lot of friends. He was terribly smart.'

Singh felt out of his depth. This girl needed a therapist.

'And he always tried to do the right thing. He was a very good person.'

The antenna went up. 'What does that mean? What does "he always tried to do the right thing" mean?'

'Just that.'

Teenagers were not his cup of tea. Give him a reluctant forty-year-old any day and he'd soon have them spilling the beans.

'Give me an example,' he growled.

Her eyes widened at the irritable tone but she did not flinch. 'He never drank Coke.'

'What?'

'He never drank Coke.'

'And how is that an example of doing the right thing?'

'He said it was a symbol of American cultural imperialism.'

'I don't suppose it was Coke that killed him.' Singh tried to remember if he'd ever had grand political principles when he'd been a young man – positions on cultural imperialism and the Western global hegemony. Somehow, he doubted it. If his memory served him right, he'd played a lot of cricket, drunk a lot of beer and eventually joined the police force against his parents' wishes.

'He did a lot of work for his professor.' Jemima interrupted his trot down memory lane. 'Important stuff,' she continued.

She carefully placed his cup on a saucer and then carried it to him with the care of a child in an egg and spoon race. He had a sip of the coffee and scalded his tongue. He grimaced – why did these machines heat up the milk too? Cold UHT from the fridge was the way to keep temperatures reasonable.

'He had a part-time job?' asked Singh.

Jemima's lips curled and he couldn't tell if it was derision or amusement. This kid was as deep as a mining pool. He would have to watch his step with her.

'Don't you know who his teacher was?'

'No.'

'Professor Luo Gan!' She delivered the information with a flourish, as if she'd just pulled a bunch of plastic flowers from a hat with a collapsible bottom.

'And what is Professor Luo Gan's unique selling point?'

'He's a Chinese intellectual. He studied and taught in Harvard for a number of years before returning to China to take up a post at Peking University.'

'What does any of that have to do with the price of fish?'

'He is well known for his criticism of the Chinese government.'

'That sounds dangerous.'

'Yes. Many people, including my brother, admired him for his courage.'

She hopped off her stool, fetched a laptop and opened it in front of him. After some busy typing while various screens flashed and Singh could only sit by and feel like a dinosaur, she turned the screen to him. 'This is his blog in English. There is also a Chinese version.'

He read it quickly, seeking the gist, rather than the detail. It was an exposé of a corrupt land deal. The professor had become involved on behalf of peasants against what appeared to be a land grab by corrupt officials in Sichuan Province. A photo had been posted of a line of villagers, locked arm in arm, in front of a bulldozer. He laboriously ran his fat finger over the touch pad and read that many officials had denounced Luo Gan for 'standing in the way of progress' and 'being stuck in the old Maoist ways of thinking'. In the end, though, thanks to the popular outcry, he'd prevented the demolition of the village from going through.

He looked at the last entry. It was brief. 'Next week I will be reporting on another attempted land grab, right here in Beijing. Watch this space.' He leaned forwards and peered at the date. The post was four weeks old.

'All right – his professor was a crusader on behalf of the people. What does that have to do with Justin?'

'Justin helped him a lot with his research. He was very proud of what he was doing. He felt that he was making a difference. My parents weren't that keen, of course.'

'Why not?'

She shook her head and her hair swung from side to side like a metronome. 'Getting involved in internal Chinese matters . . .'

Singh could see why the First Secretary of the Singapore Embassy might not have wanted a family member involved in something so controversial.

'But they didn't stop him?'

'No. But I don't think they realised how involved he really was.'

'I guess I need to chat to this professor chap,' sighed the policeman, gulping down the rest of his coffee. It seemed Justin was a good guy and a teacher's pet. That was not suggestive of a motive or a lot of Singh's schoolmates would have been in the firing line over the years. 'Although I don't see how this could have a bearing on the murder.'

'And while you're there, don't forget to look up Justin's girlfriend!'

Li Jun caught the yellow and blue bus of Beijing Public Transport – it cost less than a yuan – to his old headquarters. It was standing room only on the bus. As he stood close by the exit, clutching a post, a black limousine with darkened windows tried to cut in front of the bus with an aggressive blast of its horn. The Mercedes got past but such was Beijing's traffic gridlock that it crawled to a halt within a few meters. Li Jun smiled thinly. The wealthy and the anonymous got stuck in unmoving queues of cars just like the proletariat. It was the great leveller, capitalism with Chinese characteristics.

As he disembarked at the correct bus stop, Li Jun took a deep breath, enjoying the way the cold air from an air-conditioned shop across from him cut through the humidity like a scythe. There had been too many people on that bus and the air had become fetid with body odour and bad breath. The ex-policeman walked to a public phone and called his friend, wondering if he would be prepared to come down for a few minutes, just for old time's sake.

Li Jun sat down at a small teahouse and ordered a pot of jasmine tea for two as well as a side dish of marbled tea eggs. The undistinguished little spot he'd chosen was famous for the concoction of spices, a secret recipe, of course, in which it boiled its eggs. He peeled an egg and admired the marbling effect made by cracking the shell when the egg was only partially cooked. He was only halfway through the first when Han Deqiang walked in and took the small wooden seat opposite. He immediately reached for an egg and started peeling it before he uttered his first words.

'It is good to see you, Comrade Li. You're a stranger nowadays.'

'It is better for your career if you are not seen with a disgrace like me,' replied Li Jun with a smile. 'That is why I keep my distance most of the time.'

'Fortune has a fickle heart, my good friend.'

Li Jun knew he was alluding to the years the two of them had spent being re-educated in the country. Li Jun had been the son of the headmaster of a small school. Han had been the grandson of a former landowner. These attributes were sufficient to make the former a target as a bourgeois element and the latter as a capitalist roader. They were denounced by the

Red Guards. The sons, after watching their fathers sweep courtyards and attend ritual self-criticisms, were shipped off to the provinces for re-education. They'd met on the train and become friends, working the fields together alongside the farmers. It had, as adversity sometimes does, formed a strong bond between them.

'So to what do I owe the honour of this meeting?' asked Han.

'I have been asked to look into a death.'

This was met by a loud guffaw. 'So now you are a private investigator?'

'Just this once, my friend.'

'Well, I hope they are paying you well!'

'An honest man finds satisfaction in a job well done,' said Li Jun, a smile robbing his prim words of offence.

'And that satisfaction fills the stomach of his children as well,' agreed Han with another laugh.

Li Jun knew that Han only had one son so he did not think that he would have real difficulty making ends meet, even on a policeman's wage. Not now that his family had been re-habilitated and he was a senior policeman. Li Jun's family too had been brought in from the cold after the excesses of the Red Guard era but it had been too late for his father who had flung himself into a dark well on a dark night when the humiliation had become too much.

'So what is this case of yours?'

'That boy from Singapore who was killed by thugs.'

'Ahh – I know it. Very bad for our reputation when for-eigners are killed.'

'But the solution was reached very quickly. A robbery gone wrong, murder by an unidentified group of thugs.'

'Yes, the whole department was covered in the glory of a successful investigation.'

Li Jun smiled. He'd almost forgotten his friend's knack for making sarcastic comments sound like revolutionary-era slogans.

'So what do you think happened?'

Han's response was cautious. 'There is no evidence of any animosity towards the victim that might have made him a target.'

'Who led the investigation?'

A slight pause prefaced his answer. 'Detective Xie.'

Li Jun didn't know Xie in person but he certainly knew him by reputation. He was a man of whom it was said that he tried to feed himself rice with one chopstick. As he was a retired Politburo member's youngest son – he was protected and promoted. But he was never given a case where a solution was actually desired.

'Why?' he asked at last.

Han made a big show of chewing and swallowing his marble egg as if he were a well-mannered *gwai lo* who would not speak with his mouth full. His friend and former colleague knew he was buying time, considering his answer. Li Jun didn't mind. Han had never misled him in all the years they had known each other; he didn't expect him to start now.

'Fu ordered it.'

'Fu ordered it?'

'Are we at the Great Wall to hear such echoes?'

'But this is very interesting and thought provoking, Comrade Han.'

'That is why I am hesitant to reveal it to you, Comrade Li!

I know your penchant for trouble when you hear "interesting and thought provoking" things.'

'Fu is still the deputy head of the Bureau as far as I am aware.'

'That is correct.'

'And he does not want a solution to this case ...'

'Why do you say that?'

'My wits may have become blunt, dear friend, but credit me with some understanding. We both know Xie's reputation.'

Han remained silent, content for his retired friend to draw the conclusions that he could not be heard to speak out loud while still in uniform.

'Fu does not hand out a traffic ticket without the say-so of Dai Wei,' mused Li Jun.

'He is the right hand man of our powerful and popular deputy mayor,' agreed Han.

'And he has been the fist that has cracked down on organised crime,' Li Jun pointed out, 'but Dai Wei has been the brains behind the operation.'

'That is right. A thousand businessmen behind bars since he began the crusade.'

'All criminals?' demanded Li Jun.

'This is Beijing, my friend. All crows are indeed black. Any thousand would have done just as well.'

Li Jun slumped forwards, elbows on the table, last egg untouched and tea growing cold. His friend was right. The business community was so corrupt that it was much more difficult to find an honest man than a crook. Any thousand would indeed have done just as well.

A group of kids walked in wearing Nike trainers, headphones from their mobiles plugged into their ears. They were noisy and boisterous. The girls, in Li Jun's view, were wearing skirts that were far too short, goosebumps visible on their thighs from the sudden cool of the dark interior. He sighed and felt like the old man he was. China was changing and, despite everything he had been through, he was still not sure it was for the better.

'Is there anything else I should know?' asked Li Jun, although Han had given him plenty to ponder upon. 'Do you know of any link between the dead boy and Fu or Dai Wei?' Even as he asked the question he knew it was ridiculous. In what circumstances would a twenty-something Singaporean kid cross the two most powerful men in Beijing? He was being silly, reading more into the appointment of Detective Xie than he should have. Perhaps the detective was on the verge of retirement and they'd wanted to give him a big case to mark his departure. Maybe, with this purge of organised crime, the real cops were too busy tracking down the real criminals – street crime, however violent the ending, did not qualify as major criminal activity. Or at least there was less glory in cracking down on it.

'Your curiosity knows no bounds, Comrade Li.'

'A man is only a fool if he does not seek answers.'

'If that were true, Li, you would be the chief of the Bureau, not an outcast.'

Li Jun looked across at his friend in his smart uniform, filled out at the chest and shoulders and beginning to fill out around the belly. Han had always kept himself trim, but age and good living caught up with the best of them. He knew that, by contrast, he looked poor and ill fed. His friend was right. Sometimes it was better to look the other way, to keep one's head down. If he had followed his friend's sound advice before, he would not be in such straits now. He clasped and reclasped his hands, squeezing as he did so. The humidity was making his joints hurt. Despite the frigid cold of a Beijing winter, his joints always hurt that much more in summer. Li Jun picked up the pot of tea and poured himself some warmth into a cup. He wrapped his fingers around it and felt the pain slowly ease.

'So,' he asked again, 'is there anything else I should know?' A small smile played about his lips at the resigned expression on his friend's face.

'Men like you are the conscience of the rest of us, Li Jun.' Han cracked his knuckles like a bouncer looking for a quarrel and continued, 'Very well, since you ask, it is well known that the boy's father, Anthony Tan, was a business associate of Dai Wei.'

Li Jun nodded. It was not that much of a surprise. 'That's all you have?' He had a sense his friend was holding something back.

'I'll see if I can dig up anything else.'

'That would be very helpful.'

Their eyes met across the table.

'And you should know,' Han said at last, loyalty apparently trumping caution, 'Anthony Tan is a very good friend of Dai Wei's wife.'

Anthony Tan's mobile rang. He took it out of his pocket and stared at the number. He didn't recognise it but that really didn't mean much. He could guess who it was or, at least, on whose behalf the call was being made. His uneaten lunch was on the table in front of him – when was the last time he'd been able to eat a full meal? Not since his son had died. He was losing weight rapidly and would soon be a shadow of his former self, still shrouded in his expensive suits.

'Yes?'

'I am calling on behalf of a mutual friend. I think you know who I mean.'

'I have a lot of friends.'

'I hope for your sake that you don't owe money to all of them.'

Anthony dropped the act. 'I have explained that I just need a little more time. I will pay your boss back. I've already promised you that – what more can I do?'

'Unfortunately, he is getting impatient.'

'Look, I said I would return the money as soon as I received payment for my part in setting up this construction project. There's just been a delay getting planning permission, that's all.' Anthony shut his eyes and wondered how he had been stupid enough to get into this hole. He shifted the phone to his other ear and tried to think of something, anything that would get him a few days – a few days for Dai Wei to come good with the permit.

Anthony still couldn't believe that he'd gone to a money-lender for help, for the grease he needed for Dai Wei's palms. It had seemed a sure thing – borrow the money on a short-term loan, pay Dai Wei, get the planning permission to redevelop the *hutong* and recover a handsome fee from the Singaporean developers. But in retrospect, it was reckless to the point of imbecility. He had not factored in the possibility that Dai Wei would not come through in a timely manner. Maybe his wife's assessment of his character was the right one, after all. He was a greedy fool. Self-awareness was a bitter pill indeed.

'You told our boss that it was a done deal,' remarked the moneylender's henchman, voice dropping an octave.

'It is a done deal ... it's just taking a bit longer than we expected, that's all.'

'*Māoshǔtóngmián* – the cat and the rat are asleep together – or are they not?'

'My relationship with the principal is still good. The planning permission will be issued soon and your boss will get his money back!'

'I hear your family has suffered some ill fortune of late.'

'What are you talking about? What do you mean?'

'My boss says that your son was outnumbered in a fight. That was foolish.'

Anthony pressed his thumb and finger against his eyes and then released them. Red dots swam across his vision and he felt faint. It couldn't be, they'd promised him more time.

'You are a fortunate man and can still count your blessings. After all, everyone knows that a father's heart lies with his daughter.'

'What are you trying to say?'

'That you should pay back the money if you want to ensure her longevity.'

'How dare you threaten my daughter?'

The response was like the deep-throated bark of an angry hound. 'You have three days to find the money.'

The line was cut and Anthony stared at the phone in his hand as if he was cradling a scorpion, waiting for the fatal flash of the curved tail.

'Daddy?'

He turned to the door and saw his thin sprite of a girl

staring at him with wide, shocked eyes. How much had she heard? He tried to remember the exact words he'd spoken but it was impossible. His brain was scrambled with terror.

'Daddy, what's going on? I heard you shouting . . .'

'Nothing to worry about, honey – just an impossible client. You know how difficult it can be to get anything done in China.'

'But you said something about a threat! To me?'

'Of course not, don't be ridiculous.'

That part of Jemima's face that was not obscured by a cascade of hair conveyed disbelief.

'I met that policeman,' she volunteered. 'The one from Singapore.'

'You did?' Anthony did his best to focus on the here and now.

'Yes, he came here.'

'He shouldn't have spoken to you without my permission,' insisted Anthony.

'Mum said it was fine.'

'Did you have anything to tell him?'

'No, I didn't.'

Their eyes met and Anthony tried to read his youngest child. Did she know something?

'The thing is,' she continued, 'that policeman, Inspector Singh, is going to find the truth.'

'Why do you say that?'

'I just don't think he's the sort to give up easily. And he really wants to find out what happened to Justin.'

Seven

'Dinner time!' said Inspector Singh. 'Where shall we eat?'

These Beijing residents needed to start earning their keep. They might think of themselves as private investigators with a murder to solve but as far as Singh was concerned they were just there to point out the best restaurants.

'I have instructions to take you wherever you would like to go,' said Benson.

'When in Rome . . .' said Singh.

'I beg your pardon?' said Benson.

'Finish the sentence,' urged the inspector. 'When in Beijing . . . what should I eat?'

'Peking duck,' said Li Jun.

'Good idea,' agreed Benson. 'You can go to Quanjude or Da Dong.'

'Both are very expensive,' warned Li Jun.

'Foreigners are supposed to go to expensive restaurants and get fleeced,' said the inspector. 'Otherwise, what's the point in having tourists? As long as the food is good, of course.'

'Both are good,' said Li Jun.

'Which is better?'

'In Quanjude they even give you a diploma stating the duck number you have eaten,' said Benson.

Singh's brow knitted. 'I prefer my ducks to remain anonymous,' he explained. 'In fact, I prefer all my food to be unknown to me personally. It's why we don't eat our pets – except in emergencies.'

'All right, then it has to be Da Dong. I will bring the car around to the front and take you there,' said Benson.

He was as good as his word and in a few short minutes they were ensconced in the private cocoon that was the inside of a well-appointed limousine.

In the car, Li Jun said, 'Would you like to hear about the things I found out today?'

Singh rested his folded hands on his belly. 'Dinner first?'

'It is true that the brain works best once the stomach is full and the heart content but procrastination is the devil's tool.'

'Is that a Chinese proverb?' asked Singh. 'Confucius?'

'I just made it up,' confessed Li Jun.

'Fine – tell me what you found out.'

'I met a former colleague who is now quite senior in the police department.'

'And?'

'He said that the investigation into the murder was handed to a senior officer named Xie. He's the son of a Politburo member.'

'The First Secretary must have been pleased that the Chinese authorities took the case seriously.'

'You should know that in the Beijing police, Detective Xie only gets the cases where the outcome is not valued.'

'What do you mean?'

'He has to be kept on the force because of his father's influence, but he is known to be incompetent.'

'Who would have authority to make such a decision, to assign the case to Xie?'

'Someone senior – like Fu, the deputy head of the Bureau.'

'So the Chinese police don't want the case solved?'

'That is my preliminary conclusion,' said Li Jun primly, steepling fingers with close-cut spotless nails together.

'Great,' muttered Singh. 'Anything else?'

'There are rumours that Anthony Tan is in some sort of business relationship with Dai Wei, the deputy mayor of Beijing. My contact promised to investigate further and let me know details,' continued Li Jun.

'Still don't see how that can have a bearing on the case,' complained Singh. 'Did you ask about the earlier attempted assault? The one you prevented?'

'I forgot,' he confessed. 'I will follow up on that tomorrow.'

'Which means you have more information,' said Singh.

'Why do you say that?'

'Because you would not have forgotten unless you were distracted by something really interesting!'

'There *is* more,' said Li Jun, rabbit grin front and centre. 'Anthony Tan is having an affair with Dai Wei's wife.'

*

Forty-five minutes later, Singh was sitting in a modern, well-lit restaurant with the ubiquitous red pillars, gold lining, paper lanterns and bamboo frescos. The tablecloths were sparkling white, as were the napkins. They were ushered to the table by a waitress who spoke no English but whose cheongsam was slit high up her thigh. She was full of smiles and immediately unloaded a bunch of small appetisers from roast peanuts to seaweed in dainty porcelain dishes. Singh eyed the offerings dubiously. He hoped nothing was endangered – or poisonous. He was handed a menu entirely in Chinese, which he handed back just as promptly, grateful for the presence of his companions. Without them, the only safe way of ordering duck would have been to flap his arms and quack. The dignity of the Singapore police force would not have survived the posting of the clip on YouTube. He pictured Superintendent Chen's face when the video was brought to his attention and smiled. Wasn't that what the chief feared the most? That Singh would find some way to humiliate himself and the force? Justice wasn't at the forefront of his mind. It never was with the bureaucrats.

Li Jun was talking to the headwaiter, a tall and very thin man in a smart black suit. Apparently the girl in the revealing dress was only authorised to show them to their table and hand out titbits.

'So what are we having?' asked Singh.

'Duck!'

He wondered why it had taken so long to order.

'And beer?' he asked hopefully.

Li Jun summoned the tall waiter back with a waved hand and launched into a further order. Apparently, beer was as complicated as duck.

'So why did you leave the police force?' Singh needed to fill the time with small talk since the small snacks were unpalatable.

'It was an unfortunate misunderstanding,' explained Li Jun.

The inspector waited for clarification.

'I was investigating the murder of a woman – she was quite well known, a model worker and member of the Party.'

'You couldn't solve it?'

'Quite the opposite! I realised that the killer was an H.C.C., a discarded lover of the woman.'

'An H.C.C.?'

'A high cadre child.'

'What in the world does that mean?'

'The children of the Party and business elite,' explained Li Jun. 'They are usually considered to be untouchable, above the law. That is certainly how most of them see themselves.'

'So you were not allowed to arrest this murderer?'

'I did not ask for permission.'

'Oh!'

'Also, the press got wind of the situation.' Li Jun smiled a little wistfully.

'What happened?'

'I . . . er . . . opted for early retirement.'

Singh grimaced. Wasn't that what his superiors would dearly love him to do? However, to be fair to Superintendent Chen, he'd never actually prevented Singh from arresting a murderer – usually they just didn't like his shoes.

'And the H.C.C.?' he asked, gulping his beer and then wiping his frothy upper lip with the back of his hand.

'Because of the press interest, the authorities had no choice but to prosecute him. He was found guilty and executed by firing squad.'

'At least justice was done,' murmured Singh.

'I take some comfort from that,' agreed Li Jun. 'But things that are done, it is needless to speak about . . . things that are past, it is needless to blame.'

'You made that up too?'

'Confucius.'

The waiter arrived with a large, red, crispy creature on a tray. As he watched in awe, the waiter sliced and diced the duck, extricating slivers of skin and slices of meat and arranging them neatly in a bed of fresh lettuce. Singh was glad he had not received the duck's birth certificate or whatever they were offering. The lettuce was so green that he wondered whether the chefs had spray-painted the leaves as the organisers had done to brighten the grass during the Beijing Olympics.

Copying Li Jun, he placed a white round pancake on his plate, dipped some skin and tender flesh into the dark sauce and placed them in the centre. Singh added some spring onions, garlic and cucumber sticks, rolled it neatly, fumbled with his chopsticks, which were resting on duck-shaped porcelain holders, abandoned them, picked up his roll with his fingers and took a huge bite.

'Good?' asked Li Jun.

'Mmmm,' agreed Singh, mouth gummed shut by the duck sauce.

A waiter, waved over by Li Jun, took a photo of the two of them with Singh's phone. Apparently, a really good meal had to be recorded for posterity. Singh couldn't disagree with the principle although if he'd photographed every satisfactory meal in his long years as a connoisseur of curries, he'd have a few albums worth.

Singh scanned the round tables packed into the room – the Chinese were positively Arthurian in their fondness for a circular top. There were a number of prosperous-looking men with fat bellies, accompanied by women with low-cut dresses. By the look of things, Da Dong appealed to only two types of clients: foreign tourists and wealthy Chinese. Even the clink of glasses and the rattle of chopsticks suggested prosperity. The pitch was of fine China and thin glass.

'As you see, only tourists and businessmen can afford this place,' remarked Li Jun.

'The majority of foreigners seem to be white men in business suits,' noted the inspector. 'How do they feel, I wonder, kowtowing to China for the first time in history?'

'I think entrepreneurs are happy to do what it takes to make money,' said Li Jun. 'It doesn't matter if a cat is black or white, so long as it catches mice.'

Singh raised an enquiring eyebrow.

'Deng Xiaoping,' clarified Li Jun. His eyes narrowed. 'It seems that politicians can also afford this place.' He continued in a lowered tone, 'That man over there, in the red tie, is Dai Wei.'

Singh stared openly across the room. Dai Wei, deputy mayor of Beijing and cuckold, looked like he needed a couple of cushions to sit on to reach the table. From his pink, shiny face, it seemed that he was eating fast and well. A nubile young woman sat on his right, occupying herself with placing morsels on his plate. Even from the distance, Singh recognised the shape of a Rémy Martin bottle. Every now and then the group around the table would laugh out loud and long, usually when Dai Wei had regaled them with some apparently amusing tale.

'And the one pouring his drink is the deputy head of the Beijing security bureau, Fu Xinghua. Together they have spearheaded the crackdown on organised crime in the city.'

It was poor casting, decided Singh, when Robin was the tall, good-looking one and Batman short and dumpy.

'The same Fu Xinghua who appointed Inspector Clouseau to the case?' At Li Jun's puzzled expression, he clarified, 'Detective Xie?'

'Yes,' agreed Li Jun.

As he watched, Dai Wei rose to his feet and left with his entourage, nodding to individuals at various tables on his way out. A man with a very keen sense of his own importance, decided Singh.

He turned his attention back to Li Jun. 'There's another thing. Jemima told me that Justin's professor was well known for standing up to these land grabs on behalf of villagers,' said Singh.

'Is he Professor Luo Gan?' asked Li Jun.

Singh was impressed. 'Yes, that was the name. Jemima also said that Justin used to help this professor out with his work.'

'That could have been dangerous, I suppose,' remarked Li Jun. 'There is a lot of money involved in those transactions.'

'We can ask the professor tomorrow,' said Singh, chewing vigorously on a piece of duck and washing it down with beer.

*

He stroked her hair and wished that he were anywhere in the world but in the bedroom of another man. The silk bedding was too smooth, too cool, for his tastes. He wondered that her husband didn't mind such a feminine boudoir. The whole room was like an opium den, opulent, dark and scented.

'You seem distracted today.' She pouted.

He turned his attention back to her with an effort – and a warning to himself to be careful. She was very quick to feel a slight and he couldn't afford that. He really couldn't afford that. She was his last hope.

'I've had a rough time recently.'

'Of course, the business with your son.' She made a moue of sympathy with the painted red lips but Anthony Tan felt sick with distaste. 'The business with your son' – was that the way she saw the death of his boy? This narcissistic woman wasn't able to feel or show genuine emotion. He didn't know how he'd fallen into her clutches. Anthony Tan amended the thought – he knew exactly how he'd fallen into her clutches. The signals had been unmistakable and he'd felt complimented and valued to have caught her eye. There had been something genuinely thrilling about having the wife of such a powerful man at his beck and call, didn't that demonstrate that he too was destined for greatness? It had been easy too as Dai Wei's temperament did not allow him to suspect that he was a cuckold.

'I need your help,' he said, throwing caution to the wind. He sat up in the bed, drew the covers up to his waist and propped himself up against the deep purple velvet backboard.

She tried to drag him back down but he resisted. Instead, he gripped her narrow shoulders firmly, forcing her to turn and look at him. In the low light from a single lamp, her eyes were pools of darkness.

'What is it?' she asked. 'What do you want from me?'

'You say that you care about me . . .'

'Of course I do!' She giggled and then put thin fingers to her lips. 'Do you think I cheat on my husband with just anyone?'

Anthony wouldn't have been in the least surprised to discover that he was only one in a long line and perhaps not even the only one at that moment. Her porcelain skin, tracings of blue veins visible like fine strokes on a Ming vase, her bow-shaped mouth, the unexpectedly large eyes that suggested a depth of understanding of weakness and pain – these were all a disguise. She was as cold-blooded as a reptile. Her only interests were her face, her wardrobe and a deep desire to betray her husband on whom she depended for everything and whose generosity and wealth she flaunted like a peacock.

'No,' he said. 'I believe that you and I share a destiny.'

She leaned in closer to him and he felt his body react. He was disgusted with himself, unable to control his urges, no better than an animal.

'So will you help?'

'What do you need? I hope it's not money.' Suddenly, she was distant, the voice like a cold wind from the Mongolian plains.

Anthony guessed that a few of her outside interests had probably sought to feather their nests before she lost interest, desperate to make the relationship count where it mattered, in their wallets.

'Of course not,' he said, gripping her hands in his and trying to look as if he cared about her, about a single thing in the world other than the safety of his remaining child. The voice again in his head – 'you still have a daughter'. He would do anything to keep Jemima safe from threat. For now, he would not even consider the possibility that his actions had contributed to Justin's death.

'What is it then?' The wariness was apparent in the stiffness of her usually languid form.

'I just need you to ask your husband to ... to get me that planning permission I need. I told you about the project some time ago.'

She wasn't interested, he could see that. The eyes were inward looking, bored. She was tugging at the sheet with thumb and forefinger.

'Those are business matters, nothing to do with me,' she said. 'Do you not find it peculiar that you are asking me to intercede with my husband whom we both betray in this manner?'

He was silent for a moment, trying to formulate a response that would get her on his side.

'I am concerned that you have just been using me,' she continued.

'You don't understand my motives, my darling. If I can complete this deal, then nothing can stand between us. I will be able to keep you like a precious songbird in a gilded cage. Surely that is the future we have dreamed of together?'

She smiled and reached for him although he knew very well that she would never leave a piggy bank like Dai Wei; she just enjoyed role-playing the great romance. 'Very well then, I understand that you have our interests at heart. I will see what I can do to influence my husband to help my lover.' She found the thought amusing because the tinkling bell-like laughter rang through the room.

Singh awoke early the next morning because his phone rang.

He reached for it with a sleepy hand and growled a 'hello'.

'Inspector Singh?'

'Yes.'

'This is Susan Tan.'

He sat up straight in bed, rubbing his eyes with his free hand. What was he to tell her? So far he had intimations, no more, that all was not well. Nothing substantive enough to report to a grieving mother. How to tell her that he suspected her husband to be a crook and an adulterer? Or that the daughter was unhappy and had secrets, but whether they pertained to the case was anyone's guess?

'I had a call . . .'

This time he was awake enough to pick up the tension in her voice.

'And?'

'It was a woman, she said her name was Qing. She claimed to have some information about the murder.'

'What sort of thing?'

'She wouldn't say. She called to make sure the reward was still being offered. She saw the poster we put up at the *hutong*. I said it was, of course.'

'Did you get her contact details,' demanded Singh.

'She wouldn't give them to me. I have to meet her. With the money. She didn't come across as the trusting sort. And she had a thick provincial accent. My guess is that she's one of the migrant workers from a rural area.'

Singh paused to ponder this latest development. He reminded himself that callers for a reward were often the least credible witnesses, prepared to say anything for a fast buck. And how would a factory girl have stumbled upon important information about a killing?

'So you made an appointment?'

'She called off in a hurry, someone was coming and she had to go. She said she'd contact me again to make arrangements for payment and to hand over the information.'

'It might just be someone after the reward money, making things up,' warned Singh. It was one of the reasons he didn't like offers of compensation for information. Every crook and kook crawled out of the woodwork claiming to have seen something, heard something, done something. And Susan Tan's hopes had been raised; he could hear the eagerness in the higher pitch of her voice.

'I was sceptical as well at first,' said Susan.

'What changed your mind?'

'Her voice was trembling. I'd always assumed that was a figure of speech, but she was terrified.'

'I guess we're just going to have to wait until she calls back,' sighed Singh. 'Contact me the moment she does. Make sure you insist on meeting her and hearing the information she has in person. We need to get our hands on this girl.'

'What will you do in the meantime?' asked Susan Tan.

'Follow up other leads,' replied the policeman.

Singh had a quick shower, scrubbed his teeth with a frayed toothbrush, new ones made his gums bleed, and carefully tied his turban around his head. He'd chosen a dark blue for the day, a neutral colour signifying nothing. It was his usual choice. Singh was nothing if not a creature of habit. Why would he want to wear white and show the dirt or orange and look like his head was on fire? The six yards of dark cloth went around his head neatly. No woman swaddled a baby as efficiently as he cocooned his head. Feeling relaxed now that his head was swathed – his wife had once referred to his turban as his comfort blanket – 'Why else would you wear it? It is not as if you practise our religion! Always smoking.'

Singh bared his teeth at the mirror. It didn't seem fair that even when he was away from his wife she remained noisily in his head like a tune for which he couldn't remember the name. He'd bet the reverse didn't happen. Mrs Singh was probably gossiping with her sisters or the neighbour without a thought to what he might say, not that surprising as he hardly ever got a word in edgewise. However, her monologue in his brain had reminded him that he fancied a smoke.

'Even before breakfast, you must have cigarettes, isn't it? If you were a Muslim you would probably eat bacon sandwiches.'

There she went again – at least when he was at home, he could walk away. Or go to the office or lock himself in the loo with the newspapers. Her presence in his mind was much more insidious.

'And then the *fatwa* police would come looking for you!'

Mrs Singh had a point – he had to be grateful that Sikhs weren't so militant about punishing deviants. He decided to eschew the smoke and hasten to breakfast. Li Jun was due to meet him that morning and he wanted to make sure he was well nourished before embarking on the fool's errand that was this investigation.

He stuffed his mobile in his pocket and hurried to the buffet breakfast. To his surprise, it was so crowded he couldn't get near the food. And the food looked most unpalatable. Singh helped himself to a small pile of bread and returned to his table. He'd barely sipped his first cup of coffee when he looked up over the rim and saw a waiter indicating his table to Li Jun. He wondered how he'd been described – the Indian? Singaporean? Sikh? Short fat guy with towel over his head? It needed to be something pretty definite, the restaurant was more crowded than a Mumbai train station.

Li Jun was wreathed in smiles as he approached. Singh decided he was wearing the same clothes as the previous day. Either that or he had a cupboard full of tatty Mao suits. It was possible, he supposed. He himself had a wardrobe of dark trousers and white shirts circumnavigated by an old belt whose creases marked each year like the rings of a tree.

'Comrade Singh, you are enjoying your breakfast?'

'Come join me.'

'I have already eaten,' explained Li Jun. 'But I will have some green tea,' he continued. 'It is very good for the digestion when you have reached our age.'

The inspector was not impressed by the slur upon his age or his digestion but he held his peace.

'Susan Tan called with some information. There's a witness, by the name of Qing, offering information for the reward.'

'That is a good development.'

'Not so fast. She called off before she told the First

Secretary anything. We need to wait for her to make contact again.'

The face of the other man conveyed disappointment.

'There's someone else we need to track down,' said Singh. 'Jemima mentioned a girlfriend, suggested we talk to her as well.'

Li Jun nodded his agreement. 'What was Jemima like?' he asked.

'Thin,' said Singh. It did not sound like a compliment coming from the man with the heaped plate. 'She seems distraught over her brother's death.'

'How do we find this girlfriend?'

'I asked Benson to track her down.'

'Good idea,' said Li Jun.

'In the meantime, let's go and chat to the famous Professor Luo Gan!'

Professor Luo Gan was not entirely surprised to find that he was to be strapped to his hospital bed. He was grateful that the leather bands that bound his wrists were sufficiently long that he could raise his head and shoulders a little and look around from time to time. The ward was long and narrow. The lighting was not as bright as he would have expected in a hospital and the distant ends of the room were shrouded in darkness. It had the smell of a hospital, the sharp scent of cheap and powerful disinfectants and the underlying smell of blood and urine. He noted that the personnel, nurses and doctors, all wore military uniforms. This was to be expected; there was no way he would have been taken to a civilian establishment. He lay back down again and turned his head. His sheet, thin and worn, smelled musty and he could see washed-out stains, he didn't even want to think what they might be. He wondered again why this sudden solicitousness for his health. What was the use of beating him half to death and then sending him to hospital? The authorities moved in mysterious ways, that was for sure. It suggested that they expected to release him some day, no doubt after he had recanted. Luo Gan bit down on his lip so hard that he could taste the sharp iron of blood. He would not do that, not ever. This was his penance.

'I need a sample of your blood.' The nurse – he had not noticed her approach – held up a syringe in a bare hand; safe medical practices were not widespread in China.

'I feel fine,' he responded. This was not entirely true – his body was still throbbing with pain, sporadic bursts as if his body was a strobe light. However, he was well enough to know that given his freedom, he would be able to walk away under his own steam.

'I have to follow orders,' she said, not even looking at him, just gripping his wrist and slapping the inside of his arm, just below the elbow to identify a suitable vein.

'Who are the others?' he asked. 'Are they all prisoners?'

She looked around as if noticing the other beds and their occupants for the first time. 'Yes, this is a ward for prisoners only.' She extricated the needle from his arm and snapped her finger at the syringe as if unconvinced that he'd produced real human blood.

The professor almost smiled. He was distracted by an orderly who hurried in and said to the nurse in an undertone, 'We are looking for blood type A-negative. Anyone here with that?'

Luo Gan lay back against the hard bed and pretended that he'd lost interest.

His nurse was flipping through her charts. 'We have two,' she answered. 'Bed thirteen and forty-nine.'

'Age?'

'Both are over forty.'

'That's not good. The director was clear that the request is for a young one.'

The orderly sounded worried, as if failure to obey this instruction might have consequences.

'There is a new batch but we have not identified blood type yet.'

'Better hurry,' said the orderly. 'In the meantime, let us go with the younger of the two men.'

Luo Gan listened to the footsteps as they marched away and then turned over on his side as far as his tethers would allow. He noted that the two had approached a bed and were wheeling it towards the double swing doors. He heard the prisoner ask, 'Where are you taking me?' as they passed his bed, the voice barely audible over the reluctant squeaking wheels. They didn't bother to answer him, didn't even appear to hear him.

'There goes another,' muttered a rasping voice.

It was the prisoner on the next bed, restrained exactly as he was.

'Are you *falun gong*?' he asked.

Luo Gan nodded.

'Most of us are,' he explained. He raised a hand as far as it would go in greeting. 'They call me Xiao Ma.'

Little Horse. It was an ironic name for such a large fellow.

'Why are you here?' asked the professor, noting that the other man was younger than him by a good thirty years and didn't bear any signs of severe injury. 'Were you beaten?'

The other man laughed and Luo admired his ability to maintain good spirits. 'Of course, isn't that part of re-education? How else will we learn the error of our ways.'

'You make a valid point, my friend,' responded Luo Gan.

'How did they find out about you?' asked Xiao Ma.

'I performed the routines under the picture of Mao at Tiananmen Square.'

'So you are a martyr!'

'A martyr is an innocent,' said Luo Gan. 'I have blood on my hands.'

Seeing the other man's puzzled frown, Luo Gan changed the subject. He had no desire whatsoever to explain himself. 'Where did they take the other fellow?' he asked.

'I don't know,' said Xiao Ma. 'Every now and then they cart one of us away. We don't see them again. Maybe they have been released back to their families. I myself am waiting to go home.'

'Then why should they care about blood types? I heard the orderly ask for A-negative type.'

'For surgery?' suggested Xiao Ma.

A sense of foreboding descended over Luo Gan. He tried to blank the thought, to erase the sudden fear from his mind.

Xiao Ma must have noticed the death mask that descended over his new companion's face, thrown into harsh relief by the bare fluorescent tube on the ceiling above them. 'What is it? Why do you look like that?'

Luo Gan lay back and stared up, noting the patterns

formed by water stains in the same way, as a child, he had looked up and detected glorious shapes in the clouds. He had an overwhelming longing for his daughters, for his home.

'I think I know what they're doing,' he whispered. 'I think I know where they took him.'

'If you do not agree to make this payment, I will not be silent about what I know.'

Qing knew she was playing with fire. Her hands shook even as she tried to keep her voice firm, to project an age and a competence she did not feel.

'What can you do? Who would believe you? I myself think that you are just a lying fool who does not know that it is foolish to meddle in the business of others.'

'I know what I saw, and I am sure that there will be someone who is interested in the news even if you are not.'

Qing knew she sounded like she was reciting television dialogue. On the other hand, what other source did she have to give her guidance on how to arrange this transaction? Indeed, if it wasn't for her television habit, developed over the long winter months when there was nothing else to do back home, she would not have realised that her luck had turned so decisively for the better.

'What did you see? A man in a car? You are very naive if you think that this is worth any money to me.' His voice was deep and intimidating.

Qing was angry now. There was no way that she was going to be deprived of her windfall. And it gave her courage. 'Very well, I will take my information elsewhere. I am sorry to have taken up your time. I know you are a busy man.'

'Wait a minute,' said the man. 'Let us not be hasty. Although I think your tale is nonsense, perhaps it is better that I give you some money . . . as a donation towards improving your standard of living.'

She spotted the opening that he'd left her. 'Exactly. It is better that we agree to a solution. After all, you are a wealthy man and I am not asking for much. As you say, a donation.'

'But how do I know that you will not ask for more after I have paid you this amount? Even a deep well will run dry.'

'This is all I will ask for,' said Qing, as convincingly as she could. And she meant it as well. Only a fool would cross swords with this man on a regular basis. She would take the money and disappear forever.

He seemed to believe her because after a short pause, he said, 'Will you come here to collect the funds?'

How stupid did he think she was? She had given the practical elements of her plan careful thought.

'I need you to put the money in a carryall and leave it by the bin on the first floor next to the elevator of the Silk Market this afternoon at two pm. The bin is directly outside the shop selling fake basketball shirts. I will be watching. Once you have left, I will collect the money and you will never see or hear from me again.'

She hung up, not waiting to hear his assent. That way he would know that she meant business. Her knees, which had been locked in position to try to keep her upright, gave away suddenly and she sank to the ground. Qing leaned back and closed her eyes, trying to convince herself that what she had just proposed was the right thing to do. It had not been easy to get through to her target, to convince the lowly staffer that she had something to say that merited the attention of the big man himself. But she had succeeded by using the traditional Chinese method of warning the underlings that the buck would stop with them if they got in her way and the boss heard of it. In the end, the secretary had acquiesced.

Qing knew it would be a risk to collect the money, but the Silk Market, six storeys of small stalls selling fake designer goods, would be packed with people. She would be able to disappear into the crowds in a twinkling. She grinned suddenly, her youth asserting herself – maybe she would even be able to do a bit of shopping with her new-found wealth.

Qing rose to her feet and reached for the phone that she had bought just that morning with the ubiquitous disposable SIM card. She was about to throw it into the bin when she had second thoughts. She walked quickly down the street, a young girl, indistinguishable from the rest of the teeming hordes going about their business. When she reached a park bench, she sat down and placed her phone by her side. After a few seconds, she stood up and hurried on. She left the phone behind. She didn't doubt that someone would find it and think it was his or her lucky day. And if the call had been traced, as she had seen happen on the television, her trackers would be on a wild goose chase.

She walked directly to a small hole-in-the-wall shop selling mobile phones and purchased the cheapest available model. She took the reward poster out of her bag and re-dialled the number she had called that morning.

'Yes?'

'It's me, Qing. I called you earlier.'

The woman's voice came back loud and clear, an edge of

longing running through it. 'Yes, you have information about my son's death.'

'I do. I think you will find what I have to tell you very interesting.' Qing knew she sounded different from that morning, more confident, more assertive. But she doubted that the mother of the boy would notice. She was fixated on the words, not the tone.

'Where can I meet you?'

'At the Silk Market, at two pm. The pizza place on the ground floor.'

Singh was impressed by the sheer size of the campus. The University of Peking was not short of either space or students. However, when they reached the offices of the language institute they were told that Justin's teacher, one Professor Luo Gan, was on medical leave.

Singh eyebrows met. 'When will Professor Luo be back?' he demanded and Li Jun dutifully translated.

'Not sure,' replied the clerk. She looked harassed; glasses perched on the end of her nose, wide cheekbones flushed along the ridges and long hair hanging loose.

'Everyone is looking for him,' she continued, 'asking me when he will be back. But I am not his wife to know such things.'

'But surely you must have spoken to him?' asked Singh. 'Didn't he give any indication?'

An impatient shake of the head accompanied her words. 'The daughter is the one who has been calling me each day to say her father is not well. But she has not told me what is wrong with him. Only that he is too sick to come to the office. For three weeks! Lucky it is the semester break, but even so the work is piling up.'

It was a peculiar approach to medical leave, thought Singh. One usually had a rough idea, depending on whether one was suffering a bad cold or a mild heart attack, how long the absence would be. Calling everyday with updates? What sort of ailment lent itself to a recovery schedule that had to be gauged on a daily basis?

'And who will mark the test papers? The dean is getting very impatient.'

Singh reminded himself he was looking into the death of a Singaporean boy, not his professor's work ethic. It was peculiar though and his long experience working murder cases suggested that anything out of the ordinary might have a bearing on the investigation.

He looked around the office. It was typical of any bastion of academia. Files were piled high. Calendars dominated, two hanging on the walls and at least one on each desk. Dates were circled in red and asterisks were in abundance. What events did they mark? he wondered. End of term dates? Exams? There were grey filing cabinets along the wall. An open drawer was full to the brim.

'Are you the professor's personal secretary?' he asked.

The woman looked scandalised, although Singh was pleased to see that she was glaring at Li Jun, still translating quickly. 'Shoot the messenger' was fine with him.

'I work for the whole department. But everyone thinks that I am their servant.'

'Did you know Justin Tan?'

'The dead boy? Do you think I am like these professors

who do not know what goes on in the real world? That was very bad for the university's reputation.'

She sounded aggrieved. Getting killed while studying at the university was a sin on par with not informing her in a timely manner when intending to take a few days off sick.

'At least he was not murdered here,' she added.

Singh was forced to admit an unwilling admiration. This creature was a real piece of work. The nicest thing she could say about Justin was that his death had occurred elsewhere. It was quite an epitaph. He hoped he merited better someday.

'You knew him?'

'I saw him sometimes, he was in Professor Luo's class.'

'Your professor is quite a well-known figure – a crusader on behalf of the people in these land grabs?'

'He is too much of a big shot to talk to me about something like that.'

'But Justin used to work for him on these matters?'

'Yes, he was the blue eyed boy.'

'So the professor must have been really upset when he died.'

'He was distraught. It was as if his own son had been killed.' She smiled slyly. 'And maybe it was exactly like that?'

'What's that supposed to mean?'

Both eyebrows, plucked almost to invisibility, were raised in a knowing way. 'The daughter, of course!'

'Professor Luo's daughter?' Singh was convinced that only his tightly wound turban stopped his head from exploding. He suddenly remembered Jemima's cryptic parting remark.

'Professor Luo's daughter was Justin's girlfriend?'

There was a reluctant nod, accompanied by the drumming

sound of the secretary's long red nails against the Formica-topped table. It wasn't difficult to surmise that she was annoyed at having her bombshell pre-empted by his lucky guess.

'What is her name?' asked Singh.

'Dao Ming.'

'Where can I find her?'

'I am not her mother.'

Li Jun asked for the family address of his own volition and Singh was pleased to have a respite from the gorgon at the gate.

'Maybe if you see her you can ask her what's the matter with her father.'

'Maybe we can do that,' agreed Singh, making a vow on the spot that he would not tell this woman anything, whatever he found out. 'What did Professor Luo think about Justin being Dao Ming's boyfriend?' he continued.

'You think he would tell me?'

'Well, maybe not directly, but someone with your insight into human behaviour must have had some idea?'

Singh ignored the glare Li Jun directed at him. He didn't blame him for not wanting to translate such toe-curling praise, but it would be worth it if this woman could be persuaded to say something that was not gratuitously insulting.

'He was not keen.'

'Why?'

'The fellow was charming, big smile, kind word even for me. Professor Luo liked him very much.' She nodded at the memory and seemed almost human for a moment. 'But he was not sure that the boy's affections were really engaged and

159

he did not like it that he was a foreigner, there was no future in it.'

'He told you this?'

'I overheard him speaking to his daughter.'

'Maybe they were just young people having a bit of fun?'

'The professor is not the sort to accept that. He is old-fashioned . . . he wanted Dao Ming to excel at her studies and not be distracted by other things.'

She made 'other things' sound suitably immoral. There was no such thing as a summer romance as far as she was concerned.

Was it possible that the professor had killed the boyfriend of his daughter and now, unable to confront what he had done, had gone into hiding? It sounded like something from the literature faculty, the department specialising in fantasy.

'Do you have Justin Tan's file?' asked Singh, looking over her shoulder at the grey filing cabinets.

'Actually the police took it.'

At least they'd shown enough interest to turn up here despite what Li Jun had said about the incompetent in charge.

'Such a pity Professor Luo was not on medical leave when they came,' she muttered, eyes glinting like diamonds in the rough.

'Let me guess,' said Singh. 'You heard something . . .' How did this woman get any work done when she spent most of her time with her ear to keyholes?

'They had a very *loud* argument,' she said. 'I could not help overhear.'

'About Justin?'

'I myself only caught the last few words.'

'Which were?' demanded Singh.

'"You are a trouble maker, Professor Luo – stirring up the peasant class against its leaders."'

'And what was his response?'

'"A boy is dead and that is all you have to say?"'

'"He was very unlucky to run into a bunch of robbers." Can you believe it, that's what the police said!'

'And?' asked Singh, squinting to distinguish between her own words and those she was reciting from memory.

'And the professor said, "That's your story and you're sticking to it?"'

'"I think it would be in everyone's best interests if that was *our* story, Professor Luo."'

'"And if I don't agree?"'

The secretary lowered her voice to suggest the tone of intimidation that had been adopted.

'"You are *falun gong* – don't think we do not know that."'

'What was Professor Luo's response?' asked Li Jun.

'They shut the door,' she explained, shoulders sagging at the memory of disappointment. 'And I could not hear anything further.'

Eight

'You want to go and see the professor and his daughter?' asked Li Jun.

They were standing outside the faculty building. The sky was a clear blue with wisps of cloud like an old man's thinning beard. Singh took a deep breath and felt faint; he was not used to clean air. The usual smog was just like smoking although without the helpful shot of nicotine to the lungs. Singh looked around, squinting in the bright sunlight. His turban was attracting curious stares from the students. He watched them watch him and thought that Guru Gobind Singh, who had first demanded that his followers wear the headpiece to distinguish them from non-Sikhs, probably had not anticipated that future generations might prefer anonymity when going about their business investigating murders. The inspector really hoped that this case didn't require him to tail someone at any point. That would be a recipe for failure.

'I need time to think,' said Singh. 'Is that a Starbucks?'

he continued, looking at the familiar green sign. He never ventured into one in Singapore, much preferring the old-fashioned *kopi tiam* where they served boiled eggs and *kaya* toast with condensed milk-sweetened gloopy coffee. But beggars couldn't be choosers and the inspector was relieved to stumble upon an anonymous international brand when he didn't want to confront anything culturally challenging – like green tea that smelled of old socks.

The two men walked over briskly; the desire for caffeine had turned the inspector from a saunterer into a strider. Singh's snowy white trainers didn't provide the same assertive soundtrack as Li Jun's worn shoes but they covered the ground at the same rate. They ordered a coffee each, black for Li Jun and with milk and spoons full of sugar for Singh, and sat down with their backs to a wall. Students bustled past the glass window wearing the international uniform of jeans and T-shirts, a bagful of books hitched on every shoulder.

'So,' said Singh, 'tell me more about this "*falun gong*" then?'

As Li Jun explained, Singh's expression grew thoughtful.

'It sounds to me like Professor Luo might have decided to go into hiding,' he said, wiping the foam from his latte off his moustache and thereby reducing his resemblance to Santa Claus. 'It would explain this far-fetched illness.'

'Without telling his daughter?'

'Maybe she's covering for him?'

The policeman drained his coffee and hauled himself to his feet using the table for leverage. 'Let's go find out,' he snapped, as the caffeine hit his bloodstream.

Singh's mobile rang.

'Yes?'

'The girl called again. I'm to meet her at the Silk market, with cash.'

'What time?'

'At two pm.'

Singh's mouth thinned. Whoever this girl was, whatever information she had, she was no fool. She hadn't given much time for Susan Tan to call in the cavalry. He held the phone away from his ear and demanded to know, 'Can we get to the Silk Market in half an hour?'

'Yes, if the traffic works with us,' said Li Jun.

The policeman grimaced. The traffic hadn't worked with him yet. 'Well, let's go!'

'She said I was to come alone, no police.'

'Don't worry, no one in China will suspect me of being a police officer. And I'll keep my distance.'

'What do I do when I see her?'

'Ask her what she knows . . . refuse to pay up until you have every detail. Do you have a recording device?'

'It's an embassy, of course we do! And I've brought one with me.'

He was impressed. She was thinking like a spy. He wondered whether the Singapore embassy had a quota of spies masquerading as cultural attachés like the Americans and the Russians and decided against it. Espionage wasn't really the Singaporean way unless it was for keeping an eye on its own citizens back home.

'Use it then. I'll try to get close so I can hear what she says. Whatever it is, don't let her get away. If she's in it for the money, she deserves a good scare. If she has something to say – well then she's a material witness.'

'Where are you now?' asked Susan.

'Just leaving the university. Professor Luo Gan hasn't put in an appearance at work for a while. Apparently he's not well.' Singh waved at a taxi unsuccessfully, but Li Jun had more success with the next dilapidated vehicle. The men clambered in, phone still glued to Singh's ear. 'Silk Market,' he whispered to Li Jun.

'Justin was convinced that the professor would lose his tenure because of his activism,' continued Susan Tan.

'You think that's what's happened?' he asked, yanking at his seat belt and wincing as it snapped back against his belly.

'Or he's been asked to take a leave of absence – or he's made a decision to lie low for a while. There are so many different flashpoints in the country right now that the security apparatus might take its eye off you if you stay out of trouble for a few weeks.'

'Sounds more plausible than this mysterious illness anyway.' He remembered the secretary's lowered threatening tone as she imitated the policemen's threat. 'Might he have been arrested?'

'If he was *falun gong*? Definitely! But that would have been quite big news and I haven't heard anything.' She continued, a note of real hope in her voice, 'I've reached the Silk Market,' and he heard the sound of a car door slamming. 'I'm going to wait at the pizzeria on the ground floor.'

Singh looked out of the window at the clear roads. 'Things look good here – we might actually get there in time.' He caught Li Jun's eye and they both smiled. It made a change to progress at something other than a crawl.

Singh's pleasure turned to dismay around the next corner.

They pulled up at traffic lights and Singh could see that there was gridlock at every point of the compass.

'How long till we get there?' he demanded.

'More than half an hour,' replied Li Jun grimly.

Qing had no intention of drawing attention to herself. She arrived an hour early so as to avoid any watchers at the entrances. Now she wandered through the market like any of the hundreds of shoppers and tourists. She stopped to admire a handbag – Gucci – turning it inside and out as if seriously considering a purchase. The proprietor of the tiny shop had leather handbags in all the major brands, as many as one would find at Shin Kong Place. She ignored Qing because she was doing her best to fleece a foreigner.

Qing listened to the exchange with a half-smile.

The tourist, as broad as he was tall, perhaps a Russian, with his belly straining against his shirt, was determined to extract the best price he could. The two of them were taking turns to type offers into the large calculator the woman held. It was part of Silk Market etiquette that no one spoke a price out loud. This worked for both customer and seller. The latter could squeeze the price as hard as possible and the former could agree because it did not set a precedent.

This particular negotiation was not going well. The Russian was shouting and swearing, accusing the woman of being a thief and a cheat.

She in turn was yelling in Mandarin. Qing assumed that he did not understand the rudiments of the language or he might have objected to being called a hairy fat pig. At last they seemed to come to an agreement. The man – his buttons looked like they would pop with the ferocity of bullets – peeled off a chunk of yuan from a roll and the vendor put the goods into the type of cheap pink plastic bag that clogged every drain in China.

The tourist left, face wreathed in smiles, convinced that he'd had the better of the exchange.

The proprietor let him have his victory, but when he was gone, spared a grin for Qing.

'These foreigners think they know how to bargain like the Chinese,' she said.

'But still he paid the white devil's price?'

'Exactly.'

'And so how much is this bag?' asked Qing, holding one up.

'For you, sister, the Chinese price, of course,' she said and whipped out her calculator.

They agreed quickly at an eighty per cent discount to the asking price and Qing left the shop satisfied. She decided that even when she was wealthy she would never fall into the trap of buying original goods at Sanlitun Village. The Chinese who did this had truly lost touch with their roots.

Qing glanced at her watch. There was still ten minutes to go. It was time to walk past the drop-off point. The last thing she wanted was for some sharp-eyed shopper to steal her delivery. To her disappointment, there was nothing there. She wandered into a nearby stall selling winter coats and tried on a number of different designs, complaining in turn about the colour, the fabric, the length and the workmanship. In the end, as the discussion grew heated, she opted for the cheapest available windcheater and turned to leave, eyes automatically seeking the dark corner by the elevator behind the bin. Her heart leaped into her mouth and she almost gagged. Tucked behind the bin was a holdall, bright red in colour. She walked past it without looking back, heart pounding so loud it felt audible to shoppers. At first, it seemed every pair of eyes in the place was trained on her or the bag. It was as if she was wearing an advertising board that said 'blackmailer' in large letters. It took her a few moments to calm down and realise that, in actual fact, there was no one who seemed to be taking an interest in that corner or the red bag. Qing didn't intend to be naive though and she walked into another stall, this one selling trainers. She waited patiently, turning a shoe over in her hand, until a large group of Malaysian shoppers walked past in the direction from which she had just come. She immediately attached herself to the group and sauntered back towards her target. The Silk Market was packed to the gills, and Qing noted a group of Arab women, covered from head to toe, were making their way towards them. As the two groups converged, shopkeepers called out to them, cajoling them to have a look, the bolder and more assertive grabbing at sleeves and tugging for attention.

'Good bags for you, ma'am.'

'Best price!'

'For my friends, good deal.'

The focus was the Arabs – the Chinese stallholders knew where the money was.

When the cacophony hit a crescendo, Qing stuck out a foot and tripped one of the waddling creatures. She came down like a ton of bricks. The ice cream she'd been eating went flying and landed on a stack of jackets. The vendor, quick to see an opportunity, demanded compensation at the top of her voice even as the other women were trying to haul their weighty friend to her feet. The woman was wailing and yelling, adding to the drama. Qing took two quick steps forwards, seized the red bag, and immediately hurried down the corridor, weaving between the shoppers, maintaining a brisk pace, but not running, not drawing attention to herself.

She ducked into a bathroom and went to work with her pre-planned routine. She opened her knapsack, changed clothes quickly into jeans and a loose shirt, tied up her hair and slipped it under a cap and changed the high heels to a pair of trainers. She washed her face of the heavy layer of make-up she'd been wearing and then transferred the money – a million yuan – into her now empty knapsack. She folded her old clothes and stuffed them into the bag. She looked at the empty holdall – it was a nice bag, heavy canvas – and she decided not to waste it. Folding it in half, she shoved it into the bag as well, zipped it shut and took a deep breath. She pulled the flush and sauntered out, a young provincial without a care in the world, whiling away an afternoon at the Silk Market.

Qing maintained her slow pace with difficulty, every nerve in her body was screaming at her to hurry. As she reached the next corner, she had another look around for surveillance, but everyone seemed to be focused on shop windows and bargains, no one had any interest in a skinny girl from the provinces. Unable to control her fear any more, Qing broke into a quick trot, eyes on the escalator at the end of the passage. She reached it quickly, but hemmed in by people on all sides, she was forced to travel at the sedate pace of the escalator. As she finally stepped off, she glanced back up the way she had come. Her eyes met those of a tall man in dark clothes who, unlike everyone else, was not weighed down with shopping.

Singh's idea of a market had been formed in his early youth when his mother would take him on her weekly shopping expeditions in order to have an extra pair of hands to carry her purchases. He remembered trailing through stinking, bloody water that pooled on the uneven floor, shoulders hunched and nose wrinkled, as his mother pointed at unfortunate chickens in wicker baskets – slaughtered on request – and peered into the eyes of fish to determine if they were fresh. He remembered the slabs of meat, mutton and beef, hanging from vicious hooks over large concrete slabs. The butchers and fishmongers sliced and diced with *parangs*, splattering blood and bone over their filthy aprons and the customers who got too close.

The Silk Market, he noted, was quite different. First of all, it was not open plan but in a large six storey building. The glass cubicles within sold everything from shoes to handbags and toys to shirts. It also offered bales of silk accompanied by offers of efficient tailoring services. The only thing that bore a resemblance to the markets of his youth was the heaving crowd looking for a bargain.

The plump policeman made his way slowly through the throngs, horrified that vendors were actually grabbing his arms to physically drag him into shops, demanding loudly, 'Where you from? Where you from? India?' He found himself the rope in a tug of war between two determined shopkeepers and had to yank hard to get free, muttering, 'No, thank you. No, thanks. No, not interested,' under his breath like a prayer.

One of the more direct ones said at the top of her voice, 'You must buy new belt, sir – that one going to break because your stomach is so fat!'

He made a desperate effort to get away, but was brought to an abrupt halt as a remote control helicopter appeared out of nowhere to hover just in front of his nose. The man in the door controlling the device was a master of small spaces but Singh was convinced the rotors would slice off his nose at any second.

'For your children,' suggested the man as Singh tried to beat a retreat.

To his relief, Li Jun grabbed his sleeve and dragged him away. The vendors, disappointed that Singh was accompanied by a Chinese person who was inured to their aggressive sales tactics, transferred their attention to other foreigners.

Spotting the pizzeria, both men hurried over. Susan Tan sat at a corner table where she could watch both entrances at the same time. The place was almost deserted – why eat when one could shop? Singh met her eye, received a brief shake of the head, found a table where he could keep her under surveillance, pointed at a picture of a coffee on the sticky, laminated menu and leaned back in his small wooden chair. Li Jun sat down across from him but shook his head at the waiter. He was careful not even to glance in Susan's direction and Singh deduced that he'd spent time on surveillance in the past.

Qing the witness was late, but this was China, it didn't mean anything. Perhaps she was stuck in traffic too or had been violently dragged into a shop and forced to buy a belt.

He noted that Susan Tan was not dealing well with the delay. Her knee was bouncing up and down under the table. She clutched a briefcase to her chest – the money to pay? – and her eyes darted from one entrance to the other as if she was watching a fast-paced tennis match.

Li Jun poured himself a glass of water, gulped it down and then became engrossed in the menu.

'You want something to eat?' asked Singh, deciding that he definitely couldn't stomach a pizza. It was one thing to be deprived of a curry and quite another to replace it with fast food.

'No,' said Li Jun.

The men reverted to silence. Singh was beginning to suspect that the caller was going to be a 'no show'. He saw that Susan was staring at him, a strained question in her eyes. He indicated another five minutes with a quick raised hand and ordered a second coffee to appease the waitress who looked annoyed that two men should be sitting with a single coffee between them.

'Silk Market is very crowded,' he said to Li Jun.

'Yes, very popular with tourists.'

'Good place to meet, no one is interested in anything except shopping.'

'Yes,' agreed Li Jun. His eyes narrowed and Singh turned to follow his gaze.

A young woman had come in. She stood at the door, swaying a little on her feet as if uncertain which way to proceed. She was a slight thing, quite pretty, with her hair tucked under a baseball cap. She had a knapsack on her back that looked heavy from her listing posture. Despite the heat, she wore a dark jacket. Both her arms were folded tightly across it as if she was cold and she didn't want the coat to fall open notwithstanding the reality of the hot and humid Beijing summer. As he watched, she spotted Susan and stumbled to her table.

'Are you Qing?'

The young woman nodded and for the first time Singh could see in the dusty light that she was perspiring heavily, her thick fringe plastered to her forehead.

'You have some information for me?' Susan half rose in her chair and then sat back down again as if her knees would not support her.

Again, the nod – a creature of few words? She would have to make a better witness than that to earn her reward, decided Singh.

'I have brought what you asked,' said Susan, indicating the briefcase on her lap. 'Please just tell me what you know.'

Qing opened her mouth and closed it again.

Singh's spine stiffened. He rose to his feet, all his senses suddenly tingling. By his side, Li Jun too had risen. He was not imagining it, something was wrong. He had taken two steps forwards, arms outstretched when Qing held up a vicious-looking six-inch blade with a serrated edge.

Nine

'Qing!' Susan's voice was high-pitched.

Everything after that happened so quickly that Singh could not order events in his head, not even afterwards when he had the time and space to do so.

The girl took a step forwards, holding the knife out before her. Again, she opened her mouth. Singh leaped forwards to intercept her attack.

Susan pushed her chair back and tried to get to her feet, turning away as she did so.

The policeman got his body between Susan and Qing and turned to fend off an attack, gritting his teeth in anticipation of her lunge with the weapon. He knew he was going to get hurt. That helped. The adrenalin coursed through his system. He probably wouldn't feel a thing.

As he raised his hands defensively, he saw a trickle of blood run down Qing's chin from the corner of her mouth. For the first time, he realised that the knife and hand holding it were already covered in blood. The girl's mouth opened and shut like a goldfish in a bowl. He realised the implications of the bloodied weapon in that instance and took a hasty step forwards, hands outstretched, palms out – half plea, half offer of help.

Qing's eyes glazed over and she fell forwards into the inspector's arms. Singh caught her, she was not heavy, and lowered her gently to the ground. In the background, he could hear screaming and knew somehow, without looking around, that it was the waitress. Qing's jacket fell open and he saw that her white T-shirt was red with blood. He didn't need a second look to know it was a death wound. The serrated edge of the knife in her hand – she must have ripped her insides to shreds to remove it. Maybe in that first second when she realised what had happened, when the shock overwhelmed the pain. But who had done this to her – and why?

'Call an ambulance,' he shouted and saw Li Jun reach for his phone.

'Take her outside,' insisted a man, wringing his hands with despair. The apron suggested that he had come from the kitchen, perhaps the owner. 'This is not good for my business.' Singh ignored him.

Susan fell to her knees and cradled the girl. 'Qing, what happened? Can you speak? Please tell me what happened to my son.'

Singh, unable to understand what she had asked but able to guess, said, 'She's too far gone.'

The eyelids fluttered open. Qing was trying to comply with the request. 'I . . . I . . . saw . . . ask, ask . . .'

Her eyes shut again and her body went slack. Singh put

two fingers to her neck and he shook his head. She was gone. He looked up to where a crowd of onlookers had gathered at the entrance to the shop and met the steady eyes of a tall man with hair that looked like it had been darkened with boot polish. He was standing near the back – the only one who was not trying to get a vantage, the only one not screeching a reaction to events. All Singh's instincts were screaming at him and the policeman obeyed without question. He lay the girl down, got to his feet and lumbered after the stranger. But even as he reached the door and shoved his way past the onlookers, he could see that pursuit was in vain. There was no sign of the tall man over the bobbing crowd of shoppers. Singh closed his eyes – he needed to fix the man's face in his memory. For a second, he felt a cold chill down his spine, like a trickle of rain. The man had been waiting to see if Qing spoke before she died. When the girl had tried to utter those few words, he'd stepped forwards. What would he have done if she'd said more? Attacked her again? If she had managed a few words, a name, would he have tried to murder them all? A knife would not have been sufficient then. But perhaps he had the weaponry necessary to silence as many people as he needed to. He remembered the calculating eyes; Singh doubted there would have been any hesitation.

The inspector returned to the room and saw that Li Jun had picked the girl off the filthy floor and laid her across two tables. It wasn't best practice in a murder but Singh had some sympathy for his actions. Light shone in the greasy windows and created little rainbows against the glass. The dust in the air caught the light and looked like gold dust. Qing's face was turned towards the brightness like a plant. She was a slight thing in death, eyes still open, lips red with blood where she must have bitten down in shock and pain. Her jacket was folded over her stomach so the wound was hidden. Susan Tan was sitting on a chair by the body, sobbing without restraint – for the girl or for her secrets, now taken to the grave? A bit of both, he supposed. The owner of the restaurant was slamming doors shut against the crowds and in the distance Singh could hear sirens. Just like the Singapore police, maybe like police all over the world, they'd arrive too late to do anything except escort a body to the mortuary.

'What did she say?' asked Singh. 'At the end, what did she say?'

Li Jun translated as best as he could and Singh grimaced. She'd been so desperate to communicate, if only she'd opted for a name, a place – any word that might have led somewhere.

'There is no doubt that she did have something to tell us. This was not a hoax,' he said, his voice thin and dry as if events had exhausted him.

Singh reached down to retrieve the rucksack from where it had fallen. He opened it and removed a pair of new shoes, a handbag and a red holdall that he carefully placed on the table. Had the girl been shopping? He peered into the depths and then reached in with a hand. He brought out a thick stack of old notes, bound up with a rubber band.

Li Jun looked at the money and then the dead girl. He pointed at her work-roughened hands. 'She's just a factory girl, probably from the provinces. Where would she get that kind of money?'

'My guess? Blackmail,' said Singh.

Susan Tan had regained control of her emotions. 'She really knew something about Justin's death, something valuable.'

'It seems so,' agreed Singh. 'She was trying to sell the information to anyone with an interest. Madam First Secretary here, as well as . . . someone else . . . someone who preferred to make sure the information remained secret and was prepared to act to ensure it.'

'Greedy like a snake trying to swallow an elephant,' was the response from Li Jun.

It was a harsh assessment, decided Singh, looking at the silver moccasins the girl had bought a short while before her death. Maybe she was just poor and tired of it.

He rummaged further, convinced there was more. 'She had a rendezvous with her killer,' he muttered, 'or she'd just demanded a money drop. More likely the latter.'

'Why do you say that?' asked Li Jun.

'She took precautions – the change of clothes, for instance. She didn't want whoever it was to know who she was.'

'They took a very dangerous risk,' said Li Jun. 'If they had lost her trail in this crowded market, she would have got away with it.'

Singh shook his head. 'I doubt it.' He rummaged further, both hands in Qing's bag as if he was a child grabbing sweets at Halloween.

'Well, we're not dealing with amateurs,' he continued. He turned the holdall inside out so that they could all see the small device pinned to the base. 'A radio transmitter,' he explained. 'This must have been the bag that the money was delivered in. Whoever did this did not intend to risk losing her in a crowd.'

'But she shifted the cash to her own rucksack,' pointed out Susan.

'Yes, and decided to keep the bag anyway. I guess it's quite a nice one.' He stared at the bag —unable to decide whether it was worth squirreling away rather than discarding.

'These people, they come from such poverty, it is difficult for them to waste anything,' explained Susan, looking at the corpse with an expression of great sadness. It was the second time in less than a month she was witness to a body laid out. The last time had been her flesh and blood, and this time a woman who might have been able to help explain that crime.

'So what does this mean for the investigation?' asked Li Jun.

'It means we look for other routes to the truth,' grunted Singh, knowing without a shadow of a doubt that he wouldn't be getting home anytime soon.

Jemima sat on her bed cross-legged and ran through the dossier for the hundredth time since she'd recovered it that morning. The door to her bedroom was locked so she knew she was safe from prying eyes. Besides, her mother had gone out – she'd dashed away a couple of hours ago, looking worried and yet hopeful. The latter expression had surprised her daughter. She hadn't seen it since Justin had been killed. She'd tried to guess what might have cheered her mother and then given up. There might be an opportunity to find out when she returned. Not directly, of course. She'd tried the direct approach soon after Justin's death. She ran through that conversation in her mind.

'Mum, do you think it was just an accident?'

'What do you mean? Justin was murdered.'

'Yes, but that he just got unlucky. It was a robbery gone wrong and all that.'

'I'm not sure – that's what the Chinese police think.'

'What if they're wrong?'

'We have to trust the authorities.'

Such a Singaporean response, Jemima had thought at the time. Her mother had managed a wan smile, a half-hug and walked away, immersed in her own thoughts. If it hadn't been for the sudden appearance of Singh, Jemima would never have guessed that they shared the same doubts.

Jemima wasn't sure why her mother treated her like a child in contrast to the way she'd always treated Justin. Probably because she was younger, quieter, less successful in school, less ambitious – in fact, not ambitious at all. The opposite of her mother, a mouse compared to the lioness, which meant they'd never seen eye to eye, always had a difficult relationship. And now, when tragedy had provided an opportunity for them to draw together, they had drifted further apart. Broken-hearted from the loss of the same boy, but unable to reach out for comfort, riven with the same doubts but unable to share them.

And this dossier ensured that the gap between them remained as wide and deep as a canyon. There was no way she could go to her mother with the information contained within. Already, the relationship between her parents was angry and brittle. Jemima dashed away a hot tear and fingered the cover, feeling the texture of the rough paper. There was a very large part of her that wished she'd never retrieved it. She'd known that Justin kept a file under the mattress of his bed, deep under so that no one making the bed would run curious fingers over it while tucking in the sheets. Even before he died, she'd considered having a peek at the contents but decided against it. It would probably turn out to be pornography and she didn't want to discover that her beloved brother had clay feet.

But when he was dead, killed, she'd forgotten about it in the first hysteria of grief. Afterwards she'd avoided his bedroom, unable to bear the emptiness, the loneliness, to see the detritus of a life curtailed. But that morning she'd remembered and decided to investigate. Deep in her heart, Jemima had hoped to find something that would make her feel closer to Justin, a keepsake, like a diary perhaps, with a few kind words about the sister who had hero-worshipped him. So she'd gone looking, entered his room quietly, knowing it was untouched, unchanged from the morning that he'd left. Her mother had insisted upon that.

She'd found his file. But the contents had not been what she'd expected, not a diary, not personal, nothing about her. Instead, papers – notes in his distinct hand with the long lines and firm strokes. And there'd been newspaper cuttings too. A few photos, developed from a camera phone she guessed, because the resolution wasn't great. Various printouts from blogs, in Chinese and in English. And a series of interviews with people, they'd been identified only by numbers and alphabets, their identities preserved as a secret to any reader. It had taken her a while, but slowly she'd pieced the information together.

Professor Luo, from the blog entries and lecture notes, was a strong defender of those who were evicted from their land by government decree to make way for large-scale construction projects. She'd known this already from the admiring remarks Justin had made at the dinner table. She'd also been aware that Justin was helping the professor in his investigations and the notes confirmed it. The stories Justin had recorded in the file were always the same: 'They said we have to go'; 'They promised us some money but what is the use of that? This is our home'; 'They sent thugs – my husband was badly beaten when he refused to leave.'

Jemima read through the interviews with growing sadness. The photos were the most telling. The hordes of men, women and children, their mouths opened in protest, hands clasped in supplication. Seeking a generosity of spirit since they knew that the law and justice were not for them. In one photo, residents of a village stood with linked arms before the wrecking crew and their equipment. In another, an old man was lying directly in the path of a bulldozer.

The most recent project appeared to be a plan to requisition land from a small neighbourhood in Beijing to make way for a massive shopping complex. 'My family has lived here for generations.' 'Where will we go?' 'Are you willing to destroy history with a bulldozer?' Justin had scribbled a response ascribed to an unidentified official: 'I've seen more than enough of this place. Don't give me any more of this nonsense.'

Jemima found a photo and recognised some of the individuals – that short, well-dressed man was surely Dai Wei, deputy mayor of Beijing? She knew that her mother despised him as being a politician scrambling up the greasy pole as quickly as possible, determined to leverage his popularity with the people into a promotion to the twenty-four man Politburo that effectively ruled China and then possibly the Standing Committee, the elite group of six who presided over the Politburo. Jemima guessed that the other officious-looking men in suits were probably from the developers. They stood in the narrow lane, lined with people's ancient homes and envisioned concrete monoliths with neon lighting offering designer goods to the new rich. Justin had been spying on some very important people. Jemima could see, from an academic paper in the file, the financial implications of land grabs. Billions of yuan were at stake.

Jemima wrapped her arms around her bent knees and stared at the papers spread across her bed. There was so much information here, so much evidence, even if she had no idea what it had to do with Justin's death. Maybe nothing, of course. Maybe he'd been killed by that gang of thugs for no reason. On the other hand, she couldn't help but feel that what she'd found, what she knew, was somehow relevant. There were powerful people and powerful interests at work here. She should take it to her mother or the sleuth from Singapore and see what they had to say. Perhaps, Inspector Singh would figure out a link between the information and Justin's death.

But she couldn't. She just couldn't. She picked up the photo that she'd found at the bottom of the file as if Justin had sought to put it out of his mind by burying it in paperwork. It was the same shot of Dai Wei and his companions but taken from a wider angle so it captured both the officials as well as the protesters. There was a man standing slightly to one side, tall, well dressed, handsome. It was impossible to see his expression from the angle and distance of the shot. But there was no doubt from his position that he was there with the developers. He stood shoulder to shoulder with them, a party to the planned destruction of homes, facing the angry householders. Her father.

Her father was in league with these men being investigated by Professor Luo. What had Justin thought when he'd first seen the photo? Had he known before that his father was somehow involved in the land acquisition? Had he realised it meant that his father was in cahoots with Dai Wei? Had Justin told the professor? Perhaps he had been in denial, like she was now.

Jemima closed the file and slipped the rubber band around it again. How could she approach Inspector Singh with what she knew when it might implicate her father in something sordid and quite possibly illegal? How could she approach her mother with evidence that her father might have been involved in Justin's death?

The two men sat on opposite sides of a wooden table in a narrow dark shop with large plastic-covered pictures of food dishes taped to the walls. Benson had driven the First Secretary back to her residence. The inspector had adjourned to the restaurant at the suggestion and in the company of Li Jun. The fat man's eyes were watering. The next table was being used by staff, white aprons stained dark red, to chop a mountain of dried red chillies down to size. Every now and then one of them would sweep a pile into a plastic container and whisk it away to the nether regions from which the sound of oil sizzling and voices arguing could be heard.

'Szechuan cooking is very spicy,' said Li Jun apologetically.

Singh nodded and blew his nose into a large white hand-kerchief. He wasn't really complaining. If those dried chillies were going into anything he was about to eat, his craving for spicy food was going to be assuaged soon, and in some style. They had arrived at Jie Street long after the lunch crowd had left and well before dinnertime. The wide street was lined on both sides with tiny food outlets selling dishes from every region in China. Red lanterns hung cheerfully at every entrance, the drains reeked of rotten food and stray dogs wandered about looking for leftovers. Li Jun had led them to this particular hole in the wall and now they waited for their lunch, it had taken some persuasion for the waiter to agree to serve them so late, while Singh drank a lukewarm watery beer.

'You knew that policeman? The one who came to the scene?'

Li Jun nodded. 'I called him directly. His name is Inspector Han and he is a good person. Qing's death will be investigated properly, I think.'

'At least until someone higher up discovers it's linked to Justin's murder.'

'And you think that is certain?'

'We're investigating Justin's death, this girl calls to say she has information and the next thing that happens is she's stabbed to death in a public place?'

'I agree,' said Li Jun and then paused as a very large fish, swimming in a soup that was heaving with cabbage, was slammed down on their table. The two men spent the next couple of minutes wrestling the plastic crockery and wooden chopsticks out of the sealed plastic bags in which they had arrived.

Li Jun extricated the spine from the fish with a couple of deft slices and served Singh a large portion. 'Black river fish,' he explained.

The men ate in silence for a few moments, both thinking hard.

'Whoever did this was very afraid of what this girl had to say to take the risk of killing her.' The boldness of the move both impressed Singh and made him nervous.

'Or they did not fear justice,' said Li Jun.

'What do you mean?'

'In China, the law is not the same for everyone. Those who do not fear retribution or punishment are more likely to take such action as we saw today.'

The Sikh policeman scooped up some more soup, bubbling with heat from the fire still burning underneath. Perspiration darkened the rim of his turban. Hot and spicy. At this rate he would miss China when he left. Mind you, his exit was a quickly receding point on the horizon. He'd been sent to investigate one murder, but instead of answers, it was the body count that was mounting.

'Will Han tell us what he knows?'

'I believe so,' answered Li Jun cautiously.

Singh understood – this Han was a loyal friend, but he would not risk his badge or pension. That seemed reasonable to the policeman from Singapore. Annoying the wrong person had significant consequences in China. His thoughts turned to Superintendent Chen. Authority and impunity. He would love it in Beijing.

'I'd recognise that man again,' said Singh. 'I'm sure he had something to do with it.' He didn't bother to mention that with a population of over a billion people, he was unlikely to stumble upon his murderer. He scowled, remembering the cold eyes in the impassive face. 'Probably a hired killer anyway.'

'How shall we proceed?' asked Li Jun.

'There's not much we can do about the girl until Han finds out who she was.'

'It is better that we follow our earlier plans?'

'To go and see Professor Luo and his daughter,' agreed Singh.

'Han also told me what he'd found out about the attempted assault on Justin that I prevented.'

'What about it?'

'The bouncers at the bar recognised a couple of the thugs as being in the employ of one Wang Zhen, a high cadre child, son of a Politburo member, and a regular visitor to Beijing's nightspots. They were his bodyguards.'

Singh's nostrils flared at the appearance of another hare to chase. 'So why would this Wang Zhen have it in for Justin?'

'I do not know,' confessed Li Jun.

Singh didn't bother to explain that it had been a rhetorical question. Instead, he patted his lips with a cool, scented serviette extricated from shiny foil packing.

'The food was too spicy?' asked the rabbit-toothed ex-policeman with an expression of genuine concern.

'It was just right,' said Singh mopping his brow and draining his mug of beer.

Benson was waiting outside so they hopped into the back

of the limo, Singh with a hint of relief. He didn't think he could face another taxi stinking of stale cigarette smoke. He was beginning to understand why his wife was always complaining about the reek from his clothes – Singh's special scent: beer, curry and cigarettes.

'How is the First Secretary?' asked Li Jun.

'Shaken,' replied the driver. 'Upset about the girl and that we might have lost the chance to find out what happened to Justin.'

'There are many avenues to the truth and when one door closes, another opens,' said the Sikh.

'Confucius?' asked Li Jun.

'Singh,' retorted the policeman.

Dao Ming was very afraid. She was mixed up in things she couldn't control and had no one on her side except her six-year-old sister. Her father had not returned and she was beginning to fear the worst. Maybe he'd had an accident and no one had identified the body. Or maybe he was suffering from some form of amnesia, wandering the streets, unable to get back home. Destitute. Her imagination was going wild. That was what happened when the mind had no facts. She peered through a crack in the curtains, standing to one side so that no hint of movement would be visible. Wang Zhen was late but that was not unusual. If he was late, he expected her to wait. If he was early, he expected her to be ready. Was it his upbringing as a child of privilege that led to such visceral selfishness? She heard the roar of his car engine, a red sports car that her sister, with that unexpected flash of knowledge she demonstrated from time to time, had told her was a Ferrari.

'How do you know?' she had demanded.

'The dancing horse,' explained her sister. 'I saw it on television.'

Ferrari? All she knew was that she had learned to dread the low growl of its powerful engine, signifying as it did the arrival of the young man, her one-time boyfriend, now reinstated in that position because she needed him. Afterwards? Her mouth formed a grim line. She would find a way to walk away.

She watched Wang Zhen saunter up the front yard, looking neither to the left nor right, a cigarette dangling from his mouth. The red glow of the tip was visible in the shadows of the high walls although it was still early evening. He looked young, confident, untroubled. A real catch, she thought to herself, with that combination of cynicism and sadness which had always worried her father – 'you have an old head on those young shoulders', he would say. She didn't know a single one of her classmates that would not be delighted to change places with her, the girlfriend of a Politburo member's son. Wang Zhen rapped on the door with authority and she leaped back from the window. She walked the long way around the front room so that he would not see her shadow behind the hangings. She didn't want to give him the pleasure of assuming that she was waiting for him. If he guessed the truth – that she dreaded his presence – that would not further her plans either.

She opened the door and forced a smile. He did not seem to notice or care and immediately took her in his arms. Dao Ming hid her face in his shoulder and was glad that she had sent her sister to the neighbours for a play. She was forthright in her dislike of Wang Zhen and would undoubtedly have

189

said something that would have led to harsh words between them.

'Have you any news of my father?'

Did she imagine it or did he look away for just a second?

'No, nothing yet.'

'Are you sure? Wang Zhen, you must tell me the truth!'

The cocky young man looked uncomfortable, a rare expression for him. Dao Ming led the way to the sofa and sat down, her knees weak with fear. He sat down beside her and took her hands in his. She sensed that he was genuinely concerned and it heightened her dread.

'What is it, Wang Zhen? What have you found out?'

'I asked my father as you suggested. He had a lot of difficulty getting any information.'

'Is that unusual?'

'Yes – very few people are willing to stand in his way.'

Wang Zhen said this in a matter-of-fact way, unfazed by the realities of privilege and power. His father was a member of the Politburo, that faceless group of bureaucrats with whom all power in China rested. There were very few who were brave enough or foolish enough to contradict them.

'Eventually, my father managed to track down some information.'

'And?'

'It is not good news.'

'What do you mean? Just tell me please.'

'Professor Luo was arrested at Tiananmen Square.'

Curiously, her first reaction was relief – her father was not dead. But then the impact of what he'd said hit home. 'I don't understand – what for? Why was he there?'

'He was arrested for a public demonstration of illegal practices in Tiananmen.'

'What in the world do you mean? What illegal practices?'

'*Falun gong*.'

Dao Ming stood up, shook off Wang Zhen's attempt to hold on to her and began pacing the room. Her eyes were red with unshed tears. It didn't make any sense. She knew her father was *falun gong*. He'd been a member of the group before it was deemed an illegal organisation and continued his practice at home in the quiet evenings when the routine helped calm him down after a difficult day. But why had he gone out looking for trouble?

'Where have they taken him? Why weren't we told?'

'I haven't been able to find out exactly where – to a labour camp, that's all I know.'

She shut her eyes as if the darkness might hide the truth. Who better than her, the daughter of Professor Luo Gan, to understand the black hole of the Chinese criminal justice system? Thousands went missing, to be re-educated for the sin of having an opinion that did not exactly match that of the state.

'Did you know he was *falun gong*?' asked Wang Zhen.

'Yes – he was – but only in private. His public focus has been land grabs and illegal evictions.'

Surely it was some sort of ruse? The authorities were wary of her father because of his work on behalf of peasants who were losing their land to corrupt officials and their developer friends. He'd always known that detention was a possible outcome of his work, it had been a risk he was prepared to take. So why would he suddenly go to Tiananmen Square and provoke arrest in this way?

'It must be a lie! They made this up as an excuse to arrest him.'

Wang Zhen walked up to her and placed his hands on her shoulders. 'I don't think there is any doubt about what happened. My father looked into it carefully at my request.'

There was a sudden loud thumping on the front door and Dao Ming physically shrank from it. Had they come for her too? What would happen to her sister? Should she try to escape? She looked around the room like a trapped animal, desperately seeking a way out.

'It's all right,' said Wang Zhen. He walked to the door without hesitation. He'd never had to learn fear growing up.

The duo waiting outside didn't look like any authority figures Dao Ming had ever seen before. They were a study in contrasts. One was thin and dressed in a traditional Mao suit. His hair was sparse, grey and exposed large areas of scalp. It reminded her of aerial photos of denuded rainforests. The other man was dark, bearded and wore a turban. Since when did the Chinese authorities employ foreigners?

'What do you want?' demanded Wang Zhen.

'To see the daughter of Professor Luo,' said the Chinese man, his mild manner in keeping with his appearance. He did not appear to notice Wang Zhen's rude tone.

Hope suddenly flared for Dao, perhaps these men knew what had happened to her father. He had a lot of friends. Those who, like him, spent their days trying to push back against the overweening state, those who tried to look out for the little people. These two men certainly looked more likely to be on the side of a rebellious college professor than his enemies.

'I am Dao Ming,' she said, stepping forwards and ignoring Wang Zhen's gesture that she stay back.

'Professor Luo's daughter?'

She nodded, her chin raised defiantly as she noticed the fat one's gaze on her black eye.

'We'd like to ask you a few questions about Justin Tan.'

'Justin?' The surprise in her tone was unfeigned.

'What about him?' Wang Zhen's fists were clenched.

'Who are you?' asked Dao Ming.

'Justin's mother asked us to look into Justin's death. I am Li Jun. This is Inspector Singh from the Singapore police force who has been flown in specially to investigate further.'

'Look into his death? I don't understand. He was killed by some thugs . . . in a *hutong*. It was a terrible tragedy.'

The Chinese man was translating the conversation in whispers to the foreigner who was listening to him and watching her with the same intensity.

'We think there's more to this situation than that.' The foreigner spoke English and she understood him, of course. Her father had always insisted that she speak the language – 'We cannot only look inwards but also outwards,' he had said and she had laughed and accused him of having a platitude for every occasion. But she had studied her English diligently, knowing that it was the surest way of ensuring that she would one day be able to explore a world beyond China's borders.

'What do you mean there's more to it than that?' she asked in English.

'Our investigations suggest that his death was not a random event, someone wanted him dead.'

'Are you sure?'

The head, wrapped like a Christmas present, nodded.

'Is there anything you can tell us that might be helpful in our investigation?' asked the Chinese gentleman who had introduced himself as Li Jun.

Dao Ming stumbled back to the sofa and huddled in a corner. They followed her in as if her withdrawal had been an invitation. Wang Zhen perched on the arm of the chair next to her, his expression belligerent, his body language possessive. The turbaned man sat down across from her, but the other man remained standing. His eyes were scanning the room, taking in the modest furniture and the pictures on the mantelpiece. His gaze lingered on the shot of her father and his two daughters, taken in happier times – all three wrapped against the cold, all three grinning with delight. It seemed like another lifetime.

'About Justin's death?' She shook her head. 'I thought it was just bad luck.'

'Perhaps your father can help us?'

'He's not here,' she said helplessly. 'He's . . . he's gone out.'

'We heard he was not well.' The tone adopted by Singh had just enough surprise in it to sound like an accusation. 'Shouldn't he be in bed?'

'What's it to you?'

Dao Ming had seen it all before. Wang Zhen would act tough, and then trot out his family connections and watch the men flinch. She tried to imagine a life when one always had a 'get out of jail' card in one's back pocket. Tears welled up at the thought of her father in a prison camp and she blinked hard, trying to dam them in, hoping the men would not notice.

'Another person has been killed,' said the inspector. He looked at Dao Ming as he spoke, ignoring the interjection from Wang Zhen although it had been in English. 'She had information about the death of Justin. She was stabbed to death before she could tell us. Knowledge of this matter is a dangerous thing.'

'Are you threatening her?' Wang Zhen was in the man's face, but the foreigner ignored him. Dao Ming could see that Wang Zhen was struggling to know how to respond to being treated like a stick of furniture.

Singh's tone grew soft. 'The girl who died – she wasn't much older than you.'

Dao Ming's head was bowed as she tried to avoid meeting his eyes.

'Where is Professor Luo, Dao Ming?' asked Singh. 'Why has he not been to work?'

She hesitated and he followed up more aggressively. 'What's wrong? Is he in hiding?'

She looked up at this and, maybe reading the fear in her eyes, he added insistently, 'Has he been arrested? You can tell us. We're on your side.'

It was reckless, but she was desperate. She needed someone on her side, even if it was this ridiculous fellow in the turban with the kind eyes. She sat up, ignored Wang Zhen's half-articulated yelp, and nodded once.

Ten

He fought, of course. When they came for him, he fought. But he was tied down to the bed with leather straps. Around his wrists and ankles. Luo Gan still made it difficult for them. His thrashing body meant that they couldn't give him a sedative. The nurse held the needle while the male assistants tried to hold him down. His body arched and fell, arched and fell. He was pouring with sweat, crying and screaming. The other prisoners in the hospital wing were beginning to struggle too. His fear was infectious. Besides, now they knew. As the word was spread from bed to bed in whispers, many accepted the truth. It made sense – the fact they were in hospital despite not being in bad shape, a few cuts and bruises from beatings, but since when had the authorities cared about that?

The naive had hoped that it meant they were about to be released, the government surely didn't want them to go home with the evidence of abuse writ large on their bodies. The more cynical had assumed they were being patched up so they could take further beatings until their re-education was complete. None had suspected the reality – not even when individuals were wheeled away on their beds. Not even when they did not come back.

The nurse was frantic. 'Hold him! Hold him!'

The orderlies tried and tried again. They kept glancing up at the other rattling beds, at the screaming patients. 'What's the matter with everyone?' one of them yelled. 'Do you think this will help you? Greater punishment will follow! I promise you that if you do not settle down.' In that moment when his attention was distracted, Luo sunk his teeth into the man's hand and his howls reverberated through the ward, in harmony with the patients even as he managed to wrench free. Luo felt his jaw dislocate in the effort to hang on.

One of the prisoners, the big man known as Little Horse, successfully rocked his bed over. It fell on its side with a crash. He was still restrained and his body strained against the belts as gravity tried to have its way. His pose resembled the crucifixion. The orderlies hurried over to try to right the bed, prevent any further efforts to break free. Little Horse was strong though and he wrenched his body this way and that, fighting off their attempts to get a hold.

Professor Luo stopped thrashing as the nurse and the orderlies rushed over to Little Horse. He was exhausted and felt faint. He closed his eyes, trying to recover his breath. Points of light drifted against the darkness of his eyelids. His jaw was throbbing and twisted, drowning out the pain from the rest of his body.

He knew they would come again. They'd wanted blood type B, and he was the only one on the ward who fitted the bill. He'd heard the nurse say so in an undertone when one of the men had complained that he was too old.

Luo sensed the nurse approach from the other side. She'd seen an opportunity in his stillness. He opened his eyes a crack and watched her approach, syringe at the ready. A few feet away, Little Horse was still fighting his corner. He'd managed to bite an orderly who had been foolish enough to reach across him to hold him down by the shoulders. No surprise – teeth were the only weapons the prisoners had. He'd drawn blood and the orderly was enraged. Luo knew it was only a matter of time before they knocked the big man out. As if the thought was father to the deed, the second orderly grabbed a chair and brought it crashing down on Little Horse. His face split open and blood spurted everywhere.

'Stop it!' screamed the nurse. 'We cannot damage them – you know the orders!'

Her back was turned to Luo as she said this. He saw his opportunity. Reaching as far as the straps would allow, he grabbed her wrist, twisted it and stabbed her with the syringe in the same action. All the years of *falun gong* exercises in the quiet of his home had left him in good shape. The nurse stared at the syringe sticking out of her upper arm and then yanked at it, shouting her anger and fear. But even as he watched, he saw her eyes glaze over as the powerful narcotic kicked in and she slid to the floor. The other two men had barely noticed. They were still wrestling Xiao Ma. The big man was gasping for air through his broken nose and teeth but still he struggled like a demon. Luo yanked at his bonds despite knowing the futility, desperate to go his aid, aware that time was running out.

Time ran out – there were shouts in the corridor and the swing doors at one end of the ward burst open. Soldiers rushed in wearing the khaki green of the PLA. They were armed with machine guns and pistols. It didn't take them long, despite the melee, to identify the main source of trouble. They rushed over, boots thumping against the cement floors. One of them reversed the machine gun and brought the butt crashing down on Xiao Ma's head. The crack reverberated through the room. One moment the big man had been fighting with every sinew, the next he was laid out on his bed, as still and silent as the dead, blood soaking through the thin sheets around his head.

'What's going on?' demanded a soldier.

'They fought – we were not expecting it.'

'What happened to her?'

The orderly, still staring at the tooth marks in his arm, turned to look at the fallen figure of the nurse. He pointed at the syringe sticking out of her arm.

'This fellow must have stabbed her.'

Luo didn't bother to deny the charge. It was all over. He felt sorry for Xiao Ma, who had fought so hard. He hoped they hadn't killed him with the blow and then realised it didn't matter.

'Make sure this one gets treatment,' said the soldier, pointing at Xiao Ma. 'He's a healthy one from the fight he put up – we don't want to waste such an asset.'

A beeper on the orderly's belt went off. He looked at the message. 'They are waiting upstairs for the patient,' he said.

'Which one?'

The man pointed at Luo. 'He started this whole thing,' he complained.

The nurse on the ground stirred, but no one except Luo noticed. These men were nothing if not single-minded.

'You are a troublemaker, old man.'

'That is correct, soldier.'

'Well, your time for such activities is almost up.'

'Then I will take pride in knowing that I spent my adult life trying to save China from people just like you.'

'Will you come quietly or is my buddy here going to have to knock you out like the big fellow?'

Professor Luo shrugged. The time for fighting was over. The battle was lost, but he hoped someday the war would be won. He spared a thought for his children, for Dao Ming, beautiful and headstrong, and Dao Wu, thoughtful and kind. He wondered whether they would ever find out what had happened. He wished he'd left a note, anything really to explain what he had done and why he had done it. He remembered his last conversation with the police at the faculty office, how it had ended.

'You are *falun gong* – don't think we do not know that.'

He'd shrugged. 'Your threats do not frighten me.'

The policeman's expression had grown thoughtful. 'I believe you, Professor Luo. You are unafraid of consequences to yourself.' He paused and then continued, 'Justin Tan was helping you with your work?'

'You know he was.'

'I have heard that your oldest daughter – her name is Dao Ming? – I have heard that she also assists in this foolish crusade of yours.'

Luo grimaced and spat, the taste of blood in his mouth was disgusting. He had done the right thing, the only thing he could have done to protect his daughters – it just hurt to think that his children might never know, never understand why he had walked out the door that day and never returned. His last thought was for Justin, that likely lad beaten to death in an alley. Once again, the soundtrack of Justin's last minutes filled his memory. Was his own fate really any worse than that? And wasn't it so much more deserved? An eye for an eye, a tooth for a tooth, a life for a life. He bowed his head. It was fitting.

'I'll come quietly,' he said.

Jemima held the photo up in front of him as if she was sharing a family shot of a recent holiday.

'Justin took this. Not long before he was killed.'

He took it from her, holding it by the corner to examine it more closely, and then put it down on the dining table. She noticed that his skin was wan and fine lines radiated from the corners of his eyes like a Chinese fan. She wondered for a second whether her death would have affected him the same way as Justin's and then shook her head as if to physically dislodge the thought. Her father loved her, she was confident of that.

'What are you trying to say?'

'He was investigating a land acquisition in Beijing.'

'Don't be ridiculous – why would he be doing such a thing? He was just a kid.'

She sighed and wondered when their father would accept that his children had grown up with opinions and principles of their own.

'You know his professor at the university, Professor Luo – he was very interested in these sorts of things. He wrote a blog that publicised land deals that he thought were unfair on the residents.'

'What does this have to do with Justin?'

'He always asked his students to help him, those who were interested.'

Jemima was sitting at the head of the dining table, talking to her father as he wandered around the room, straightening ornaments and flicking at his nails. A third of the time she was addressing remarks to his back. His restlessness was infectious and Jemima began to nibble on her fingernails, up and down, up and down, as if she was playing a harmonica.

'How do you know all this?'

'I found a file of his investigations, hidden under his mattress … and the photo.' They both turned back to the picture. A man standing in the corner. This man. Thinner now that he had been then. But back then his only son had been alive.

Anthony Tan turned abruptly and pulled out a chair so he was sitting at right angles to his daughter. 'I still don't understand what you're trying to say?'

She wanted to look him in the eye, to be brave like her brother, but the strain was too great and she lowered her gaze to the shiny surface of the wooden table. An impractical and expensive antique rosewood piece. Her mother was always nagging them not to place hot or cold drinks directly on the surface. Such a trivial concern it seemed now.

'I think you're involved in the land deal that Justin was investigating. The one to seize that place −' she tapped the picture − 'for a construction project. Even though the residents are against it.'

'That's nonsense!'

The words were decisive but the limp tired tone was like a confession.

'According to his notes, there was a plan to clear people out of the *hutong* to make way for a shopping mall.' Again, she nodded at the picture. 'I guess that must be the *hutong*, right here in Beijing. I thought this sort of thing only went on in rural areas.'

'The paperwork is in order,' said her father. 'The people are being well compensated. The transaction is completely legitimate whatever Justin – or his professor – thought.'

Could one protest too much?

'We are just waiting for Dai Wei to issue the permit,' he continued.

'Mum says he's a crook and can't be trusted.'

'Your mum sees everything in black and white. There's a lot of grey in this world. Dai Wei is a businessman who wants to see Beijing developed properly. There is no place for sentiment in these sorts of decisions.' He was growing animated, pacing the room with even strides. 'People like your mother and this professor fellow would prefer to keep China in the dark ages.'

'I think this had something to do with Justin ... getting killed.'

This stopped him in his tracks. He walked over and reached out a hand, took one of hers. 'Jemima, how could you think something like that? How could you think I had anything to do with it? He was my son!'

'I don't mean you had anything to do with it on purpose, Dad. But think about it. Justin is looking into this land grab and then he's killed? These men are dangerous. Mum says Dai Wei is very ambitious and won't let anyone stand in his way.'

'It's a coincidence, I promise you. Justin would never even have crossed paths with Dai Wei. Besides, what threat could he have posed? It was a land acquisition – you're right, some of the residents objected, but so what? It's the price of progress!'

'Then what about the call?'

'What call?' He would not meet her eyes and she knew that he remembered all too well that she'd overheard the tail end of his conversation.

'The call where you warned someone to leave me alone.' She said it in the most matter-of-fact voice and gave herself a mental pat on the back. She was doing her best for Justin, not shirking the truth, not running away from confrontation. In a nutshell, she was behaving completely out of character. A lump at the back of her throat stopped her speaking for a moment. Justin would have been proud of her.

There was complete silence except for the gentle hum of the air conditioning.

'Dad, you have to be honest with me. I need to understand what's going on.'

He was angry now. She'd seen it before when he was quarrelling with her mother. If he was in the wrong, he began by blustering, became defensive and eventually convinced himself of his 'rightness' and adopted a tone of weary indignation. But he was her father and she loved him.

'There is nothing going on for you to worry about,' he said, rising to his feet and walking to the door, signalling that as far as he was concerned, the conversation was over. 'We all miss Justin. We all want to understand what happened to him. But that is no reason to come up with these half-baked theories about his death.'

She might have agreed with him once upon a time. The old Jemima would have selected the path of least resistance without hesitation. But Justin was her brother and Jemima had loved him too.

'It sounded like they were threatening me!'

'You just misheard. You're safe, I promise you. These Chinese businessmen like to talk tough, that's all. It doesn't mean anything. I'd never let anything happen to you, you know that.'

'Like you never let anything happen to Justin?' she asked, as he stepped out the door and shut it firmly behind him.

'Arrested?'

'Wang Zhen just told me.'

Singh turned to the youth who was sitting possessively by Dao Ming.

'This is Wang Zhen?'

'Yes,' said Dao Ming.'

The young man maintained a surly silence. There was no denying that he was a handsome fellow, but there was something about the shape of his mouth – a permanent pout? – the inspector did not like. And he was dressed in an expensive downmarket way, patched jeans and a faded checked shirt, which also contrived to annoy the inspector. If one drove a Ferrari, surely there was no need to wear intentionally ragged clothes?

'How do you know that Professor Luo has been arrested?'

'I have my sources.'

Singh eyed the petulant mouth again. He was pretty sure that Wang Zhen's sense of self-importance was tied up with his sense of self-worth.

'A kid like you? What are your sources? Picture books?'

He'd read the boy right, he was steaming already at being so readily dismissed. The tips of Wang Zhen's ears turned red and he leaned forwards as if debating whether to get up and punch the plump policeman in the mouth. Singh didn't fear violence from him. Although Wang Zhen was trim and muscular, the policeman was an expert at spotting the difference between gym muscles and those that had been tested on the street. It frequently kept him out of dangerous situations. Besides, surely Li Jun would step in to rescue him? He glanced at the frail former policeman and decided his intervention might be willing and timely but inadequate to the task.

Dao Ming released the tension by saying hurriedly, 'Wang Zhen's father is senior in government, a member of the Politburo.'

'I can speak for myself,' growled Wang Zhen. Singh wondered at the relationship. Wasn't this girl supposed to have been Justin's girlfriend? Which stage of grief involved finding a replacement in less than a month? And this model, although more expensive, struck Singh as decidedly inferior. And what about her cut cheek and black eye? Was this aggressive young puppy responsible for that?

'So you ran to Daddy for help?' asked the policeman.

'None of your business.'

The Sikh policeman noticed that Li Jun's herbivorous face wore an expression of extreme nervousness. It was probably time to dial back the antagonism a little bit. Superintendent Chen would be preaching caution at this point. On the other hand, that was just not Singh's way.

He looked over at Dao Ming and noted her expression. 'I'd

speak up if I were you or you might end up in the market for a new girlfriend.'

Wang Zhen followed his gaze and decided on a semblance of co-operation. 'I was told he'd been arrested. What's it to you, anyway?'

'We're looking into the death of Justin Tan.' He saw the boy's mouth twist with dislike and added provocatively, 'Dao Ming's boyfriend.'

'*I* am Dao Ming's boyfriend.' The statement was aggressive and he outlined his ownership, because that was clearly how he thought about it, by putting his arm around the girl. She shrugged him off immediately, unthinkingly, all her attention focused on Singh.

'But I thought he was killed by thugs? It was in the newspapers.'

'Yup, but now it seems it wasn't random, someone hired those thugs.' He wondered whether to accuse Wang Zhen there and then of being responsible and then decided to keep his powder dry for a few moments while he figured out Professor Luo's story.

'And the girl? You mentioned a girl?' she continued.

'Stabbed at the Silk Market – she was on the way to tell Justin's mother what she knew.'

'Oh God . . .' She buried her face in her hands and he could hear the muffled sobs. He was impressed with her resilience when she took a deep breath and raised her head again. 'Who would have done such a thing?'

'That's what we're trying to find out.'

'Do you think it has anything to do with my father's arrest?'

There was no point misleading the girl. 'This is the first

time we've heard of that,' he explained. 'I suppose it depends on why he was arrested.'

'Being *falun gong*,' she answered. 'Nothing to do with Justin.'

Nothing to do with Justin. Nothing to do with his murder. In a world of infinite potential outcomes, it was possible, of course, but the plump policeman had never been a fan of coincidences. And what had the gorgon at the gate said – that the police who'd been investigating Justin's death had also mentioned Professor Luo's ties to the *falun gong*. As a threat, as leverage. His gut insisted there was a connection and Singh was not one to ignore its insights.

'My sources did not mention the arrest of Professor Luo so it cannot have been through traditional channels,' said Li Jun.

'He's ex-police,' explained Singh in answer to Dao Ming's questioning look.

'So who took the professor?'

'Security apparatus – he was arrested at Tiananmen Square. He was practising *falun gong* in public.'

'Most likely he has been taken to a re-education camp,' explained Li Jun, looking away from the man's daughter. No one in China was under any illusions about the conditions in such detention centres for enemies of the state. Especially for *falun gong* practitioners. The websites that detailed their punishment, the torture, were taken down as quickly as they were put up, but everyone had seen something, heard something, or known someone. In China, where rumours were currency, information on the treatment of *falun gong* was the gold standard.

'Re-education?' asked Singh.

'Through labour.'

Singh shook his great head and tried to understand the Chinese dynamic. Re-education through labour? What next? Whatever happened to evening classes and Open University?

'But why haven't the family been told?'

'This is China, Inspector,' said Li Jun, 'not Singapore. The security forces do not feel obliged to keep family informed.'

But there was still one huge puzzle at the heart of the enigma. 'He was picked up exhibiting his *falun gong* tendencies at Tiananmen?' Singh remembered his brief stop – the gawking tourists and the security personnel. Hardly a private spot.

'Yes,' said Wang Zhen.

'He was courting arrest. Why?'

'That's what I don't understand,' said Dao Ming, tears running unchecked down her face. 'He didn't tell me anything, didn't warn me. It is such strange behaviour. He went out that morning . . . he must have known what he was going to do. I almost can't believe it – except for the fact that he's not been home for more than three weeks.'

'Guilt,' said Singh, his face a grim mask. 'Only guilt could drive a man to such extremes.'

'But what did he have to feel guilty about?' demanded Dao Ming, her voice rising in anger at the implied accusation. 'He was a good man. He helped people, he fought corruption, he tried to stop the illegal land seizures . . . and he would never have left my sister and me in such a way . . . not knowing . . .' Her voice trailed off as she uttered the last part of her defence and found it threadbare. The fact of the matter was that that was precisely what her father had done.

Singh cracked his knuckles together. 'I can think of only one plausible reason – he felt guilty over Justin's death.'

'Are you accusing Professor Luo of murdering Justin Tan?' asked Li Jun.

Dao Ming opened her mouth to protest but the only sound she emitted was a soft moan. 'It cannot be,' she said at last. 'He would never do such a thing.'

'The killing was done by a third party,' pointed out Li Jun in an almost inaudible voice.

'He hired the thugs and was then overcome with guilt?' suggested Singh, one eye on Wang Zhen to watch his reaction.

'We have to find my father,' whispered Dao Ming.

The man being wheeled into the operating theatre was overweight. The large hump of his stomach under the green hospital covering would have done a camel proud. He was still awake, sedation would only occur in the theatre itself.

'You are sure? You have found me a good heart?'

The orderly nodded but did not speak, just continued with the job of pushing the trolley bed through swing doors at a measured pace. This wasn't an emergency or a television drama so there was no need to rampage through the corridors at top speed, shouting out incomprehensible medical terminology. This fellow was sufficiently heavy that such speed would have been impossible anyway. The wheels of the bed protested squeakily.

He noted that the man in the bed was red faced and sweating. Most likely he was nervous, although a man that fat did not need an excuse to perspire. The orderly didn't envy the surgeon. The procedure would take hours; a heart and lung transplant was not a walk in the park. For a patient like this one, with the layers of fat to cut through and the already heightened blood pressure, it would be a close-run thing.

'The donor is young?'

'Young enough,' replied the orderly calmly. He didn't want to deliver him to the OT on the verge of a heart attack. The doctors and administrators would not be amused. It would be exactly like killing the golden goose.

'Soon you will be up and about and twice the man you used to be.' He added this last with a wink that seemed to reassure the patient and even provoked a smile.

They reached the theatre and the man was wheeled in and then quickly transferred, although not without a grimace from the nurses, onto the cold steel table. The operating surface was one of three. The far end was occupied as well, although this patient, young, thin and tall from his profile under the sheet, had already been sedated. The orderly noted the patient look over and flinch at the sight of the tube running into his mouth.

'Is that the donor?' he asked in a whisper, as if afraid to wake the sedated man.

'No, he is also here for a transplant.'

'How come – what do you mean? I thought this was for me.'

'Yes,' said the doctor, as he walked over for the first time, all in green and with a white shield over his mouth and nose. It muffled his voice, but the eyes behind the spectacles were alert, albeit underscored by dark shadows and bags large enough to go on holiday with. 'You are due for a lung and heart transplant. That guy just needs a couple of kidneys.'

'Nothing goes to waste, eh?'

'That's right,' agreed the doctor. 'In fact, we will even keep parts like the cornea in deep freeze for a later transplant . . . so if you ever have trouble with your vision . . . '

The man stared upwards at the ceiling and the bright lights that made the room seem like a waiting room for hell. No secrets could be kept here; there were no dark shadows where the lies could hide. He shivered suddenly and goosebumps popped up all over his luminescent flesh.

'Cold?' asked a nurse.

He shook his head but did not articulate his fears.

'Are you ready?' asked the surgeon.

The patient nodded, turning once more to look at the other patient waiting for his transplant. The squeaking of wheels informed him that another trolley bed was coming through the doors. He tried to squint in that direction, eager to catch a glimpse of the donor. He'd been assured of a young and virile man, exactly the sort of person from whom you would want to receive a heart and lungs. He paused to regret a life-time of good living and the dozens of unfiltered cigarettes that had left him at this medical last resort. The trolley was wheeled into the space between the two men just as the doctor held the anaesthetic mask to his face. He inhaled deeply, felt his eyes roll back and descended into oblivion.

'You're late,' complained the doctor, 'that guy has been out for half an hour already.'

The orderly didn't disagree. 'Problem upstairs, some of the donors were not too happy.'

'He must be at least sixty,' pointed out the surgeon.

'Patient won't know.'

'He might guess when he has a heart attack in three years.'

'Would have paid in full by then.'

The surgeon shrugged. The man was right – besides, that aspect of the business was not his problem. He just had to conduct the transplants and in that he was an expert. He'd lost count of the many hundreds he'd performed as medical tourism turned China into a popular destination for those whose life expectancy did not match their ambition. The nurses deftly shifted the donor onto the spotless table.

'Ready?' asked the surgeon.

'Ready,' agreed the team of doctors and nurses in unison.

'We'll do the kidney transplant first. That procedure should be relatively quick. Then we will conduct the heart and lung transplant.' He glanced at the patient, naked now, his belly like a limestone hill. 'Not sure if this guy will survive it. He's a mess.'

'Wasting the organs,' said the nurse primly.

'He paid,' said the doctor, holding out a hand. 'Scalpel,' he barked and was handed the steel-coloured instrument with the viciously sharpened blade.

'Here we go,' and he made a short but deep incision.

The kidney removal proceeded without complications and he left it to his assistants to perform the transplant into the waiting man. He needed to focus on the removal of heart and lung. The surgeon made an incision starting above and finishing below the sternum, cutting all the way to the bone. He retracted the skin edges neatly.

'Bone saw,' he urged, turning to the nurse so she could wipe away the sweat on his brow. Despite the cold temperatures maintained in the OT, he was sweating like a pig.

Using the bone saw, he cut the sternum down the middle.

He let the nurse utilise the rib spreaders to give him access to the heart and lungs of the patient. His patient had undergone a similar ordeal and was now hooked to a heart–lung machine to circulate and oxygenate blood. The donor, chest open and soon to be empty, didn't need that, there were no replacement organs waiting for him. The surgeon carefully removed the heart and lungs and then turned to the obese man, positioned them in the cavity and began the delicate job of sewing them in place. It would be hours before he would be sure that the donor organs were functioning normally so that the heart–lung machine could be withdrawn and the chest closed.

He instructed the other doctors to harvest whatever else could be preserved from the donor before his empty chest and removed heart destroyed the value of the remaining organs. Death was quick to render all it touched useless. He wondered for a moment how the donor had ended up in front of him. He seemed a healthy if slightly elderly man. The doctor dismissed the thought as pernicious and continued with his work on the patient who was doing better than he'd expected. Perhaps the freshly harvested organs that he'd been bequeathed would not go to waste after all.

A short distance away, the nurses began the job of stuffing the empty cavities and sewing up the cadaver, a nicety the surgeon insisted on although in all likelihood the donor body, which had once been Professor Luo, *falun gong* practitioner and civil rights activist, would be cremated so that the family never became aware of his fate. Ashes to ashes, dust to dust – the best way the surgeon knew to disguise missing organs.

Eleven

'So that was Wang Zhen ...'

'Yes,' said Li Jun. 'According to Han, it was *his* bodyguards that tried to beat up Justin.'

'That time you intervened outside the nightclub,' agreed the inspector. 'At least we know the connection between Justin and Wang Zhen now. Presumably, it was some sort of altercation over the girl, Professor Luo's daughter.'

'It seems the most likely explanation,' said Li Jun. 'She was Justin's girlfriend, now she is with Wang Zhen. You think he ordered a second attempt on Justin and succeeded in having him murdered?'

'It's possible, I suppose. It seems that he got what he wanted anyway.' Singh was not wholly convinced. Surely, there were other ways to get the girl. Whatever happened to flowers and poetry?

'So maybe this is a simple case, after all,' remarked Li Jun. He continued with real feeling, 'And I know very well that the H.C.C. believe they are above the law.'

'So Wang Zhen might not expect to face any consequences even if he was responsible for Justin's death?' asked Singh.

'That is correct. There are some who think that the father might be elected Premier the next time the People's Congress meets.'

The men reached the front gate and stopped to admire the red Ferrari parked outside. Singh had no doubt that his wife would be shocked at such indulgence of a child. Any hypothetical child of his would have had to beg to borrow the car key or been told to use public transport. And that was the way it should be, argued Mrs Singh, from her temporary residence in his head. How will they learn discipline and hard work if they are given everything they want without having to earn it? The plump policeman chewed on his lower lip ruefully. It was never a good sign when he agreed with his wife's remarks, imagined or real.

'Are you hungry?' asked Li Jun.

Singh abandoned his efforts to bite off his lower lip. 'Who do you think gave Dao Ming the bruise on her cheek?' he mused. 'It looked fresh.'

'I have no idea,' said Li Jun.

'Well, I think it was Wang Zhen,' insisted Singh. 'A young man who treats women like possessions finds it much easier to give in to violent instincts.'

Li Jun looked dubious.

'Also,' he added, 'there was a small cut in the centre of the bruise.'

'Why does that matter?'

'Because Wang Zhen was wearing a signet ring.'

'I too saw the ring,' said Li Jun, 'but I do not have your ability at deductive reasoning.'

Singh stared at his colleague suspiciously. Was he being sarcastic?

'Why would she run straight into the arms of such a nasty piece of work right after the death of a fine young man like Justin?' he demanded.

Li Jun shrugged. 'Who can understand the young?'

'The young are exactly the same as us except with less facial hair,' said the Sikh, scratching his beard. He turned his face to the last of the evening rays and enjoyed the warmth for a second.

'She must feel very lonely after Justin's death and her father's disappearance,' suggested Li Jun with lugubrious empathy.

'Or she might have hoped to get information from him,' suggested Singh. He was always happy to credit ulterior motives to unlikely romances. He'd seen too many corpses of wives and girlfriends to be a romantic. 'And it worked. He found out what happened to her father.'

'I will ask my colleagues if they can find out anything further about the fate of Professor Luo,' said Li Jun. 'It will be easier now that we have an idea why he has been taken.'

'Do they ever get released?' asked Singh.

'Those who have been sent for rehabilitation? Sometimes.' He grimaced. 'But they are not always in great condition – the food is bad, the work hard and there are rumours of torture and much worse.'

'What's worse than torture?'

'Death.'

Singh felt as if he was standing on the edge of a precipice. Everything that he believed about justice and law enforcement was turned on its head in China.

'But how do they get away with that?' he demanded.

'Accidents, suicide, killed attempting to escape, fighting with other inmates, sickness – there are so many different ways to die in custody.'

The Singaporean sighed. Was it so different in any other country? Death in custody was a blot on many penal systems.

'And for *falun gong*, it is worse.'

Singh looked up expectantly. What could be worse than death?

'There are a rumours that prisoners are being used to make profits for government officials.'

'What do you mean? Some sort of free labour scam?'

'Their organs are being harvested for the black market.'

Singh shook his head as if trying to clear his ears. 'I beg your pardon?'

'There is a huge organ transplant business here in China. People come from all over the world for new kidneys, hearts or lungs. Executed prisoners were a source of organs. But now there are rumours that officials are using live prisoners – especially *falun gong* – because there is so much demand but not enough supply.'

The policeman closed his eyes. Was this a further example of China's new capitalism?

They both heard the front door slam and knew that Wang Zhen would soon be upon them. Singh tried to get his mind back to the matter at hand and forget, pretend he'd never heard, what Li Jun had just told him. He ran a hand down the smooth bonnet of the car. If he'd been a teenager he would have considered scratching the paintwork with a coin, a blow for the oppressed masses against the capitalist freeloaders. In the circumstances, he merely wondered what Mrs Singh would think if he ever came home in a car like this one.

The bonnet was still warm – Wang Zhen had not been at the house for long when they had barged in and interrupted the tête-à-tête and he was leaving already. Whether he'd arranged Justin's murder or not, all was not well between him and Dao Ming.

'You're still here?' Wang Zhen spat the words out like orange pips.

'Admiring your car,' said Li Jun.

'I prefer them in black,' said Singh.

Wang Zhen leaned against the vehicle, the epitome of confidence, and said, 'Is this is how you investigate, smoking cigarettes and gossiping like old women?'

'I've had a lot of success with it,' replied Singh.

'If you were Chinese, my father would arrange for you to be dismissed. There would be no iron rice bowl for one such as you.'

'Is that how you solve your problems? Run to Daddy?' The policeman leaned forwards until his face was level with Wang Zhen. 'But with Dao Ming I see you prefer the direct approach.'

'What are you talking about?'

'You hit her.'

To his credit, he didn't deny it. 'I was angry – it was a mistake.'

'So let me get this straight. You usually run to your father to get you out of trouble. But once in a while you prefer to take things into your own hands. Curiously, I know of another similar situation.'

Wang Zhen was silent so Singh pressed on. 'Let's see, you disliked a young man because Dao Ming preferred him to you. Not something Daddy could help you with really ... so did you take matters into your own hands? Employ a little violence?'

'Are you accusing me of murdering that fellow?'

'Hiring a bunch of thugs to do your dirty work sounds like something right up your street.'

Unexpectedly, he laughed. 'Someone like me doesn't need to kill anyone to get the girl.'

'But we know for a fact that your bodyguards tried to attack Justin once before. They would have succeeded if Li Jun here hadn't stopped them.'

'I don't know what you're talking about!'

Wang Zhen flung open the car door and slid inside. In a moment the low rumble of the powerful engine filled the street. He leaned out of the window. 'And you should be careful what you say to me – I think you do not wish to offend my father unless you want the cell next to Professor Luo!' On this parting note, he accelerated away, taking the first corner low and hard, tyres screeching in protest.

'I'd love it if he did it,' said Singh wistfully.

'Be careful what you wish for,' warned the other man. 'It doesn't matter if the Ferrari is red or black, it still belongs to trouble.'

Singh decided to ignore this latest in Chinese aphorisms. Instead, he said, 'But sadly, I'm not convinced.'

'Why not?'

'You said the men cornered Justin outside a nightclub?'

'Yes, they were pushing him around when I told them that I was a policeman and the uncle of Fu Xinghua.'

'The place was crowded?' asked Singh.

'Yes, that area of Beijing, Guomao, is famous for its nightlife.'

'You see, that makes sense – Wang Zhen having Justin pushed around in a public place, a way of humiliating him as well as warning him away from Dao Ming.'

'But not the murder?'

'That was a quiet alley after midnight. No witnesses. It wasn't a warning or a lesson about messing with Wang Zhen's possessions. If it was planned, intentional – not a robbery gone wrong – then it was a very cold-blooded murder indeed.'

The inspector contemplated the angry young man and his generally hot-headed behaviour. He'd struck a girl he claimed to care about and lost his temper with them after what Singh would have characterised as mild provocation.

'But you think Wang Zhen's blood is hot?' asked Li Jun.

'Exactly,' agreed Singh, nodding his great head. 'As hot as Szechuan food . . .'

The police chief flicked a speck of dust from the boot that was crossed over his knee. If he leaned forwards, he would be able to see his reflection in the leather – his servants were definitely worthy of their pay. He attracted the odd curious stare, but the few people who were about mostly minded their own business – it was not the Chinese way to get involved in the affairs of others. At most, he speculated with some satisfaction, they would wonder who he was and why he looked familiar. One or two, maybe more, might even recognise him, the sharp blade of the axe in the fight against black. Fu was, on balance, pleased with the way things were turning out. A few hiccups but they had constituted a warning, not a problem. And Fu had not made it to the pinnacle of his career, to the cusp of greatness even, without heeding the warning signs. It was the difference between him and other men who had risen fast only to fall back down again even more quickly. Chinese prisons were full of success stories awaiting execution by firing squad.

The vast grounds of the Temple of Heaven were still relatively deserted so early in the morning and still shaded from what promised to be a bright and intense day. He watched the old men and women conduct their t'ai chi exercises, like a slow-motion action movie. Curious really that this form of a workout was acceptable while *falun gong* practices were not. The ruling elite was prone to panic when they perceived a threat to their well-being and logic and common sense went out of the window.

Without looking around, he sensed that the man he was waiting for was close, striding towards the appointment, indifferent to the slower pace around him, like a twig caught in the current of an otherwise languid river. Fu Xinghua smiled, revealing even white teeth with a hint of yellow at the roots. He liked the metaphor. In many ways, it described him, surging ahead in the fast waters while others were left behind.

'Good morning, Jie,' he said.

The other man was dressed in black jeans and a black T-shirt with the characters for 'handsome' emblazoned in red. He was at least forty, but dressed like a much younger man and had the lean muscularity of someone who took pride in his physical condition. Jie sat down next to him and said abruptly, 'It is done. Exactly as you requested.'

'I know that.'

'And my payment?'

'You are impatient today, Jie.' He raised an arm and

indicated the expanse of the horizon. 'Relax, take in the view. It is going to be a beautiful day, one for poets and artists to savour.'

'I am a simple man, sir, unable to appreciate the finer things.'

Fu laughed but reached into his briefcase and removed a brown envelope that he placed on the bench between them. Jie grabbed it, undid the seal with a long fingernail and ran his thumb over the thick wad of notes within. He smiled. 'With enough money, the devil is your servant,' he remarked. He slipped the envelope into his backpack and asked, 'Any other tasks for me?'

'We are planning an arrest this afternoon. A big fish who runs a state-owned manufacturing enterprise whose family has mysteriously amassed great wealth during his tenure at the top.'

'A worthy target,' said Jie.

A curious choice of words, thought Fu. Did this man in his ridiculous T-shirt think of himself as some sort of hero of the people? Did he feel regret when his targets were, for lack of a better word, innocent? He had never turned down a job on moral grounds which suggested that any principles were held in a loose grip to be set aside when necessary.

'But these rich men,' said Fu, shaking his head, 'first sign of trouble and they call the best lawyers and cause trouble for everyone.'

'So you prefer it if the suspect dies resisting arrest?'

'You know me, I like to see justice done quickly.'

'It will cost more this time.'

'And why is that?' Fu's nose wrinkled in distaste. Jie was sweating like a man who had worked hard to screw up the courage to ask for a raise but was not confident of the outcome.

'The last two jobs – the danger was quite great.'

'Surely not for a man of your talents!'

'I was on the roof of the building. But there was not much cover. I was not at all certain that one of your policemen would not spot me. If they had, I would have been as dead as that fat bastard you were trying to arrest.'

Fu folded his arms and gazed at the other man through narrowed eyes. 'I knew you were there and I could not see you.'

'I was lucky to get away with it.'

'How much do you want?'

'Double!'

Again Fu caught the animal scent of fear. The fox outside the hen house knows the pay-off if he gets it will be huge. But it also knows the farmer might be lying in wait somewhere with a shotgun.

'And what if I do not agree?'

'I do not think a man of your stature would make such an error of judgement.'

'Very well,' agreed Fu. 'A good workman is always worth his wage. I will double your fee for this job.'

Jie's face creased into a big smile.

'Same thing – we arrest the guy, you open fire from a hidden location.'

'And your policemen will return fire and the suspect will die in a hail of bullets.'

'That's right. And what speaks to guilt more clearly than resisting arrest violently?' Fu chuckled out loud. He opened a notebook, tore out a page and handed it to the other man.

'Here is the address of the takedown. Make sure you're in position beforehand.'

Jie pocketed the address without looking at it. 'Of course, have I ever let you down?'

He was rewarded with a thin smile and a shake of the head. Jie rose to his feet and hurried away. Fu watched him retrieve the address and have a quick look at it as he walked. There was no hesitation in his step and Fu was confident that Jie was up to the task. He'd proved to be a conscientious worker and had not failed so far. The policeman cracked his knuckles and sighed. It was a shame Jie was getting greedy. It always happened. Human nature, he supposed. The underlings worked hard and did well and then they began to think they were indispensable. Having inflated the sense of their own importance, they eventually screwed up the courage to ask for more. And that was when they received a reality check.

He leaned back against the back of the bench and watched the sun emerge from behind the magnificent circular building that was the Temple of Heaven. The blue roof tiles glowed in the bright light. It was admirable what the ancients had achieved, thought Fu, building such an edifice without using a single nail. It was more difficult in modern times to be so pristine in one's methods. He pondered the question of Jie again. He had to admire the fellow, for an illiterate hatchet man, his threat had been subtle – 'I do not think a man of your stature would make such an error of judgement.' Jie was right, a man of his stature would not be so careless of his reputation as to let himself be threatened by a know-nothing gangster.

Fu extracted his mobile phone from the pocket of his coat and rang the station. He was immediately put through to his deputy, a hard-working fellow with limited imagination, the perfect sidekick.

'Yes, sir?'

'An informant has told me that there will be an assassin waiting at our planned arrest. He has been paid by our enemies to kill me. Tell the men to look out for him ... and shoot on sight.'

'Would it be better if I handled this arrest so that you are not at risk, sir?'

'I trust you, my friend. I have no doubt you will get him before he has a chance to fire a shot.'

'It shall be as you say, sir.'

Fu Xinghua snapped his phone shut and grinned at no one in particular although it did earn him an answering smile from a young woman jogging past.

'Good news!'

Anthony Tan did not bother to hide his relief. 'You will issue the planning permission?'

'I always said I would.'

'That's right,' agreed Anthony quickly. 'And I never had any doubt. The only problem was that some of my investors were not as familiar with your power and influence here in Beijing, and the whole of China.'

Could he lay it on any thicker? For a moment, Anthony Tan despised himself almost as much as he believed his wife despised him. But there was no point thinking about that, the past needed to be left in the past. And now, maybe he was in a position to do so, having finally secured the future.

With the planning permission in hand, he would be paid

his finder's fee by the Singapore developers, pay off the gangster from who he had borrowed money and still have a decent sum left over. Enough to make a fresh start? Away from his wife? Away from the city that had taken his son from him? These were questions he would contemplate at leisure.

'You will inform your backers?' asked Dai Wei.

'The minute I leave your office.'

'I do not have to remind you that my financial involvement in the development project must remain a secret ... between friends?'

'Your participation is appreciated and there is no difficulty about your preference to remain a sleeping partner,' agreed Anthony. 'The other investors are grateful for your confidence in the success of the project.' Even in China elected officials, who provided the licensing necessary to evict households for commercial developments in which they had a financial interest, were best kept under wraps. Especially so when they had also demanded a bribe for the permit. A mere share of the project held through shelf companies registered to distant relatives was not enough for Dai Wei.

'Nowadays there's always some intellectual with a blog popping up to complain about the necessary steps we have to take for the advancement of Chinese interests,' explained Dai Wei as if Anthony Tan was a reporter for the *China Daily*.

'But you seem to do a good job suppressing such unhelpful attitudes,' said Anthony. He remembered his daughter's insistence that the project he was involved in was one that Professor Luo had been investigating with Justin's help.

'The vast majority of the people agree with my vision for Beijing,' agreed Dai. 'But there will always be outliers.'

'Did you have any particular difficulty with this project?' asked Anthony casually. 'I know the residents were not too pleased when they first heard about it.'

'There are always those who complain.'

'We are fortunate that their story hasn't been taken up by any of those crusading intellectuals,' said Anthony.

'Yes. They are a huge problem, using their positions to undermine our quest for economic growth. After all, which is more valuable, an old *hutong* or a twenty-first century shopping mall that attracts huge foreign investment to Beijing?'

'I've heard of one called Professor Luo from Peking University.'

'An activist?'

'Yes, who specialises in fighting what he calls "illegal land grabs",' explained Anthony, crooking his fingers to indicate inverted commas and wondering why he was risking antagonising the other man. It was as if Jemima was at his shoulder, prompting him to continue. 'Apparently, he's investigating this transaction as well.' He sipped his tea from the fine china cup decorated with flying cranes, determined to keep his hands steady.

'Never heard of him,' said Dai Wei. 'These intellectuals shout from the windows of their ivory towers but no one listens to them.'

Anthony hadn't realised how much his daughter's suspicions had weighed on him until he experienced the relief of knowing they were unfounded. Dai Wei had never even heard of Professor Luo. And if he had never heard of Luo, there was no way that he could have known that Justin had been helping him – which meant in turn that there was no way he was involved in Justin's death. A weight of guilt was lifted off Anthony's shoulders and he sat straighter and taller, a new man. A small voice in his head demanded to know if he was so sure he could tell whether Dai was dissembling but he ignored it. He'd always prided himself on being a good judge of character.

Dai noted the change in demeanour and smiled. 'I can see you are pleased with this outcome!'

'I am indeed,' said Anthony. He decided that he would have to end the affair with Dai's wife. This man was much more useful to him than any pleasures to be found in the arms of his wife.

'And don't worry about troublemakers, whether it is this Professor Luo or anyone else.'

'I'm sure there is no problem,' said Anthony hastily.

'Even if there is, there won't be for long. You can inform your investors that we will not allow anyone to get in the way of a successful enterprise.'

'Thank you,' said Anthony and stood up to take his leave. Dai Wei did not stand and Anthony suspected it was because he did not appreciate the height differential between the men notwithstanding the platform shoes. Anthony stooped to shake his hand and regretted that he was effectively bowing to the official. But the bottom line was always the bottom dollar, and unlike the planning licence, this bow was costing him nothing.

Singh stared at the young girl as if she was an exotic species of butterfly. He wondered if he'd have a better time understanding teenagers if he had one of his own. He'd asked to see

Jemima, hoping that she'd shed some light on Justin's girlfriend or his relationship with Professor Luo. In his experience, a curious, lonely younger sibling was the best detective cum spy whether in real life or in fiction. Benson had driven her over with Susan Tan's permission, but so far their conversation, or lack thereof, had been unproductive. Not even the information that Professor Luo had been arrested had provoked any disclosures, although he'd seen the shock in her wide eyes.

Jemima continued to pick at the tablecloth, showing no inclination to speak. Singh decided that a coffee might help, especially if it was hot, milky and sweet. He was prepared to be patient as long as he was well lubricated. In his experience, family often knew things, it just took them a while to realise it and a little while longer to decide to share it. He waved to a waitress and ordered a drink. He raised an enquiring eyebrow, like a caterpillar on the move, at his companion but she shook her head. He sighed, looked around, wondered whether in a parallel universe somewhere, he was a businessman trying to climb on board the Chinese gravy train. If that were the case, his doppelganger would undoubtedly be in this ostentatiously gold lobby. His coffee arrived and he sipped it slowly, slightly horrified at the price. Superintendent Chen was quite likely to assume he'd been imbibing beer with breakfast and refuse to cover his expenses.

'So you're quite sure that you have nothing further to tell me about his relationship with Dao Ming?'

'She was his girlfriend, that's all. I mean I don't know any *details*!'

'She was also the daughter of his professor – the one you said he admired and was working for!'

The shrug of the shoulders again. Singh had lost count after they reached double figures.

'Maybe Professor Luo was involved?' he suggested.

'With Justin's death? Don't be silly.'

'He disapproved of the relationship.'

She bristled at this, probably because of the insult to her beloved brother.

'It's true – his secretary told me so.'

There was no response and he decided it was necessary to be more provocative, although, truth be told, he didn't want to upset her, she seemed so fragile, sipping her water with nervous regularity. He allowed himself a mental shrug, murder investigations were not for the unduly sensitive.

'You're probably right, it wasn't as if the liaison was that serious. She's already found a replacement. Some well-to-do kid with a red Ferrari.'

'I don't believe you.'

'Well, it's true. I met him. Nasty piece of work.'

'Justin . . . Justin really loved her.'

'How do you know?'

'He told me,' she whispered.

'The new guy is the son of a Politburo member.'

'I can't believe it,' she insisted. He assumed it was the new relationship she doubted rather than the status of the father.

'Do you know what I think?' he demanded and then didn't wait for an answer. 'I think Dao Ming is pretending to get back together with that horrible fellow in order to get his help to find out what happened to her father. She's in despair. She has a younger sister and she has no idea why her father has been taken.'

'I thought you said he was *falun gong*. My mother says the government always cracks down on them.'

'He went looking for trouble, revealed that he was *falun gong* in a public place.'

'Why would he do that?'

'Because he feels guilty about something ... something, I would hazard a guess, that's connected to Justin's death.'

'You really think he might have something to do with it?'

'It seems out of character, but I have only two facts to work with. One, he didn't approve of the relationship and two, he felt guilty about something.' He sensed uncertainty in the girl and decided it was time for some emotional blackmail.

'Justin always tried to do the right thing. Dao Ming, his girlfriend whom he loved, is putting herself through hell trying to find out what happened to her father. I think you know something, and I think you're as strong a person as either of them.'

Jemima rubbed her eyes with the palms of her hands.

'For Justin,' added Singh.

She finally spoke, her voice trembling with emotion. 'I have something to show you.'

'OK.'

'I found it.'

'That's good,' he said, wondering if he sounded encouraging like he intended, or dubious, like he felt.

'It belonged to my brother. He didn't know I knew where he hid his stuff, you see.'

At this, two hairy ears perked up. She reached into a capacious bag and retrieved a file that she slid tentatively across the table. It was thick, professional and bound in a rubber band. He almost smiled. If she'd brought the file along she'd always meant to share it, she'd just needed some persuasion.

He opened it and stared blankly at the documents within. 'What is this?' he demanded. 'I assume you've been through it.'

It didn't take her long, now that she'd decided to speak, to fill him in. Singh listened intently, allowing his coffee to grow cold and his biscuit to remain uneaten.

'So what you're saying is that Justin might have been in trouble because of the work he was doing for Professor Luo? Helping investigate dodgy land acquisitions?'

The nod brought a curtain of hair over her eyes and she pushed it away as a matter of habit. This was more plausible – Singh hadn't for the life of him been able to think why a university professor would have a student bludgeoned to death in an alley whether he approved of the relationship with his daughter or not. But if Luo felt indirectly responsible for getting Justin involved in something that had let to his death, it might have led to the public display on Tiananmen Square. He grimaced. It still seemed an extreme reaction to abandon his two daughters without a word.

'And your father is involved in this land grab of the *hutong*?' continued Singh.

'He calls it a "land acquisition". He says it is necessary to create a modern China and people who are not in a position to understand the bigger picture should not be allowed to stand in the way.'

'And your mother?'

'She thinks Dai Wei is a crook and representative of everything that is wrong with China.'

Her resemblance to Susan Tan was startling when she pursed her lips and echoed her words. Singh had a sudden premonition that this shy creature would turn out as formidable as her mother some day.

'So do you think this has anything to do with Justin?' demanded Jemima. She gestured at the papers on the table with a slim hand. 'You know, all this stuff.'

'I don't know,' he replied, rifling through the file and admiring the methodical nature of the dead boy. And he meant it. After all, whether Luo, and by extension, Justin, were researching the project involving Dai Wei and Anthony Tan, that didn't seem to be any reason for someone to kill the boy. From the file, Luo had been standing up for peasants for years without anyone being murdered in back alleys.

He picked up the photo, the one that tied Anthony Tan to this particular land grab, and stared at it.

'That's how I knew my dad was involved,' she explained. 'He's in that picture.'

'So who are the rest?' asked Singh. 'I know that's Dai Wei.' The comical and yet intimidating figure was hard to miss. 'And the man behind him is Fu Xinghua.'

'Yes,' she agreed. 'The others are probably Singapore developers.'

That made sense. 'And the angry residents,' he muttered, staring at the line of distant figures, their anger discernible in the stiff bodies and bowed heads.

'But I guess there's still no way of knowing if this had anything to do with what happened to Justin,' said Jemima.

He'd heard so many euphemisms for violent death from

family members – from Jemima it was 'what happened to Justin'. He couldn't blame her. Language was a powerful tool, a window to memory. And who wanted that when contemplating murder of a loved one? But family still needed closure, justice, penance. And that was his role.

'It's a big coincidence otherwise, isn't it?' he muttered. 'After all, it's the same *hutong* where he was killed.'

Her head snapped back at this. 'The same *hutong*? I didn't realise that! I've never been … to where he was killed. My mother wouldn't let me go.' She paused to take it in. 'But that means this *must* have something to do with Justin's murder!'

'Anyone wanting to kill Justin for any other reason might still have wound up at the same place. From the file, he spent a lot of time there, gathering information for his professor,' pointed out Singh.

'There's more,' Jemima added at last, her reluctance to divulge anything further manifest in the long pause.

'What is it?'

'I heard my dad on the phone – it seems like he owed someone money. He was asking … begging for more time to pay it back.'

So Li Jun's policeman friend had been right about Anthony Tan being in the clutches of moneylenders.

'And then he said, "How dare you threaten my daughter!"'

'I see,' said Singh. 'And you think whoever it was he owed money to might have previously threatened Justin?'

'It's possible.'

'Yes, it is,' agreed Singh, wondering whether Anthony Tan's fecklessness had actually resulted in the death of one of his children.

'I guess we'll never find out.' Jemima spoke and her words were barely audible and wrapped in a sigh.

'Never find out?' Singh looked up at her in surprise, jolted away from his own thoughts. Her eyes were wet with tears, which she hurriedly blinked away, fighting to maintain her composure in such an open place, a teenager's horror of a public display of emotion writ large on her face.

'Of course we're going to find out. What do you think I'm doing here in China?'

He was rewarded with a half-smile from his young companion.

Indeed, he'd been so convincing Singh had almost believed his own propaganda for a moment.

The man in the red apron was dripping sweat. His hands were calloused and grubby, nails black and short. Neither man at the breakfast joint noticed. Instead, they nodded their thanks as he added a stack of bamboo containers containing spinach and pork buns in front of them, adding a sprinkling of sweat to the open dish at the top. Li Jun reached for his chopsticks and snapped the ends apart. He dipped the *pau* into soy sauce and crammed the whole thing into his mouth, he was very hungry and this was the sort of budget establishment where he felt comfortable.

His companion followed suit, but then held a hand over his face briefly as the smell from the narrow drains outside wafted into the shop. Li Jun didn't doubt that the proprietor dumped all the entrails into the shallow water – he'd caught a glimpse of rainbow-coloured grease as he walked in – but it did not seem necessary to share the information with Singh.

The inspector stuffed a *pau* in his mouth and waved the man over to indicate he needed more tea. It was poor quality and rancid but still cleansed the palate after the rich salty buns. Besides, what could you expect from a place that charged less than two yuan for a hearty breakfast?

'My ex-colleague, Han Deqing called me with some updates. The dead girl, her name was Qing. She was a factory worker from Hunan province. Been in the city for about six months. Before that she worked in Dongguan for a while.'

Singh felt a pang of loss for this girl who had come to find her fortune like so many others before her. This one had only found death.

'I spoke to the parents. The last time they heard from her was the day before she was killed. She was in a good mood and promised them that they would soon be seeing the benefits of her work. She promised them the biggest television in the village. Their chief emotion seemed to be disappointment.'

Singh's chewing slowed down a notch. 'I still don't see how she could have crossed paths with Justin or found out anything about his death.'

'There's more,' said Li Jun. The two men ignored the scowl of the proprietor as he topped up their tea. It was a tiny outlet with four small tables and wooden stools. The turnover was rapid as shop and office workers raced through breakfast before hurrying to work. Two men indulging in a leisurely conversation was a recipe for a bad morning for the business.

'What is it?'

'Qing had an aunt.'

'So? I have more aunts than I can count. A number of them

are dead and I haven't spoken to the rest of them in decades.'

'She lives in that *hutong* where the boy was killed. We probably met her when we did the door-to-door. Apparently she is very old and does not leave her house much.'

Singh, perched on a stool like an overfed vulture, sat up suddenly. This was crucial information – the link between Qing and Justin's death.

'She must have seen something or heard something while visiting the aunt,' he exclaimed. The tragedy was that she'd decided to try to cash in instead of going to the police. But it seemed they finally had a lead.

'That appears quite likely,' agreed Li Jun.

'Any pressure not to look into this carefully?' he demanded.

Li Jun shook his head. 'Not yet according to Han. If there is no interference, does that mean there is no link between the two deaths?'

'I think that would be drawing unwarranted conclusions. Anyway, we know there is a link – the aunt at the *hutong*. Possibly whoever is keen to sweep this under the rug does not know about the connection yet. You should urge your colleague Han to be discreet about committing his findings to writing.'

'Do not worry – he has always been hopeless at paperwork and I will urge him to continue in this manner.'

Both men laughed and then quickly sobered at the memory of Qing.

'What about the professor?' asked Singh. 'Any news on his whereabouts?'

'Han has promised to sniff around today. But if he's been swallowed up by the security apparatus, he might as well have never been born.'

'Well, he was indeed born and has two daughters who are worried sick about him to prove it,' replied Singh tartly. He didn't doubt that Li Jun's bleak assessment was accurate but he didn't want to lose sight of the man behind the crusader and supposed *falun gong* practitioner. It might be the Chinese way to label a person – terrorist, communist, capitalist, anti-government activist – and then forget about his essential humanity, his inalienable rights. He wouldn't fall into that trap.

'I still don't understand why he went out of his way to get himself arrested,' complained Li Jun. 'Someone like him, with his track record, he must have known there was no way they would let him get away with it. The authorities were probably watching him already, looking for a reason to pick him up.'

'Guilt – he felt responsible for what happened to Justin, I'm sure of it.'

'Guilty enough to just leave his daughters?'

It was the question that had bothered Singh earlier too and he nodded to acknowledge Li Jun's point. He'd filled Li Jun in about Jemima and the file and now he added, 'It must have something to do with the land deal.'

He retrieved a serviette, carefully cut in half by the owner to double the available quantity, and wiped his mouth. The red chilli looked like bloodstains against the white and the seasoned policeman felt suddenly nauseous. He wasn't sure whether it was the general presence of death, or the sure and certain sensation of someone walking across his grave.

'There's one more thing we need from your friend,' said Singh.

Li Jun raised a sparse questioning eyebrow.

'Track down the moneylender . . . find out what he knows about Anthony Tan's business dealings.'

The camera lights flashed. Fu Xinghua beamed. His boss was centre stage at the press conference but he didn't mind. He knew that his appearance of deference would go down well with the public. And he towered over Dai Wei, a looming presence that suggested to viewers at home that he was the power behind the throne.

'I am here to announce that Goh Yuan, former member of the Chongqing central committee was killed resisting arrest this morning.'

More light bulbs flashing. Questions being shouted by reporters. 'What was his crime?' 'How many suspects have died resisting arrest now?' 'Are you satisfied with the outcome?'

'We would obviously prefer that men like Goh Yuan, who betray the public trust to line their own pockets, are tried for their crimes before a court of law. However, Goh was determined to fight his way out. No doubt, he knew that the evidence against him was overwhelming.'

'Is it true that there was an assassination attempt against Fu Xinghua?'

Dai Wei stood back and gestured for the deputy chief to answer the question.

Fu stepped forwards and waited until the hubbub had descended into total silence.

'Yes,' he said. 'I'm afraid that Goh Yuan, anticipating this crackdown, had placed a sniper on the roof of his office building. That man had instructions to kill me.'

'But we are pleased to see that the attempt on your life failed,' said a sycophant from the *China Daily*.

'That's right,' agreed Fu, offering up a smile. 'Fortunately, my men spotted him on time. After a brief struggle, he shot himself rather than face arrest. His name was Jie and he had a criminal record as long as the Yangtze.'

He paused and looked slowly around the crowded pressroom, making eye contact with individual reporters and looking deep into the various cameras trained on him. 'But everyone in Beijing needs to be aware that the fight against criminal activity does not rest with me alone. The police, and our political leaders who have courage and determination such as Deputy Mayor Dai Wei, are like the emperor's terracotta soldiers. Too many to kill, too many to thwart. We will ensure that no one in China is above the law. So they can try their best to kill me and some day they may succeed, but the fight against black will go on!'

Fifteen minutes later, he was sitting behind his desk feeling satisfied at a good morning's work. One potentially troublesome fellow was out of his hair and he'd certainly burnished his reputation with the fighting talk.

His phone rang and he reached for the receiver.

'I have some news, sir. Wang Xi is asking around after the professor,' reported the head of the corrections department, in charge of re-education.

'You mean Wang Xi from the Politburo?'

'That's right.'

'What is his interest?'

'He did not provide any explanation. Just said he was looking into the matter of the disappearance of Professor Luo.'

Fu Xinghua leaned back in his chair and made a conscious effort to loosen his grip on the receiver. This was not good information. It never was when the Politburo started sticking its nose into matters. And he was puzzled too. Fu had been aware of Luo's activities for some time and had never known him to have any contact with senior party members or government officials. He was, as far as Fu knew, unprotected. It made him a brave man in his quest to seek justice for the peasant victims of land grabs, but also a vulnerable one. Fu ran a finger along a line of light coming in through the blinds and forming stripes on his desk. He needed to think, to understand the consequences and advantages. The policeman was a talented amateur chess player and he liked to apply the same approach, thinking forward five or six hypothetical alternative moves, to consider his approach.

'What do you want me to say, sir?' The glorified prison guard sounded afraid, which was no surprise. No official wanted to hear questions from the Politburo, especially when they didn't have the answers.

'The truth, of course. Professor Luo was a *falun gong* member who defied the authorities with a public demonstration of his faith. Does Wang Xi expect us to allow such people to make trouble for us?'

'No, sir.'

'What is the status of Luo anyway?'

'Unfortunately, he was weak and did not survive the attempts to re-educate him about the error of his ways.'

'That is unfortunate, but maybe it is for the best. Why don't you return the body to the family and announce the reason for his arrest at the same time? That way we can draw a line under this business. After all, he was an elderly man, it is not surprising that he did not survive.'

The security chief cleared his throat. 'Professor Luo was an organ donor, sir.'

Fu slammed his open palm on the desk in front of him. 'I did not authorise that!'

'There was an urgent requirement. Also, Professor Luo had been causing a lot of trouble, fomenting rebellion amongst the other detainees.'

The chief sounded nervous and for good reason. The consequences of crossing Fu were never good. And he had a reputation for biding his time when it came to payback, so underlings never knew when the axe would fall. There were many tales of subordinates who had assumed they had weathered a storm only to find themselves on traffic duty in Ulaan Bator or worse. Much worse.

Fu Xinghua, however, was of a mind to be reasonable. All things considered, this might be the best outcome. Professor Luo had been arrested for being a *falun gong* practitioner. There was no suggestion in the records that his detention had anything to do with his investigation of land transactions. Which meant his death was effectively a dead end for those who might seek to follow his trail.

'You know what to do,' he said.

'What is that, sir?'

'Send him home in an urn.'

Twelve

'So all roads lead back here,' said Singh.

They were standing close to the spot where Justin had been killed, heads turning to scan the four narrow lanes that ran off that small central junction. The rewards posters, faded and torn, still adorned the walls.

'We are assuming that Qing knew something,' said Li Jun, nodding at the posters. 'But how do we know she was not just making up a story, hoping to get some of the reward money?'

'If she'd only approached Susan Tan, I'd agree with you,' said Singh. 'But she must have tried to blackmail someone with the information she had. And it was damning enough that whoever it was had her killed. She knew something all right, we can be sure of that.'

'Something to do with the acquisition of this land?'

Singh grimaced. 'I have no idea.'

'They told us about it – do you remember? A group of

women said that they feared they were going to lose the land to a development project.'

'Impossible to have known that it was relevant then,' said Singh. Truth be told, impossible to know if it was relevant now.

'I wish I had paid more attention,' said Li Jun, sucking in his already hollow cheeks.

It was the mark of a good cop, Singh believed, to feel each mistake personally. It was the mark of a bad cop to wallow in self-pity and not move on and try to correct the error. 'Well, we should visit this aunt now and find out if she knows anything,' he said, proving that he himself fell into the latter category.

Li Jun pointed down one of the streets. 'It's this way.'

They walked in silence, not hurrying, both policemen trying to puzzle out the implications of everything they knew before adding another layer of complexity from a witness.

Li Jun stopped in front of an entrance to a small cluttered courtyard and cross-checked the address against the piece of paper in his hand. 'This is the place.'

'I remember it,' remarked Singh. 'I think we met the aunt.'

Li Jun knocked loudly and when there was no answer, crossed the threshold into the courtyard and picked his way through the debris, Singh following in his wake like an ocean liner being guided by a tugboat.

At the inner entrance to the dwelling, Li Jun shouted, 'Hello!' and then rattled on in Mandarin. Singh assumed it was some version of 'Hello, is there anyone at home?' After a long silence, they heard the shuffling of feet and the same old woman they had met the last time, stooped over almost double, appeared at the entrance. She was leaning on a cane and Singh didn't doubt that she would topple forwards without it.

'Whatever you are selling, I don't want it,' she grunted.

Singh smiled at Li Jun's quickly whispered translation. Old, but with spirit. He'd have to remember that when he was as ancient as this creature. Not that either his wife or his doctor gave him much hope of living to a ripe old age.

'We visited you last week, Old Aunt,' said Li Jun.

'And I didn't want what you were selling then either.'

'We were not selling anything,' said Li Jun, sounding defensive even in Mandarin. 'We were looking for information about that boy who died – who was killed – in this *hutong*.'

At this she craned her neck so that she was looking at him like a baby bird in a nest waiting for a worm. 'I remember,' she said with satisfaction, as if memory was a triumph, and it probably was at her age. 'But I had nothing to tell you then and I still don't.'

'We are here about Qing this time,' said Li Jun, reaching out a hand as if he expected the mention of her niece to cause the old woman distress.

The cataract-filled eyes moistened, but her words were harsh. 'Silly girl,' she said.

'Why do you say that?' asked Singh after Li Jun had translated in some surprise.

'What was she up to? It must have been boy trouble. And it got her killed!'

'Is that what you really think?'

'What else?' Suddenly the wrinkles deepened and darkened.

246

'She was the best of us.' The grief, temporarily hidden in anger but now revealed, cast a shadow across the courtyard. 'Prepared to work, to earn a living, to send money home to her feckless parents, to make something of herself . . .'

'Tell her we think it might have to do with Justin's death,' whispered Singh.

'Old aunt, we think that Qing's death might have had something to do with that boy – the one who was killed last month.'

'What are you saying? I don't understand?' This time the cane wobbled, and Singh took a hurried step forwards. She steadied herself, glared at him and continued, 'Why should these two deaths be related? She did not know him.'

'Qing called the mother of the boy,' explained Li Jun, acting entirely as Singh's mouthpiece now. 'She said she had some information about Justin's death. She was killed on the way to deliver it. Someone didn't want her to tell what she knew.'

'Why would she get involved? It had nothing to do with her.'

'There was reward money. She believed it might help your family.'

The old woman turned a full circle and moved with surprising speed back into the house. The two men followed her hurriedly, afraid that she was about to slam the door in their faces. For a moment both were jammed in the doorway like extras from a lowbrow comedy but then they achieved ingress with Singh in the lead. He blinked, trying to adjust his vision to the gloomy interior. It was an effort to control the gag reflex – the place stank of boiled meat. Qing's aunt lowered herself onto a three-legged stool and turned to face the two men who stood above her like the sharp end of an inquisition.

'She was always greedy for money,' she acknowledged. 'She loved nice things – clothes and shoes. And her parents never stopped nagging her for funds, for her brother, for her village home.'

'So you're not surprised that she would have approached the mother of the dead boy?'

'Not if she knew something and thought there was money in it.'

'There are reward posters pasted to the walls outside,' explained Li Jun.

'That would have been like putting a bone in front of a starving dog.'

'But what did she know?' demanded Singh. 'What did she know about the death of that boy?'

The old woman faced him for the first time as Li Jun translated his agitated words. 'I have no idea,' she replied with complete certainty.

'She must have said something?' Singh was almost begging.

'That day – the day she was killed – she was excited.'

'She only visited on weekends?'

'Just for the day on Sunday most of the time. And not every weekend. If there was overtime at the factory, she would take it. She was always keen to make a little bit more money. But four weeks ago, when the boy was killed, she stayed the week-end.'

Singh pondered the information, stroking his beard as if it was a pet cat. Justin had been killed on a Saturday night, or the wee hours of Sunday to be precise – so she must have seen something. At least, they now had evidence placing her within a street of the murder.

'Did she go out that night? That Saturday night?'

The brittle shoulders shrugged. 'Possibly. I am an old woman and I need my sleep. Do you think it is my job to watch her every movement?'

'No, of course not,' he replied. 'We just want to work out if she could have seen something.'

'Did she say why she was excited?' asked Li Jun.

'No, but I guessed it was either a new job or a boy.'

And it had turned out to be neither.

'It was nice to see her happy,' volunteered the old woman, hunching her shoulders and appearing even smaller. 'She enjoyed her lunch – beef noodle soup. I cooked it especially for her.'

Singh was touched. The poor old bat showing what affection she could for her niece. He'd bet his bottom dollar she'd nagged the girl about her eating habits, clothes sense and work ethic even while stuffing her with soup. Shades of Mrs Singh really.

'If Qing knew something, why did she wait for almost a month before doing anything about it?' asked Li Jun.

'Maybe she didn't realise the significance of what she saw?' suggested Singh. 'Or maybe she only saw the reward poster at a later date.'

Li Jun nodded lugubriously to acknowledge that both suggestions were plausible.

'We need to remember,' said Singh, 'that Qing didn't just see something – she saw someone.'

'Why do you say that?'

'Because otherwise she wouldn't have had the identity of someone to blackmail.'

'But she's a factory girl from the provinces – who could she have seen and recognised?' Li Jun sounded unconvinced despite the incontrovertible evidence, that of her murder, that she had tangled with the wrong person.

'Someone from this *hutong*?' suggested Singh.

Li Jun quickly explained their thinking and then asked Qing's aunt, 'Did she know the people around here?'

The old woman shook her head. 'She kept herself to herself when she came to visit. There are not many young people left in this neighbourhood. Besides, no one from around here has money to pay any blackmail. We are all poor folk.'

Singh looked around the mean residence and knew that she was right. The marks of poverty were everywhere, staining the small residence like the soot from the coal stove.

She must have seen his quick glance around because she added bitterly, 'And even this might be taken away from us soon.'

'Because of the land acquisition?'

'Yes, we have just been told by the resident's organisation that licensing has been awarded for the construction. But they will have to carry me out feet first, I tell you.'

'Did you know the boy who was killed was trying to help?' asked Singh.

'What could he do? What can anyone do to stand up to the powerful here in China?'

'He worked for a Professor Luo from the University of Peking.'

'I know him,' she said unexpectedly. 'He came here and

spoke to the residents. A while ago. Before the boy died. He was trying to find out who was behind the project. He showed us pictures. Asked us to identify anyone we had seen around the place.'

Immediately upon translation of this piece of information, Singh rummaged around his file until he found the photo that Jemima had given him. He held it out to her and she took it in a hand that trembled like the last leaf of autumn in a mild breeze.

'Do you know any of the people in the photo?'

She peered at it through rheumy eyes, holding the picture so close it almost brushed her nose.

'It is hard for me to be sure,' she said, causing the inspector's heart to sink down to his white trainers.

'Except for him, of course.'

Han Deqing cornered the moneylender in his lair, a small pawnshop with grilles across all the windows. The possessions of the desperate were laid out in orderly rows in glass cases, mostly watches and gold, but, this being China, a few brush-stroke paintings and jade bangles.

'A visit by the police is bad for business,' complained the moneylender, putting down his newspaper and stubbing out his cigarette in a small ashtray that was already brimming.

'An arrest by the police will be worse for business,' replied Han.

At this, the fellow glanced around the shop quickly as if taking a quick inventory of possible illegal activities. 'Why are you threatening me, Han? You know I run a legitimate commercial operation.'

'I know this pawnshop is a cover for your illegal money-lending concern.'

'If you had evidence, you would have arrested me already – in fact, anytime in the last ten years!'

'That's right,' agreed Han. 'But maybe I've finally grown impatient of waiting for proof to take you into custody.'

'Everyone knows you are a clean cop.' The man's wheedling tone stuck in Han's craw and for a moment he was tempted to drag the man into the station in cuffs and beat some truth out of him. He took a deep breath and waited for the anger to pass. It was not his way and this foul creature was not going to tempt him into compromise. Besides, Li Jun and his friend from Singapore had asked him to ferret out information, not put this fellow in hospital.

'Even clean cops need something sometime,' he said.

'You want money?' The moneylender sounded genuinely surprised but also hopeful. The conversation was now within parameters he understood – loans and bribes were his lingua franca.

'No, I want something more valuable,' said Han. 'I want information.'

'Which him?' demanded Singh, ungrammatically.

'The short fat one with the silly shoes.' At this she glanced over at the Sikh and he wondered whether she'd realised that her description suited him too. She asked suddenly, 'Why does this man have a cloth on his head? Is he injured?'

Li Jun grinned as he quickly translated and then answered, 'No, Aunty. He is from Singapore and the turban is part of his culture.'

'And you told Professor Luo that you had seen this man?' Singh was like a dog with a bone.

'Yes, he had a picture of him too.' She rose to her feet as slowly as a plant growing towards light. She rummaged in a drawer and pulled out a small head shot and passed it to Singh. 'He said that he was not surprised that this man was involved.'

Singh pondered her identification – Dai Wei. A short man in silly shoes, who had the power to dispossess people of their land. And Luo had known about his involvement. Which meant Justin had as well. But they would have known anyway from the photos and research – it was not news that Dai Wei was involved. After all, he was the deputy mayor of Beijing. All they had discovered was that this old woman knew that too. Which raised the critical question.

Singh said slowly and carefully and listened to Li Jun adopt the same pedantic tone in translation, 'Did you show Qing this picture?' He held up the one that she had produced of Dai Wei, the one that Professor Luo had left with her.

'No, why should I? This was not her property. What do the young care about the troubles of the old?'

Singh rocked back on his heels. He'd been so sure that Qing had somehow tied Dai Wei to the murder. Seen something, heard something, and then been in a position to identify him because the aunt had shown her the picture. He took a deep breath and got another whiff from the entrails boiling on the stove.

'So there was no way that Qing knew about Dai Wei?' he asked.

'Is that his name? I couldn't remember, although I see him on television sometimes singing old Mao songs as if those were good times.' She spat on the floor and Singh leaped out of the way with the agility of a much younger man. 'My family starved to death because of Mao and his stupid policies, but now they are trying to make him a hero again.'

She was lost in angry memories and Singh cleared his throat and tried again. 'So Qing did not know Dai Wei by sight?'

Li Jun translated at increased volume, trying to recall the old woman from her contemplation of the past.

'Why are you shouting at me? Do you think just because I am old and stooped that I am also deaf?'

No one responded. Singh hoped for the sake of justice that it never became necessary to put this grouchy old thing on a witness stand.

Having cowed them all into silence, she said, 'The night before Qing died, we were watching television.' She gestured to an old square box with two antennae on the top. Flat screens hadn't reached this *hutong* yet. 'The fellow, Dai Wei, was on the news talking about some crackdown on black.' She snorted. 'Crackdown on black? When he is the biggest crook?' She looked as if she was going to spit again and Singh retreated warily.

'I saw the same news programme,' said Li Jun.

'I said to Qing, "That is the man who wants to destroy my home."'

'What was her response?' asked Singh.

'She said, "Not to worry, Old Aunt – 'kind deeds pay rich dividends, evil is repaid with evil.'" As if the thin strands of information had finally knotted into a rope, she turned to stare at them in turn. 'You think this man, Dai Wei, had something to do with her death?'

Thirteen

'You see – it must have been Dai Wei. Qing saw him that night and she tried to blackmail him and he had her killed. This is not a good development. He is a very powerful man.'

Singh sat in the back of the car and felt the back of his shirt stick to the seat with perspiration. The air conditioning hadn't done enough to cool the car yet. He ignored Li Jun's conclusions. He was grateful to be away from the old woman and her claustrophobic home. And she had certainly given them information to ponder – but he wasn't prepared to leap to conclusions. It was not what fat people did. Leaping to anything was just not their forte. 'There are a lot of gaps,' insisted Singh, determined to be contrary.

'What gaps?' demanded Li Jun, turning sideways so that he could catch Singh's eye. 'You should be happy – you've solved the murder, although I am not sure how we will catch the murderer.'

The fat policeman glared at his sidekick. He was definitely

placing the cart before the horse or the bullock or whatever the Chinese equivalent was.

'What's the motive?' he demanded.

'Qing saw him at the crime scene.'

'We don't know that. If he outsourced the job of killing Justin to a bunch of thugs, why was he hanging around the crime scene?'

'To make sure the task was completed?'

'But, more importantly,' continued Singh, 'what's the motive for Dai Wei, deputy mayor of Beijing, to kill Justin Tan?'

'Justin knew something . . .'

'What?'

'Something about the land deal.'

'But according to you, such land grabs are common. Dai Wei has authority to issue permits if he wants to, he's well know for supporting the development of Beijing into a modern city – why kill anyone? This situation is no different from all the others that Professor Luo writes about.'

He'd given the enthusiast a pause for thought, noted Singh. It was time to throw him a bone. 'Unless Justin found out something that was specific to this transaction and to Dai Wei – something that took it out of the norm.'

'What sort of thing?' Li Jun was cautious now.

'What would get a man like Dai Wei into trouble?'

'Well, he's famous for his crackdown on corruption and his revival of Mao worship,' said Li Jun. 'He's very ambitious so he has enemies who fear his rise to power and his populist streak. I have heard that even the Politburo members are afraid of him.'

'There must be more … I don't see how any of that can have involved Justin.'

'There are many who insist that Dai Wei is as corrupt as those he targets, but there is no proof.'

'I've got it!' said Singh, smacking his hands together in triumph.

The face turned to him was hopeful. It made a change not to be confronted with Superintendent Chen's incredulity.

'Anthony Tan took a loan from a moneylender. What could he have needed it for?'

Li Jun raised both shoulders to communicate his ignorance.

'What if it was a bribe for Dai Wei?' suggested Singh. 'To get the planning permission.'

A slow grin spread over Li Jun's face, creasing his cheeks like old parchment.

'Evidence of such an inducement would be seized upon by Dai's enemies as a means to undermine him, maybe even remove him from office. It would be a good motive for a killing.'

'But what's the evidence of money changing hands?' demanded Singh rhetorically. 'It is possible, I suppose, that Justin found out something – maybe linking his father to the payment of a bribe. He might have seen something or heard something.'

'So what should we do?' asked Li Jun.

'We should not forget our other suspects,' pointed out Singh. 'There's Wang Zhen – who might have killed the boyfriend in a fit of jealousy.'

'Or to persuade Dao Ming to return to him,' agreed Li Jun. 'But you said that you didn't think he'd done it.'

Singh cast his mind back to their interaction with the high cadre child. 'I still doubt that he was behind Justin's death. He'd have assumed that his wealth and status would have won him the girl in the end. I'm sure his plan to have Justin beaten up in a public place was just a warning ... with a bit of revenge thrown in. Besides, how would Qing have identified him as someone to blackmail? He's not a public figure – what are the odds?'

'One in a billion?' responded Li Jun, provoking a grin from the fat man.

'There's Professor Luo, who felt sufficiently guilt about something that he went looking for trouble,' continued Singh. 'Most likely it was getting Justin involved in his crusade against land acquisitions in the first place, but his act of penance does seem a trifle extreme. Maybe there's more to it.'

'And the moneylender was threatening the daughter if Anthony Tan did not pay up – maybe he killed the son first,' added Li Jun.

'And if Anthony Tan did bribe Dai Wei and Justin found out, he had a motive to kill the boy too.'

'You think Anthony Tan might have killed his own son?' Li Jun sounded sick to the stomach.

'I've seen worse,' said Singh.

Li Jun's phone rang loud and sudden in the quiet interior of the car and he reached for it.

There followed a rapid conversation in Mandarin. Singh watched the Chinese man's face for clues but was unrewarded. His foot was tapping with impatience by the time Li Jun finally hung up. 'Well?' he demanded.

'That was my colleague from the police force, Han,' he

said. 'He went to see the moneylender in question as you requested.'

'Let me guess, the money was for a bribe?'

'According to Han, the moneylender was initially reluctant to lend Anthony Tan such a large sum of money without surety. So Anthony told the moneylender that the money was a short-term loan to "facilitate" Dai Wei's issuance of the planning permission. Anthony Tan would be paid a commission by the Singaporean developers and return the money with interest.'

'"Facilitate"?'

'I think there is not much doubt that it was a bribe.'

'Not much doubt and not much evidence,' growled Singh.

'When Anthony Tan did not pay the money back, the moneylender threatened him and Jemima.'

'And murdered Justin before that?' suggested Singh. His life would be made much easier if the murderer was a known criminal rather than a Beijing bigwig.

'Han says the moneylender denies any involvement in the murder of Justin and he believes him. It is not consistent with his methods to murder – not at first. Only after threats, broken bones and destroyed property.'

Singh acknowledged the point with a nod. Moneylenders who murdered people as a first rather than a last resort soon ran out of customers.

'Also,' said Li Jun importantly, 'Anthony Tan repaid every penny this morning.'

'The old woman did say that the planning permit had just come through,' said Singh.

'I wonder why there was a delay in the first place?'

'The investigation by Luo and Justin might have caused Dai Wei to hesitate,' said Singh. It was a reasonable hypothesis. The deputy mayor had probably been reluctant to hand out a controversial licence when there was trouble about. But once Justin was dead and Luo incarcerated, he had felt confident to proceed.

Singh ran a tongue over his teeth and made an annoyed clucking sound. 'Even if Dai Wei is involved, from what I've seen of China so far, that will not be the end, not even the beginning of the end, but perhaps the end of the beginning.'

'Mao?' asked Benson, who had been listening avidly from the front.

'Churchill,' said Singh and Li Jun in unison.

'How is the investigation going?'

Han stood to attention in the other man's large and well-lit office and wondered why he had attracted the notice of the deputy chief of the security bureau, Fu Xinghua. It was not a good sign, he decided. It was the first time he had appeared before one of the big guns in a long time, since Li Jun had been forced to resign in fact, and no good ever came of it. Furthermore, this man was Dai Wei's hatchet man. And according to Li Jun, the deputy mayor was climbing up the suspects chart quicker than a Korean pop song.

'So far so good,' he said, keeping any inflection that might hint at his fears out of his voice. Despite his best efforts and the cool room, he felt the beads of sweat pop up along his upper lip.

'Very peculiar incident – a young girl stabbed at the Silk Market. Do you have her identity?'

'Her name was Qing.'

'Factory girl?'

'Yes, from Hunan province.'

'Any leads?'

'We have found an aunt who lives in a *hutong*. I have not had an opportunity to interview her yet.' This was probably no time to tell Fu that he'd outsourced the job to a Singaporean policeman and a Chinese copper who had resigned in disgrace. Or that, according to Li Jun with whom he had just got off the phone, the aunt had implicated Dai Wei in the killing.

'So what do you think – a jealous boyfriend?'

'That seems the most likely scenario,' he agreed, perhaps too quickly. The largest window in the room was directly behind the senior man and the bright light cast his face in shadows. Despite that, Han could feel the intensity of his gaze, like a predator in the undergrowth sizing up the weakest member of a herd.

'Have you written up a report yet?'

'No, sir. I haven't made much progress yet, you see.'

'That strikes me as quite puzzling – you have a reputation for being a diligent policeman.'

Han did his best not to fidget but it was difficult. His wide-spaced eyes, almost birdlike, focused on the deputy chief as he tried to decide on the best response – treat the remark as a compliment and ignore the undertow?

'In fact,' said Fu, getting to his feet and walking round the desk briskly, until he was eyeball to eyeball with Han, 'I have taken a personal interest in this case.'

'And why is that, sir?'

'Can't have our young girls feeling unsafe in this great city, can we?'

Han Deqing nodded vigorously as if the safety of factory girls was a well-known police preoccupation. It seemed to him that Fu had summoned him on a fishing expedition. Maybe he was trying to find out if Dai Wei had been implicated in any way. Perhaps he was debating whether to hand over the Qing investigation to another Politburo member's idiot son so that cold trails led only to dead ends. Li Jun popped into his head, expression mournful rather than accusing. Han had always known that the rebellious streak he shared with Li Jun would get him into trouble one day. He'd dodged a bullet on more than one occasion but now the lifeless corpse on the pizza restaurant table demanded action from him – and courage. It was time to do a little fishing himself.

'In fact, I do have a few thoughts,' he said.

'And what are they?'

'Firstly, Qing's death was connected to the murder of that Singaporean boy last month. She was on the way to sell her information to the mother when she was murdered.'

'That is interesting if rather far-fetched. What could a greedy tramp from the provinces know about such a thing?'

'She must have witnessed something – her aunt, the one I mentioned, lives at the *hutong* where Justin Tan was killed.'

'That is interesting . . .'

'Further, she must have approached someone other than the boy's mother, most likely the killer, hoping to blackmail him. Like all these girls, money was tight and she could not resist the temptation.'

'And?'

'And whoever that person was had her murdered before she could speak of what she knew or had seen.'

'That is a fascinating theory,' said Fu, placing both his palms face down on the desk. 'If you are right,' he continued, 'it is doubly unfortunate for your investigation.'

'Why do you say that, sir?' asked Han, meeting his superior's eyes with as much courage as he could muster.

'Because none keep their secrets as well as the dead.'

'You'd better go back to the Embassy with Benson and brief the First Secretary.'

'What should I tell her?' asked Li Jun.

That was a good question, decided Singh. Was it still possible to protect Susan Tan from the worst of their discoveries? Did she need to know that her husband was having an affair with the wife of the deputy mayor of Beijing? Was it necessary to tell her that Anthony's bribe to Dai Wei was probably at the root of Justin's murder? He thought of the First Secretary, greeting him in front of her desk with the firm handshake and later, her shoulders shaking as she cradled Qing's body at the Silk Market. Was it really his decision or duty to protect her or should he rely on the courage and resilience she'd shown to date and trust her with the facts?

Singh's thoughts turned to Jemima. She too had done the best she could for her brother, even to the extent of implicating her own father in the land deal that might have played a part in Justin's death. Her mother deserved to know that both her children had determination and moral strength – a strength they must have inherited from her if their father's track record was anything to go by.

'Inspector?'

'Tell her everything we've found out so far,' said Singh. 'She has a right to know.' He paused for a moment. 'Except about the affair – that has no bearing on the case as far as I can see.'

'Very well,' agreed Li Jun. 'It shall be as you say. What will you do in the meantime?'

Singh glared at the man. Since when did he have to explain himself to sidekicks?

'I will return to the hotel – I need to think. Murders are not solved with legwork alone, you know.'

If Li Jun was unconvinced, he didn't show it. Instead, they set out together and in a few minutes were dropping Singh at the lobby entrance.

'Are you sure you don't need the car,' asked Li Jun as Singh clambered out with difficulty.

'No,' said the inspector and raised a hand in farewell.

He waited for a few minutes until the car had turned the corner and then, instead of sauntering inside and in the general direction of the restaurants, Singh immediately flagged down a taxi. He was determined on his next course of action – the time had come for confrontation. He explained to the doorman where he was going and waited while the destination was translated for the driver.

In twenty minutes, the taxi drew up outside a large mansion. Why was it that when he was in no hurry the traffic cleared as if by magic and he reached his destination in the shortest possible time? The policeman climbed out of the taxi and watched it speed away. The late afternoon sunshine caused him to squint against the glare that originated low on the horizon. He stopped to admire the grey walls embossed with reliefs derived from Chinese mythology and guarded by squat stone lions at regular intervals. The doors and windows, too numerous to count, were picked out in red and gold. It looked more like a palace than a home.

Taking a deep breath, Singh strode towards the front door. He'd sent Li Jun away because his present mission was fraught with danger. He knew Li Jun would have insisted on coming along if he'd told him his plans and it just wasn't worth the risk for a native Chinese, entirely susceptible to the machinations of the state. But he, Singh, was a foreigner. What was the worst that could happen to him?

Re-education through labour? suggested the voice in his mind.

'I'm sure they'll just deport me,' he retorted out loud, more in hope than in faith.

It took some persuasion on Singh's part before a servant agreed to summon the boss. The policeman suspected that the underling had beat a retreat largely because he'd been so taken aback by the appearance of his visitor. Swarthy, turbaned men with excessive facial hair clearly didn't drop in that often. Mostly likely the fellow had assumed he was some sort of foreign potentate with a personal harem and a fleet of Bentleys.

Singh kicked his heels in a waiting room, choosing not to sit on the square rosewood chairs that rested on rich carpets. The walls were covered in fine art, artfully framed, vases sat in lighted alcoves and slightly more peculiarly, a grandfather clock complete with swinging gold pendulum stood tall in a corner. He didn't have long to wait. The deputy mayor of Beijing traipsed in, still wearing his fine suit and platform shoes.

'Who are you and what do you want?' The accent was pronounced but the meaning was clear. There was going to be no time for niceties.

'My name in Inspector Singh and I'm from the Singapore police. I was asked to look into the murder of the son of the First Secretary of the Embassy of Singapore, here in Beijing.'

'I remember,' said Dai Wei. 'He was killed by some thugs in a *hutong*. Not good for the reputation of China. I ordered a full investigation.' He looked Singh up and down as if puzzled by his appearance. 'So I do not see why you are involved?'

'The *hutong* where he was killed has just been designated for redevelopment – by you.'

'So?'

'The boy who was killed and his professor were investigating the transaction . . . representing the residents who did not want to move.'

Dai Wei shrugged and his silk suit shimmered. 'Anthony Tan did say something to me about that. Whatever the project and wherever it is, the residents never want to move, but China's progress cannot be held hostage to individuals.'

The conversation was not going as Singh had intended. Dai Wei was brusque but he wasn't defensive. Was it because he was so convinced of his immunity from trouble that he could afford to relax? It was time to light a fire.

'I know you took money, a bribe, from Anthony Tan to approve the land permit.'

Silence filled the room as completely as the incense from joss sticks. As if to emphasise the accusation, the grandfather clock began to toll the time. It was six in the evening. Singh was sweating profusely despite the cool. He remembered what Li Jun had said – torture and death were not uncommon in Chinese custody. He felt a bead of sweat trickle from under his turban and down his neck.

'How dare you come here and accuse me of such things? Do you know who I am?'

'I know exactly who you are. You're the man with authority to issue planning permissions and you did so for money. So much for your anti-corruption drive, eh? I am sure your constituents, and your enemies, will be interested to know about your crooked activities.'

'What proof do you have?'

It was too late for cold feet and caution. 'The testimony of Anthony Tan and the moneylender.'

Dai Wei snorted. 'It is nonsense to say that these men might implicate me in your lies because they would implicate themselves as well.'

'Anthony Tan holds you responsible for the death of his son. And I *know* that you had that girl, Qing, murdered at the Silk Market as well because she saw you the night of the murder.'

Even as he said it, he suspected that he'd overreached. Dai Wei's sudden spontaneous laughter confirmed his fears and caused Singh to take an involuntary step back. 'Is this what the Singapore police do? Run around making wild accusations? In China, even the traffic police in the provinces are more competent than you!'

'It's the truth,' said Singh, mouth pursed in a stubborn line.

Dai Wei was still wiping his eyes. 'It is a fascinating tale, worthy of a Chinese opera. But now, if you don't mind, you will leave my house immediately instead of wasting my valuable time with your fables.'

Singh knew it was time to withdraw as gracefully as possible. Part of him was relieved that he was to be allowed to walk away. He hoped his trembling knees were up to the task.

'But my advice, Inspector Singh from the Singapore police, is that you catch the first plane out of here tonight. Otherwise, I cannot be responsible for any accidents that befall you. In China, we try to provide a hospitable environment for foreigners, but even our best efforts fall short sometimes, as you very well know.'

Singh made his way back to the Embassy by taxi and in silence. He lit a cigarette and sucked on it as if his life depended on an infusion of nicotine. It didn't make him feel much better. Dai Wei had been worried, until he'd brought up Qing, and then he'd relaxed and regained his confidence. Why? What had he missed?

Li Jun was waiting for him at the entrance and he said in a hurried whisper, 'The First Secretary is waiting for you. She's not very happy.'

'What did you tell her?'

'As you suggested, I described all the elements of the investigation to date except the personal matter regarding her husband and the wife of Dai Wei.'

Singh exhaled sharply and wished that he was back in Singapore, waiting for his wife to put dinner on the table. He missed the inconsequential abuse about his personal habits and hygiene, the steaming rice, the spicy curries and the cold beer. He'd settle for a dressing down from Superintendent

Chen. Even that was better than knowing that he'd placed himself squarely in Dai Wei's sights and achieved nothing for it. The policeman stubbed out his light with a sneaker-clad foot – the shoes were still pristine white he noted glumly – and lumbered after Li Jun.

This time the First Secretary did not stand up or walk around the desk. Instead, as the two of them stood across from her, she snapped, 'You fools! Do you know what you've done?'

She didn't even know about the interview with Dai Wei and she was already fuming. That didn't bode well. Singh knew full well that he was about to be put on a plane, but he hoped she would extend Li Jun any protection she could manage if his involvement in the investigation became known. He really didn't want to leave his associate within Dai Wei's reach. Was it possible for Li Jun to ask for asylum? Sadly, Singh didn't think the Singapore government would risk their relationship with China to protect one man – least of all on the say-so of one of their least favourite cops.

'We know Dai Wei was involved in Justin's death,' he insisted. And then added plaintively as he remembered the deputy mayor's apparently genuine astonishment, 'He must have been. All the evidence points that way.' He ticked off his points on stubby fingers, not sure if he was trying to convince the First Secretary or himself. 'We know your husband bribed him from the moneylender's evidence, we can extrapolate that Justin might have found out about it. After all, he was investigating the land deal in question on behalf of Professor Luo. Besides, who has better access to a father and his secrets than a son? Somehow, Dai Wei got wind of it – maybe Justin accused him, maybe Professor Luo did. On the night of Justin's death, we can guess Qing saw him because her attempt at blackmail led to her death.'

'If it was Dai Wei, why did Qing wait so long to approach me ... and him?'

'Because she only realised who it was she had seen the night of the murder from the television some time later – we have that information from the aunt.'

'So let me get this straight. According to your theory, the deputy mayor of Beijing was at the *hutong* the night Justin was murdered? And Qing saw him there, tried to blackmail him and was killed?'

Singh nodded. It was an efficient summation in an icy tone and no more than he had outlined to Dai Wei earlier. It still wasn't clear why Dai Wei had felt obliged to supervise his thugs in person, but no other explanation fitted the available facts.

'I suppose we should be grateful that you came to me first and haven't accused Dai Wei of anything,' said the First Secretary. 'Otherwise, I'd be looking at a diplomatic scandal, Li Jun would be facing jail and you would be on the next plane.'

Singh opened his mouth and closed it again.

Susan Tan rubbed her forehead with her thumb and index figure. She seemed suddenly deflated. 'I guess it is not your fault, Inspector Singh. It was too much to ask that someone outside the system, who didn't know China, could get to the bottom of Justin's death.'

'Madam First Secretary?'

'Yes, Inspector?'

'I went to see Dai Wei before I came over here.'

'What?' Susan Tan and Li Jun exclaimed together.

'I decided to go on my own to try to keep anyone else out of trouble,' he added with an apologetic glance in Li Jun's direction.

'What did you say to him?' she asked, her expression one of deep foreboding.

'I ... err, I ... accused him of murder,' said Singh. 'Both Justin and Qing. And accepting bribes as well,' he added. There was nothing to be gained from not making a clean breast of his transgressions. 'Besides,' he added stubbornly, 'I still think he was behind the deaths of Justin and Qing.'

Li Jun leaned against a wall as if his legs were no longer strong enough to hold him upright. Susan Tan stood up for the first time and walked right up to Singh until she was well and truly in his personal space.

'Do you remember I mentioned that we had an Embassy function the night that Justin was murdered, which went on until the small hours?'

'Yes.'

'Well, just for your information, Dai Wei was a guest at that event. He didn't leave until late, well after the supposed time of Justin's death.'

The fat policeman felt the blood drain from his face and could only hope that his dark skin disguised his shock. By his side, Li Jun uttered a sound like the yelp of a small dog.

'In other words, Inspector Singh,' she continued, 'I can alibi the man, the very important man, you've just accused of my son's murder.'

Fourteen

'We have a problem. A policeman from Singapore came to see me. He accused me of accepting money from Anthony Tan for the *hutong* development planning permit.'

Fu Xinghua was pleased that he was at the other end of the phone line so Dai Wei could not see the expression of disgust on his face. The deputy mayor of Beijing was not happy unless he was feathering his nest at every opportunity. And it was turning into a source of real trouble. How much money did Dai Wei need anyway? Or was his wife, whose domestic spending was enough to prop up the economy of a small country, the source of the problem?

Fu didn't bother to ask whether the accusation was true but Dai Wei seemed oblivious to this omission. Instead, he demanded, 'How did he find out?'

'The moneylender from whom Tan got the money.'

'He is not a credible witness – not when it is his word against the famously incorruptible deputy mayor of Beijing.'

Fu hoped that the sarcasm in his voice was not evident to the other man.

'There is also Anthony Tan.'

'Why should he back up such a story? He has as much to lose as you if he was to support such a tale.'

'There is more to it, I'm afraid.'

'You must tell me everything if I am to make this problem go away. What else did this policeman say?'

'He accused me of the murder of Anthony Tan's son! He says that Tan will be prepared to testify because of that . . .'

There was no mistaking the panic in Dai Wei's voice. And Fu couldn't blame him. A moneylender from the underworld was not a threat. The businessman husband of a foreign dignitary was another matter entirely.

Fu Xinghua ran a thumbnail between his front teeth, trying to dislodge a sliver of chicken from his early dinner. The deputy head of the Beijing security bureau ran through his options quickly, all the while wishing his benefactor was less of a fool. Why didn't he understand that real influence came from power, not money? He made a decision.

'There's something you should know,' he said.

'What is it?'

'There is another reason why Anthony Tan would be pleased to have you out of the way.'

White sheets, white pillowcases, white quilt and a blue turban or at least five yards of blue cloth thrown carelessly over the coverings. Singh dug his nails into his scalp. He'd been metaphorically scratching his head; it felt good to have the physical relief of more direct action. He'd been so sure, and in fact, he was still so sure. The evidence against Dai Wei was circumstantial but credible and consistent. Except for the tiny matter of the alibi that the victim's mother had provided his suspect. The irony was almost too much to bear. The policeman poked a fork into the remnants of his dinner – he'd ordered everything marked on the menu with three chillies for spiciness but he'd finished his meal dissatisfied. He wouldn't have given any of the dishes even a single chilli.

Was there a way round this evidential hurdle? Singh gritted his teeth so hard he thought they might shatter into a thousand pieces of slightly yellowish enamel. It was highly unlikely that Qing would have been able to tie someone like Dai Wei to the crime unless he'd been there, at the scene of the murder, in person. Where else and how else would a factory girl find incriminating material tying a senior political figure to the killing of a foreigner? And there was the incontrovertible fact that she'd been at that *hutong* the night of Justin's death visiting her aunt. She *must* have seen something involving Dai Wei. Which meant the alibi still mattered. And it was airtight.

Singh lumbered over to the fridge and grabbed a beer. He stuck a finger through the metal clasp and ripped it back, enjoying the fizzing sound of the frothing beer. He hoped the hotel bill was not itemised, he'd hate to have to pay for the beers himself, but he doubted that Superintendent Chen would sign off on alcohol, however much he insisted it lubricated his brain cells. After his efforts that day, accusing the deputy mayor of Beijing of murder, the chief would have some grounds to dispute his assertion anyway. Singh's index and forefinger twitched; he needed a cigarette but was too lazy to reassemble his turban. And there was no way he was going out without it. He'd feel less exposed naked than without his headgear. The policeman wondered whether to risk a smoke in the room and then decided, with one eye on the smoke detectors, that it wasn't worth the risk.

There was only one thing to do really. He assembled his plates and side dishes in a heap and dumped them on a table. He yanked back the covers and clambered into bed, shivering slightly. Even the sheets were icy cold in the vicious air conditioning. Singh slumped back against the stacked pillows and reached for the remote control. He switched between channels in a desultory fashion, hoping for something that would soothe his agitated spirits. A cooking show? Cricket?

To his irritation, he realised that Dai Wei was on all the local news channels. He was giving some sort of news conference although Singh couldn't for the life of him figure out what it was about. It must have been earlier in the day because the sun was shining brightly. It had involved some violence because there was a split-screen image of a couple of bodies under sheets. No doubt another episode featuring Dai Wei's apparent crackdown on organised crime. You had to admire the man's gall – one hand clenched into a fist on behalf of the people and another reaching into their pockets.

Singh turned the sound down to silent and watched as Dai Wei played the press like an expert, all smiles, hand gestures and bonhomie. He stood aside after a while and ushered forwards the tall man who had been standing behind him. Singh recognised the dominant figure as Fu Xinghua – Li Jun had pointed him out that night of their duck dinner. Dai Wei's right-hand man. This man did not waste his time with smiles.

Instead he stared directly into the camera when he spoke, eyes flashing with passion. He was a convincingly heroic figure, unlike the squat deputy mayor.

Singh was distracted by his phone. He grabbed it, recognised Li Jun's number and held it to his ear.

'Li Jun?'

'I am just calling to enquire how you are feeling, inspector?'

'Are you in jail?'

'No.'

'Then I'm feeling all right.'

The Chinese man laughed. 'You need not be concerned about me, Inspector Singh.'

'A significant number of people associated with Dai Wei appear to be dead or have disappeared so I think there might be some room to worry.'

'But he has an alibi for the murder ...'

'Yes,' agreed Singh. 'We know he received a bribe though, can't anything be done about that?'

'I spoke to Han about this matter. He said that no one would be prepared to proceed with such a charge on the word of the moneylender alone.'

And despite what he'd told Dai Wei, there was no way in hell that Anthony Tan was going to back up the accusation, not without some evidence that Dai Wei had been involved in the death of his son.

His attention was caught by the television again. Dai Wei was smiling broadly. 'I'm watching Dai Wei on television now and he looks as if he doesn't have a care in the world. Although it must be a recording from before I went over and made a fool of myself.'

'I saw him on the news earlier,' agreed Li Jun. 'There was another attempted arrest this morning but the target was killed. Dai Wei increases his popularity every day with these types of incidents. He is untouchable.'

'It's that policeman stealing the limelight now.'

'Fu Xinghua? Yes, there was an attempt on his life but he survived. The assassin was killed.'

Singh was tempted to shake his fist at the television but he didn't have the energy. Suffice to say, these two left a large number of bodies in their wake, many of whom might otherwise have had something interesting to say.

'Any word on Professor Luo's whereabouts? He seems the only person who knows something who might actually be alive!'

'There has been no trace of him so far.'

'At this rate we'll never get to the bottom of this,' grumbled Singh.

'A fat person didn't become so with just one mouthful,' said Li Jun.

'Are you calling me fat?'

'Of course not,' said the other man hastily. 'You might have said that Rome was not built in a day.'

'I'm not sure that applies here in China,' complained the policeman. 'Dai Wei and his henchmen seem keen to build Beijing in a day.'

He noticed that the television was now showing the *hutong* where Justin had been murdered. 'Li Jun, are you near a TV?'

'I will switch mine on,' said Li Jun, always co-operative.

'The news channel – isn't that our *hutong*? What's going on?'

He guessed at almost the same time as Li Jun answered. 'They are talking about the planned development.' The screen shifted to a computer mock-up of the proposed shopping mall and Singh watched little pixelated figures marching through shops weighed down with bags.

'It is sad that so much of Beijing's history is being lost,' said Li Jun, echoing Singh's thoughts. Who would have thought he'd feel a pang for those narrow grubby streets?

As Singh watched, Dai Wei was shown shaking hands with a number of self-important looking men. The Singaporean developers, he guessed. The video was time-stamped the previous afternoon. One of the men provided Dai Wei with a hard hat emblazoned with the company logo. He put in on his head to much enthusiastic applause. And then, no doubt fearing that he looked ridiculous, he took it off and passed it to Fu Xinghua who was as ubiquitous as always. He wondered how the right-hand man felt about being used as a butler cum valet. Knowing Dai Wei, it was probably part of the official job description.

'Nothing can prevent this development now,' said Li Jun.

Singh grunted his agreement and reached for the remote. He was about to switch off the television, eager to erase the images of a smug Dai Wei, when he sat bolt upright, eyes gleaming with excitement in the reflected light of the wide screen.

He reached for his turban with an impatient hand. 'Li Jun!' he shouted.

'What is it, Inspector?'

'Li Jun! I'm not going to bed. We've got work to do.'

'What?'

'I need you with me. I've got an idea!' He barked out a few instructions and then tossed the phone away from him. With two dexterous hands, he wrapped his turban neatly around his head.

'Did you pay him?'

Anthony Tan sat on the edge of a deep chair, his elbows resting on his knees. The living room was lit with lamps and shadows criss-crossed the floor.

Susan asked again, more prosecuting counsel than wife, 'Did you bribe Dai Wei?'

He looked up and nodded once.

His daughter, watching from a corner of the room, whispered, 'Oh, Dad.'

Susan was not finished. 'And you borrowed the funds from a moneylender?'

'Yes, but I've paid him back.'

'Was he the one that threatened me?' asked Jemima.

Anthony Tan rose to his feet and walked slowly to his daughter. He hugged her tight. 'I'm so sorry, honey.' He released his daughter and turned to face his wife. 'Look, I know what I did was wrong. But at least remember, despite everything, this didn't have anything to do with Justin's death. Dai Wei was right here at the Embassy – you said so yourself.'

'Where did you get the cash to pay the moneylender?'

'Dai Wei issued the planning permission. So the Singaporean developers paid me a fee for facilitating the project.'

'But, Dad – Justin was working to stop people from being thrown off their land. He and Professor Luo tried to prevent this deal.'

'I know, honey. And I'm sorry.'

'But you could have pulled out! Told them you didn't want to be involved any more instead of dishonouring Justin's memory.'

'I had to pay the moneylender – otherwise you might have been in real danger. I had no choice but to go ahead.'

The three of them stood, staring at each other. All that was left of the family of four just a short month before. In the silence was the acknowledgement that although his words were true, they provided cold comfort.

'Can you forgive me?' he asked. He spoke to them both but he was looking at Jemima.

There was silence. Susan looked as if her face had been hewn from rock. At last, Jemima nodded, although her eyes remained bleak.

Anthony Tan's phone rang and he reached for it instinctively. Even as mother and daughter listened to the faint tinny sounds of a hurried speaker on the other end, the blood drained from his face like sand through an hourglass.

'You were right!' Li Jun was smiling broadly and the full moon lit up his teeth so that he looked uncharacteristically vicious.

Singh acknowledged the compliment with a nod but rather wished he'd had his insight twenty-four hours earlier. That would have saved him a whole heap of trouble.

They stood at the small *hutong* junction, a few yards from where Justin had been killed. Singh turned a hundred and eighty degrees until he could feel the wind in his face. It probably presaged a violent storm and an uncomfortable drenching but it felt good after the clammy humidity of the last few days. Maybe the weather breaking predicated a break in the case. It certainly seemed that way from their late-night conversation with Qing's old aunt.

'What do you think our next step should be now that we have made this discovery?' asked Li Jun.

'Confront our suspect?'

'That is a good idea, but perhaps we should take our latest information to the First Secretary before we decide on the direct approach? It might be prudent to do this.'

Singh grinned – it was the closest thing to a criticism of his previous efforts that he was likely to hear from his loyal sidekick.

'Very well,' he said, prepared to humour the man. Singh turned to face the wind and sniffed suddenly. 'I smell rain,' he said.

'Yes – after it has been hot for a few days it always rains in Beijing,' said Li Jun, taking the diversion into meteorological matters in his stride.

They watched the heavy clouds approach the moon in a pincer movement as if determined to snuff out the light. A metaphor for Beijing, slowly swamped in pollution and crime? Singh remembered Dai Wei's warning that he get on a plane that evening or face the consequences. He shrugged, as the first few drops of rain landed on his face. He wasn't going anywhere when he was so close to a solution to Justin and Qing's murders. Beijing and its inhabitants would just have to put up with the continued presence of one angry but determined Sikh copper for a couple more days.

Fifteen

By the time Fu reached Dai Wei's mansion, it was too late. The house was bathed in light. He could hear screaming and crying from within. Two police cars were already at the scene, engines running, red lights cutting swathes in the pre-storm darkness. He stood outside for a moment, gathering his thoughts, preparing for whatever he might find within. He could smell the air, heavy with impending rain.

A policeman in uniform appeared at the door. He was speaking into his radio. Fu couldn't hear the words but the tone was high-pitched and rushed. It was time to take charge. He hurried towards the door, coat billowing, accompanied by a crack of thunder that sounded as if the ground beneath his feet had been ripped asunder. The junior policeman at the door looked as if he might burst into tears of relief at the appearance of the senior man.

'What is it?' demanded Fu.

'It is not good.'

'What do you mean?'

'Do you know whose house this is?'

Fu nodded. 'Yes.'

'Come and see what has happened.'

Fu followed him in. Every light was on and the interior was so bright that it reminded the deputy chief of a film set, or the stage for an elaborate Chinese opera. Through a doorway, he could see uniformed staff huddled together around a sofa. Some were stony faced but most were weeping and at least two were in hysterics. Fu Xinghua didn't spare them a second glance. He continued after his guide who led him up a wide staircase with increasingly reluctant steps. When they reached the landing, he pointed at a door that was slightly ajar. Even if he hadn't indicated the entrance, Fu would have realised it was ground zero from the whey-faced policeman standing outside. He too recognised Fu. Without a word, he pushed the door open. Fu stepped forwards and looked in. Even for a seasoned policeman, it was a shock. He took a small step back and closed his eyes.

The second policeman was made of sterner stuff than the first. 'It's the wife,' he said. 'The servants identified her from her clothing. It's Dai Wei's wife.'

Fu nodded. He hadn't expected anything else although only a DNA sample would provide proof beyond reasonable doubt. Her own mother would not have recognised the former socialite – her face had been beaten to pulp, features completely destroyed in a mess of raw flesh and splintered bone. Her sheets were soaked in blood and the splatter on the walls looked like a display at a museum of modern art.

'Where is the deputy mayor?'

'He has gone out.' The policeman cleared his throat as if he was having difficulty uttering the rest. 'The servants heard screaming. One of the braver ones came to investigate – she was the personal servant of Madame Dai and felt great loyalty to her.'

'And?'

'And Dai Wei told her to "clean up the mess". Then he had a shower and went out. The servant called the police and we were the first car to respond.' The policeman paused as if seeking to formulate a sentence in a foreign language. 'I have not put out the alert for Deputy Mayor Dai Wei in case the authorities choose a different approach to his apprehension.'

Fu Xinhua met the other man's eyes, pupils wide with fear and shock, and nodded. Which junior policeman wanted to be responsible for seeking the arrest of the most powerful man in Beijing? And it was quite possible that the higher-ups might decide on a "different approach" – in other words, a cover-up. This young man had an effective antenna for the politics of China. He would go far. Fu glanced once more at the remains of Madame Dai Wei. There were not going to be any easy solutions here – too many witnesses, too much of a mess.

'Did Dai Wei say where he was going?' he demanded.

'No.'

'It doesn't matter,' said Fu. 'I think I know.'

Anthony Tan and his wife stood side by side, a couple of feet, and a lifetime, apart. They were bathed in the ghostly glow of a street light that heightened the blackness in every direction. The two of them had walked out of the Embassy and down the street until they reached the corner. Dai Wei was waiting for them, leaning against the Embassy walls, facing the deserted road, as if he was a vagrant deciding where to bed down for the night.

'So you came . . .' The deputy mayor sounded pleased but not ecstatic, as if he had picked the right number on a roulette wheel but not put all his chips down on the table.

'You said on the phone that I had to meet you – that you were considering withdrawing the planning permission?'

'That's right.'

'Why? I don't understand.'

Next to her husband, Susan tried to process the information, tried to understand the implications. When she had heard that the rendezvous was with Dai Wei, she had insisted on coming along. She wasn't sure why exactly, but she knew her husband's dealings with this man posed a threat to what was left of her family.

Dai Wei cackled suddenly, his mouth opened like a gash. Dai was not lost or drunk or confused, realised Susan, he was enraged to the point that his self-control hung by a thread.

'Please, Dai Wei, don't do it,' whispered Anthony.

'Why not?'

'Because the developers will want their money back, and I don't have it any more.'

'Because you repaid the moneylender?'

'Yes.'

Susan Tan understood why her husband sounded as shocked and broken as the day they heard that Justin was dead. Beijing was a very bad place in which to owe people money.

'Comrade Dai, we ask you this favour. I'm not involved in the transaction, but I beg you not to do anything that would endanger my daughter. I have already lost one child.' Susan's voice was trembling like the last leaf of autumn.

'You think that revenge from a failed transaction might threaten your child?'

'That is what I fear.'

'All the better,' snapped Dai Wei.

Anthony Tan swayed on his feet as if he'd been hit by a heavyweight. 'Why? Dai Wei, why are you doing this?'

'Because you were having an affair with my wife.'

In the empty space after his words, Susan Tan gasped. She had discovered many truths about her husband in the last forty-eight hours, but not this last one. She didn't even turn to look at Anthony for confirmation. Instinctively, she knew that it was true. A man with something to prove would have been susceptible to the charms of a trophy bride.

Dai Wei reached into his pocket as nonchalantly as someone looking for loose change to tip a waiter. But instead of a wallet, he extracted a vicious-looking revolver. Susan stared at the dark shadow in his hand, an inkier black than the stormy night sky.

'I am going to kill you,' said the deputy mayor.

He raised the gun.

Singh and Li Jun reached the Embassy well after midnight but the First Secretary's residence was lit up like a skyscraper in a banana republic. It was as if someone within was trying to chase away fearsome night terrors. Jemima answered the door, her eyes wide, her cheeks tear-stained.

'Jemima, what is it? What's the matter?'

'My parents – they walked out, down the street. To meet Dai Wei.'

As Singh stared at her blankly, trying to process the reason for this post-midnight rendezvous, she continued, 'They wouldn't let me go with them. They said it might be dangerous.'

'We'll go after them,' said Singh.

'Would it not be better to wait here?' asked Li Jun. 'It might be a confidential matter between them –' he looked at Singh meaningfully – 'and they may prefer privacy.'

Singh knew Li Jun was alluding to the affair, but he shook his head. 'I have a bad feeling about this.'

They hurried out into the night, waving away Jemima's request to come with them, and past the main gates with its puzzled-looking security officer. The rain was coming down in an unbroken sheet now and both men were drenched immediately. Even as they hesitated, trying to decide which way to turn, a police car came screeching around the corner. It skidded to a halt in front of them, spraying both men from a puddle of water. Fu Xinghua leaped out, all lithe motion and indifference to weather, the people's hero. He stopped when he saw the two men, both watching him warily.

'You are the inspector from Singapore,' he said. 'I've heard about you.'

Singh grimaced. He knew the source and he doubted the reviews were good. He noted that Li Jun was standing a couple of feet behind him, head down, trying not to draw attention to himself.

'What are you doing here?' demanded the inspector, unwilling to be intimidated.

'There has been an incident.'

'What's that supposed to mean?'

Fu Xinghua did not answer directly. Instead, he said, 'I am on the trail of Dai Wei, have you seen him?'

Singh's answer was drowned out by gunshots.

'But first, I intend that you too understand the pain of losing everything you care about.' He turned the weapon towards Susan Tan. 'And when I am done with the two of you I will return to the Embassy for your daughter.'

Dai Wei pulled the trigger, once, twice, three times. Claps of thunder echoed the gunshots. But it was Anthony Tan who hit the ground. In that last second, he'd flung himself in front of his wife and taken the bullets meant for her. His collapse was lit up as lightning crackled across the sky. Susan screamed. She fell to her knees beside Anthony, trying to see in the darkness, feeling for a pulse, trying to spot the bullet entry points.

Anthony Tan was as pale as death and not far from it. His eyes flickered open, shut and then, with an act of will, open again. A hand trembled and then found a place to rest on his stomach, covering the wounds but not the spread of blood.

'Susan . . .' He met her eyes. 'I'm sorry.'

She didn't say that it was all right. He was dying, had tried to save her, but how could she forgive him? Justin was already dead and Jemima was in danger. Nothing was ever going to be all right again.

'I just wanted to be prove myself . . . that I wasn't just a husband . . . I could be a success too.'

She nodded. A small part of her understood. A large part

of her found the ability to blame herself. Could she have avoided this reckoning? Were there forks on the road that she had missed because her eyes were always on the horizon, the next posting, the next promotion? Susan had no thoughts at all for the man holding the gun in the shadows. She could only think of her dying husband, her dead son and what might have been.

Anthony reached out a hand and she could see that it was covered in blood, black as tar in the night. Susan hesitated and then took it. His eyes remained open but she could have sworn she saw the moment when Anthony Tan's spirit left his body. It was fanciful, but she had seen the terror ebb in the dying man's eyes.

Susan reached over and closed them – did she see an accusation there? At least her husband had suffered an easier death than her son.

Susan turned around and saw that Dai Wei still had the gun although he was not pointing it at her with any singularity. The deputy mayor was lost in his own thoughts and she sensed that the rage that had fuelled him had died along with Anthony.

Like spectres out of the shadows, they came – first Fu Xinghua, followed by Li Jun and then, trailing a few feet behind, Singh.

Li Jun fell to his knees beside Anthony Tan. The inspector came to a stop beside him, hands resting on knees, wheezing and panting. The rain plastered Li Jun's hair down until it looked like a tonsure. In his dark Mao suit, Singh thought the Chinese man looked like a priest administering the last rites. But it was too late for any attempt to save Anthony Tan's soul.

Li Jun turned to face them and in that sudden lull that punctuates all tropical storms, his voice was loud. 'He's dead.'

'What happened?' asked Singh, straightening up and taking in the tableau, his heart rate calming down for the first time since they'd heard gunshots ring out further down the road. Fu Xinghua had led the cavalry and Singh had brought up the rear.

'He's been shot.'

Singh had already noted the gun limp in the deputy mayor's hand. But Dai Wei did not appear a threat. His expression was dazed, his shoulders rounded with defeat.

'Dai Wei – he shot Anthony.' Susan's voice sounded almost disembodied. 'He was trying to kill me – he said that he'd go for Jemima next so that Anthony would lose everything he cared about.'

'Then how come it's him that's dead?'

'Anthony . . . Anthony got in the way.'

'Do you know why?' asked Singh although he thought he could guess. Fu, in a movement so quick that none of them anticipated it, stepped up to Dai Wei and in a quick efficient twist of the wrist seized the weapon. He retreated two steps and pointed the gun directly at the chest of his former boss.

'Anthony was . . . was having an affair with Dai Wei's wife.' Susan Tan was still crouched next to the body of her husband. Her hands were covered in blood, her words barely audible.

'I have just come from their residence,' said Fu Xinghua.

Dai Wei appeared to wake from his gaze. 'You saw?' he asked, the upward tilt of the head indicating some pride in his handiwork.

'Yes.'

'She deserved it.'

'No one deserves what you did to your wife,' responded Fu. And then in a formal tone, 'Dai Wei, I arrest you for the murder Anthony Tan, Madam Dai . . . as well as Justin Tan.'

Singh opened his mouth to protest and then shut it firmly again.

'Are you sure?' asked Li Jun.

'Without doubt,' said Fu.

Singh had been watching Dai Wei, curious as to his reaction, but the deputy mayor remained impassive, indifferent or oblivious to being arrested on three counts of murder.

Fu gestured with the gun and Dai Wei obediently turned and headed back in the direction of the Embassy entrance. Fu followed behind. Singh bent over the dead man and hooked his arms under Anthony's shoulders. Li Jun hurried over and grabbed his feet. With difficulty, they raised him off the ground and stumbled slowly after Fu with Susan forming an escort. They left a trail of blood and rain behind them on the pavement.

Sixteen

Mother and daughter were huddled together on the sofa, one tearful, the other dry-eyed. The two policemen, Singh and Li Jun, sat across from them. A deep silence reigned and had done for some time, punctuated by the occasional audible sob from Jemima. Singh stood up and went to a window, easing the curtains to one side so that he could have a quick peek. Outside, the Embassy grounds were a hive of activity. A squad of police cars were parked at random angles, their headlights reflected in the pools of water, the only evidence of the stormy weather earlier that evening. As he watched, Dai Wei, hand-cuffed and with his head bowed, was bundled into a squad car, presumably to take him to police headquarters. Singh's head was spinning like an out of control merry-go-round.

An ambulance was present although it was too late to rush Anthony Tan anywhere – his next stop would be a cold autopsy room, maybe even the same one that was used for his son. Embassy officials scurried around trying to limit the damage to reputation. The press, who had somehow got wind of events, were pressed against the main gates like a lynch mob. Singh was glad he was indoors.

The doorbell rang and it was like a bell tolling for Anthony Tan. Li Jun looked at the First Secretary and she nodded once. The slight creature hurried away and returned a few moments later with Fu Xinghua.

He immediately went over to the widow and took her hands in his as she rose to greet him. 'I am sorry for your loss.'

'Thank you.'

'You will be pleased to know that Dai Wei has been taken to police headquarters to be charged with the murders of your husband and son. And his own wife, of course.'

'And you should know that I will not sit quietly by if there is any attempt to cover up what he has done.'

Singh could only admire the woman, in the throes of loss, still determined to see justice done for Justin.

'I give you my word that will not happen,' said Fu Xinghua. 'My expectation is that Dai Wei will face a firing squad for the murders.'

Singh, who had been listening quietly to this exchange as translated by Li Jun, now asked loudly, 'What about his alibi for the night of Justin's killing?'

'The murder was committed by hired killers. He did not have to be there.'

'But Qing saw something, and was killed before she could talk. Except that she couldn't have seen Dai Wei, because he was here at an Embassy function.'

'The factory girl? We are not convinced that her murder had anything to do with this case.'

'But she called me, said she had information,' insisted Susan.

'She was a factory girl – she probably thought that there was some easy money to be made pretending she knew something. Your reward posters around the aunt's *hutong* were too tempting.'

'But she was killed!'

'These girls – so far from home, they often get into trouble. Relationships gone wrong, moneylenders, prostitution.'

Singh pondered this explanation. If one took Qing out of the equation, then there was no reason that Dai Wei could not have ordered Justin's murder. But it was completely contrary to what he'd believed to be the truth a scant three hours earlier. It was possible that he was wrong, of course. Even in Singapore, he was sometimes fallible. Why not here, far from home, operating in a strange culture and without the ability to communicate directly?

'What was Dai's motive?'

'You are able to ask such a question?' Fu's disdain for the foreign policeman was there for all to see in the curled lip. 'Anthony Tan was having an affair with his wife. Everyone knew that Dai Wei was obsessed with that woman.'

'How did he find out?'

Fu Xinghua met his eyes and they were reptilian in their lack of emotion. 'I told him. Of course, I could not have predicted the consequences.'

'Of course,' said Singh, allowing the sarcasm he felt to infuse his tone.

'But why would you tell him such a thing?'

Fu altered his tone to speak to the First Secretary, derision replaced with courtesy. 'I worked closely with Dai Wei in the crackdown on organised crime in Beijing. I knew he had ambitions for higher office. I feared that his wife would become a liability. It was intended as a friendly warning to get his house in order.'

Singh looked across at Li Jun to see how he was taking the information. His sidekick's expression was one of bovine placidity but his eyes were bright and alert.

'His motive for killing his wife and lover are clear,' said Singh. 'But what about Justin?'

'What better way to punish a man than to kill his son?'

Singh wasn't buying it. The killing of Anthony and his own wife had been the classic crimes of passion. He remembered Dai Wei's dazed expression when they had reached the crime scene – his rage exhausted, he'd been docile and co-operative, seemingly indifferent to his fate. That didn't square with the suggestion of a complex long-term strategy of revenge beginning with the murder of Justin a few weeks earlier.

'When did you tell him about the affair?'

'Yesterday.' Fu added quickly, 'But he might have known earlier.'

'He didn't,' said Singh emphatically. 'You saw how he reacted – he killed two people, for God's sake – do you think he could have kept up appearances if he'd known about the affair since before Justin's death?'

Fu sighed but acknowledged Singh's point with a brief nod. 'You are right,' he said. 'I will tell you what I know but there must be agreement that it remains confidential.'

Singh and Li Jun nodded in unison.

'We are not sure of the exact details but Justin found out about the bribe that Anthony Tan paid to Dai Wei. He told the professor he worked with, Professor Luo. He was not sure what to do with the information because it implicated his father. But the professor went ahead and threatened Dai Wei that if he didn't refuse planning permission, he would ensure the matter became public.'

This was a whole lot more plausible, thought Singh. If Luo had gone behind Justin's back and it had led to the boy's death, it would explain the professor's profound sense of guilt. He nodded to indicate that Fu should continue his hypothesis.

'As a consequence, Dai Wei had Justin killed and the professor arrested to protect his reputation.'

'You know this for a fact?'

'Professor Luo confirmed the story. After he was arrested for *falun gong* practices, he explained to the security personnel that he felt guilty because his work on land grabs had led to the boy's death.'

'But why was this information not acted upon?'

'It was assumed that Professor Luo was lying to distract from his own deviant behaviour. It was only after recent events that his story has gained plausibility.'

'And the professor will testify to this effect, that Dai Wei killed Justin to keep information about the bribe a secret?'

'Professor Luo is dead.'

'What happened?'

'Prison is a dangerous place . . .'

Singh's eyes closed, but the image of Dao Ming was not so easily shut out. He remembered what Li Jun had said just a few days earlier. Deaths in custody were common in China. It seemed that he'd been right. And Dao Ming and her sister would never see their father again.

'I should tell you that senior figures would prefer that the motive for the murder of Justin be connected to the affair between Anthony Tan and his wife.' Fu Xinghua's expression was wooden.

'Why is that?'

Li Jun's voice was filled with bitterness. 'So that they can pretend that Dai Wei was not a corrupt official lining his own pockets at the expense of the Chinese people.'

'The fight against black must not be compromised,' stated Fu.

Why wasn't he surprised? This man's reputation and career were also tied up with Dai Wei. How much better for the government if the killings had been a crime of passion rather than a crime of Mammon? That way, the facade of law and order remained intact.

'And if we won't keep quiet?' asked Susan.

'Dai Wei won't be charged with Justin's murder, just the other two.'

When she didn't respond, he became almost animated. 'Isn't it better that Dai Wei face justice for what he did? What does it matter if *why* he did it remains a secret?'

Deep indentations were visible between Singh's eyebrows.

Jemima buried her face in her hands. Susan Tan put her arms around her daughter and glared at the policeman. 'It is better if you leave,' she said. 'I need to take Jemima upstairs.'

Fu Xinghua nodded and rose to his feet. 'I will keep you updated of progress,' he said.

Singh watched him go, a thoughtful expression on his face, and then hurried after Susan Tan.

'Where are you going?' asked Li Jun.

'Just to say my goodbyes, then I'm going back to the hotel for a well-deserved sleep. Why don't you do the same thing?'

'What about the new information? What we found out from Qing's aunt?'

'That'll keep for another day.'

Li Jun looked doubtful but he did not protest.

Forty-five minutes later, contrary to what he'd told Li Jun, Inspector Singh was not at the hotel but back at the *hutong* where Justin had been killed. He stood leaning against a wall and kicking his foot into the ground as if trying to dig a small hole. He was a still figure except for the rhythmic sucking on his cigarette and the puffs of smoke exhaled through his nose. The lone tree beneath which Justin's body had been found was the only shelter along the street so Singh was grateful that the storm had done its worst and moved on to douse some other part of China in torrential rains. The night was clear and mild now, the air as fresh as it had been since he'd arrived in Beijing less than a week earlier.

The policeman inhaled smoke deep into his lungs and admitted to himself that he was afraid. It had been a long time since he feared a meeting with a criminal; usually he antici-pated it with pleasure, knowing that he was close to finding justice for a victim of violent crime. And it had seemed to him, against all the odds, perhaps because the fates were determined to annoy Mrs Singh, that he was destined for an old man's quiet death. So why was he afraid this time? He realised suddenly that it was failure that frightened him. His fears this time were on behalf of Justin – that their best efforts would not find him justice. That China's elite would once again prove that they were above the law. He had sent Li Jun, scrawny and determined, away because he feared for him as well. It was never prudent to entice a tiger down from the mountains, but that was what the two of them had done with the case. And if he doubted that the consequences were real, he had only to remember Professor Luo who had not survived his guilt-induced encounter with the country's security apparatus.

He heard the sound of boots on cobblestones. It was a firm, even stride. Singh turned to face the newcomer, hoping his doubts were hidden from view.

'Inspector Singh?'

'Comrade Fu, I am glad you came here to meet me.'

'I found the message you left under my car wiper asking me to come this way because you had important information.'

The fat policeman had to look up to meet Fu's eyes. The deputy chief of the Beijing security bureau was a good head taller than him. As he stood there, impassive, unruffled, his long coat slapping around his knees in the wind spirals, Singh fought the desire to walk away. He allowed himself an internal grimace – it was too late now anyway. He'd shown his hand merely by demanding a meeting.

'What do you want? I am in a hurry, there is much work to be done to close this case.'

'I have some important information that I thought you might like to know.'

'And what is that?'

'That the girl by the name of Qing left a note with her grand-aunt before she was murdered.'

There was a brief pause and then Fu said, 'So?'

'She named her killer in it.'

'What do you mean?'

'In the letter, Qing explained what she was about to do, *whom* she was about to blackmail ... and why. Undoubtedly, the victim of the blackmail was also her killer.'

'If it is as you say, it will be further good evidence against Dai Wei.'

Singh almost smiled. The Chinese policeman was fishing for information, always a sign of weakness.

'It was not Dai Wei she was attempting to blackmail.'

Fu was watchful, cautious. 'Who was it then?'

'It was you.'

'You bring me out to this godforsaken spot to tell me fairy tales?'

'If you do not wish to hear my stories, you have only to walk away.'

'And what will you do?'

'I will see if I can find a more willing audience elsewhere.'

The moon slipped out from behind a cloud and the darkness beat a retreat into the corners. Singh did not blink or retreat as the other man took a purposeful step forwards. Instead, he tossed his cigarette on the road, ground it out with his heel and then took a step closer himself so that he was face to face, nose to nose, with Fu.

'Show me this letter then if you think it might be of interest to me.'

'Do you think I am a naive twenty-something from Hunan province to have my evidence with me?'

'Then why should I believe you?'

'Because you know it is the truth – that is why you haven't walked away.'

'It was Dai Wei who ordered that youth killed. He will be charged with the murder and does not deny it.'

'I expect you put pressure on him to accept the outcome. Li Jun explained to me how the system works in China. Maybe you will threaten his family or offer to keep his corruption a secret so that his relatives do not lose their positions. Dai Wei has nothing to lose, so he will agree. After all, he will definitely face the death sentence for the other two murders.'

'If you have this letter, why have you not taken it to the First Secretary or directly to the police? Why approach me?' asked Fu.

'I prefer a more . . . financially rewarding solution.'

'This is an odd choice for you,' said Fu. 'The reputation of the Singapore police for honesty is widespread.'

'Let's just say I have developed an admiration for the Chinese way of doing business.'

'I don't believe you.'

Singh was suddenly impassioned. 'You think everything is fine in Singapore? Do you know how much pressure I am under to resign because my bosses don't like my methods? Every chance they get, they send me off on dangerous missions like this one. Not long ago, I was almost killed on an investigation in Cambodia. My wife is worried because we have not saved much money for retirement. The police in

Singapore are honest – *when* they are in Singapore. But when in China, when opportunity presents, why not do things the Chinese way?'

'What about your friend, Li Jun?'

'He does not need to know anything about this. He is incorruptible . . . and see what it has cost him. I do not want to end up like him.'

'All right, let's say I agree to play this game of yours. How much do you want for the letter?'

'Five million yuan.'

He laughed. 'The girl only wanted a million.'

'Inflation,' grunted Singh.

'How do I know that you will keep your word, destroy the note?'

'Again, I remind you that I am not a naive factory girl looking to make a quick fortune. I merely want to . . . retire in more comfortable circumstances, back in Singapore where I belong.'

'What about Li Jun?'

'What about him?'

'Does he know of this evidence?'

'Of course not.'

'Very well, I will make the necessary arrangements for payment in exchange for the letter.'

'You show excellent judgement,' said Singh, turning away. 'I am at the Hyatt. If you arrange for delivery of the money, I will fulfil my part of the bargain.'

With the speed of a mongoose, Fu leaped forwards and wound an arm around the fat man's throat.

'You are a greedy fool,' hissed the other man.

Singh struggled but Fu seemed impervious. He stood rock solid, feet apart. His grip tightened, and Singh felt his vision start to darken around the edges. He stopped his fight and let his body go limp, hoping to lull the man into easing his grip but to no avail. A small rational part of him knew that he'd underestimated the Chinese man. He'd expected trouble, but not there and then, in a crowded neighbourhood. So far, Fu had always acted through intermediaries; thugs to kill Justin, the hit man with the cold eyes for Qing. But it seemed that the security chief was not afraid to get his hands dirty.

'Let him go,' shouted an angry, familiar voice and he felt rather than saw someone leap at Fu, knocking him sideways and causing him to loosen his grip for a moment.

Singh sucked in oxygen and felt his legs go weak with relief. But the respite was brief, the grip tightened again.

'You cannot kill both of us in time. Let him go or I run for help.'

Singh was coherent enough to spot the flaw in Li Jun's analysis. It was true that he would get to a residence before Fu could reach him, but that would leave one Sikh copper very dead indeed. Was he supposed to take comfort from the fact that his murderer would face justice?

The situation deteriorated immediately. Fu pulled a gun from a holster in the small of his back and pointed it at Li Jun.

'It seems you are mistaken and I can kill you both before you have time to summon help.'

Why hadn't he produced the gun in the first place? Probably because he preferred to dispose of annoying Sikh coppers quietly. Singh didn't doubt for a moment that he would choose the noisy option if necessary.

Li Jun was standing with his hands hanging loosely by his sides. His eyes appeared to measure the distance between the two men.

Fu let go of Singh and shoved him in the small of the back so that he stumbled towards Li Jun. He straightened up and turned around so that he was facing Fu Xinghua, one hand massaging his neck.

'What are you doing here?' croaked Singh through his damaged windpipe.

Li Jun smiled. 'I'm afraid I did not believe you when you said you planned to return to the hotel, not after the previous time. So I watched you, followed you and kept my distance.'

'Enough talk,' countered Fu. 'Where is the letter?'

'There's no way you will get away with this,' said Singh.

Without warning, Fu shifted his aim and shot Li Jun in the thigh. The ex-policeman fell to the ground clutching his leg.

'Give me the letter or the next bullet will be in his head.'

Singh knew he was out of options. Moving quickly for a man of his size, he flung himself at Fu's gun arm. It was sufficiently unexpected behaviour that he closed the gap before Fu shot him. Or maybe he didn't want the inspector dead until he'd traced the letter. Singh jerked Fu's arm into the air, trying to prise the gun from the other man's grasp. It was a futile effort. Even as he fought with all the strength he had, he could feel the weapon slowly but surely turning towards him as the greater strength of the other man began to tell.

He didn't see it, certainly never anticipated it but Li Jun rose to his feet, stumbled forwards and then flashed into a scissor kick that caught Fu Xinghua on his left side. Fu stumbled and caught his foot on an uneven paving stone. As he crashed to the ground, the gun spilt from his hand and slithered across the ground. In that second, while he was down, Singh launched himself at the weapon. The other man, still shaken but no less effective, grasped Singh's ankle and brought him crashing down. The wind was knocked out of him as abruptly as a bursting balloon. He gasped and tried to get up. Fu was reaching for the gun. With a desperate yell, Singh launched himself forwards and knocked Fu's legs out from under him, an ungainly bowling ball against the last two pins. The fat man reached the gun first. He didn't even bother to try to get up. He rolled over on his back and pointed the weapon directly at Fu.

Li Jun struggled to a sitting position, a palm pressed against his leg. The inspector reached into his breast pocket and extricated the handkerchief he always kept there. He handed it to the other man who tied a tourniquet.

A few men appeared out of the darkness, coming cautiously to investigate the gunshot. Li Jun said something and a man reached for his phone. Singh looked at his friend and hoped the cavalry would hurry. The wound was bleeding heavily and he feared Fu might have nicked an artery.

Singh rose slowly to his feet, gun still pointed steadily at Fu.

'What letter is he talking about?' whispered Li Jun, pale but determined to get to the bottom of things.

'There is no letter,' admitted Singh.

'If that is so, how did you know it was me and not Dai Wei?' demanded Fu.

Watching him, Singh knew the question was not asked out of idle curiosity. The Chinese security chief, at the wrong end of a gun now, still believed he would walk away. And that meant ensuring that there were no loose ends.

'Qing identified someone on the television as the culprit. Her aunt thought she meant Dai Wei. That is why we were sure it was him. But it turned out Dai Wei had an alibi for the night of the murder. She couldn't have seen him.'

'So?'

'I was watching television in my hotel room, and there you were standing right next to Dai Wei at some press conference. And I realised that I had never ever seen Dai Wei without you – you two are the public face of Beijing law and order. This evening we asked the aunt. She confirmed that you were on television at the same time, standing behind Dai Wei. And that's when we realised Qing had been talking about you all along.'

Fu nodded to acknowledge the explanation.

'What did Qing see?' asked Singh.

The policeman shrugged. 'I was waiting in the car near the *hutong* to ensure the job was done. Qing saw the murder and then spotted my man stopping to report to me. She recognised me later from the television. The price of fame.'

'But why did you need to kill Justin? It was Dai Wei that was corrupt, not you!'

Fu shrugged. 'Dai Wei was very useful to me in my career. I did not want to lose that advantage.'

'But when the evidence could not be suppressed, you decided to use Dai Wei as a scapegoat – told him about the affair between Anthony Tan and his wife,' said Singh. 'You knew how he would react. As a bonus you would get rid of Anthony Tan as well and all first-hand evidence of the corrupt land transaction.'

Fu didn't look in any way discomfited to have his crimes laid bare.

'That is correct,' he agreed. 'And if there is no letter, then it is the word of a disgraced ex-policeman and a foreigner against the people's hero.'

'That's not all, I'm afraid,' said Singh. He reached into his pocket and pulled out the recording device he had borrowed from Susan Tan before leaving the Embassy. He rewound it for a few seconds and pressed play. Fu's disembodied voice repeated, '. . . *it is the word of a disgraced ex-policeman and a foreigner against the people's hero.*'

Singh glanced down at Li Jun and saw that his friend was grinning from ear to ear.

Epilogue

The remnants of the Tan family came to the hospital to say their goodbyes to Li Jun and Singh. They'd been grateful, but Singh had shrugged off their thanks. There was gratitude and blame to go around, enough for all of them. And enough death as well. The *China Daily* was on the hospital side table and Susan looked at the headlines and smiled ruefully. The authorities – and Singh would have loved to be a fly on the wall at that meeting – had decided that Dai Wei bear the brunt of the censure. The papers were full of tales of his lavish lifestyle, corrupt activities and expensive wife. Alive, the powers-that-be had feared him. Dead, they enjoyed their posthumous revenge. Fu had disappeared into the system; no one knew where he was or whether he'd been charged with any crime. But Han had told them that rumours were rife within the force that he had been removed from his post and detained. It was justice, Chinese style.

Once Li Jun had been discharged, the two men met again.

They had one more task to complete. It was Singh's last assignment. He was booked on the late flight that very night. He decided he would not miss China but would definitely miss Chinese food. He wondered if Mrs Singh could be persuaded to learn Szechuan cooking.

Benson drew up outside the Luo residence. This time there was no Ferrari parked outside. Singh rather suspected that Wang Zhen had received his marching orders. The two men got out and made a sombre procession, Li Jun still on crutches, Singh bearing their offering. Singh saw a curtain twitch and knew that Dao Ming had been waiting for them. As they reached the front door, she opened it slowly and stood waiting. By her side, there stood a younger girl who bore a striking resemblance to her sister. Singh tried to smile at her but it was too hard.

There were tears in Dao Ming's eyes and, as he watched, they spilt over and rolled down her cheeks. 'My father has come home?' she asked.

Singh took a step forwards and held out the small urn that they had retrieved with Han's help from the labyrinthine security apparatus that China used to control its citizens. 'Yes,' he said. 'Your father has come home.'

Do you love crime fiction?

Want the chance to hear news about your favourite authors (and the chance to win free books)?

Kate Brady

Frances Brody

Nick Brownlee

Kate Ellis

Shamini Flint

Linda Howard

Julie Kramer

Kathleen McCaul

J. D. Robb

Jeffrey Siger

Then visit the Piatkus website and blog
www.piatkus.co.uk | www.piatkusbooks.net

And follow us on Facebook and Twitter
www.facebook.com/piatkusfiction | www.twitter.com/piatkusbooks

This book must be returned or renewed on or before the latest date shown

Mrs Hale R2